GHOSTCLOUD

MICHAEL MANN

hodder

First published in Great Britain in 2021 by Hodder & Stoughton.
This edition published in 2022

1 3 5 7 9 10 8 6 4 2

Text copyright © Michael Mann, 2021
Illustrations copyright © Chaaya Prabhat, 2021
Map by Samuel Perrett copyright © Hodder & Stoughton Limited, 2021

A CIP catalogue record for this book
is available from the British Library.

ISBN 978 1 444 95930 7

Typeset in Vendetta by Avon DataSet Ltd, Arden Court, Alcester, Warwickshire

Printed and bound in Great Britain by Clays Ltd, Elcograf S.p.A

The paper and board used in this book
are made from wood from responsible sources.

Hodder Children's Books
An imprint of
Hachette Children's Group
Part of Hodder & Stoughton Limited
Carmelite House
50 Victoria Embankment
London EC4Y 0DZ

An Hachette UK Company
www.hachette.co.uk

www.hachettechildrens.co.uk

To Grandad Luke for the coal

and little J for the naps.

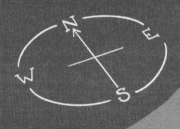

HAMPSTEAD HEATH

NORTH LONDON

HOUSES OF PARLIAMENT

PIMLICO

LONDON
OLYMPIC STADIUM
TOWER BRIDGE
NEW THAMES BARRIER
DEAD ZONE
DOCKLANDS
BATTERSEA POWER STATION
SLUMS

PREFACE

This book is set in London, but not as we know it. It is a London where Big Ben beeps and Battersea Power Station belches out smoke; where bustling river markets float on the rising water and kidnapping is rife; where the Channel Tunnel lies closed, ever since the old war ended.

And far below, hidden underground, children are shovelling . . .

CHAPTER 1
COAL DUST

Spade down. Scoop up. Lift. Pass forward.

Luke Smith-Sharma lived beneath Battersea Power Station. It was a gloomy place with towering chimneys and blackened bricks. A treacly darkness oozed from its walls and at night the corridors were stalked by shadows.

'Come on, speed up!' hissed Ravi, from behind. 'You're spilling the coal.'

'Sorry, I was thinking.'

'Well, don't. Less sleuthing, more shovelling, mate.'

Luke was a shoveller for the station's first chimney. He kept the fuel coming in the great furnace room, feeding the fires till they glowed white-hot. Lines of children, one hundred kids long, snaked across the hall to the hungry flames, each passing coal dust to the child in front. Hidden from the millions of people above they powered all of London: from Big Ben's beep to the robot-horse carriages, from Buckingham Palace to London Zoo.

'You know, I miss homework. And detention. And sprouts.'

'Focus, Luke.' Ravi wiped his glasses. 'They say she's visiting today. She's giving amber tickets to the hardest shovellers . . .'

'. . . and it's our only way home. I know. I know.'

Luke tightened his grip on the rust-iron spade. He ignored the chafe of his coalsack collar and the tickle of sweat on his neck and brow. He had to keep shovelling. Nobody ever stopped shovelling. Not unless they wanted to be fuel themselves.

Iron scraped carbon. Lungs panted hot air. Dancing flames hissed and crackled. These were the sounds of the furnace room. The same sounds he'd heard for over two years. But each week, on Sunday, he heard a different set of sounds. And you had to be ready.

A door creaked. A deliberate creak he knew well. It was followed by a hush that rolled up the line, silencing guards and children alike, then the echo of heels on a hot stone floor.

'Don't look back,' Ravi said. 'Keep your eyes on the spade!'

Spade down. Scoop up. Lift. Pass forward.

Black nails tapped, on a black clipboard. A black lab coat

swished, over black leather boots. A black heart beat, closer each second.

Spade down. Scoop up. Lift. Pass forward.

Luke tried to think happy thoughts: eating ice cream under a warm blue sky; flying kites with his sister Lizzy; his dad sifting through his police files on the kitchen table. Or the day – maybe today, if Ravi's intel was right – when they'd earn their amber ticket and leave this miserable place for good.

But the good thoughts wouldn't stick. Instead, he found himself looking up at the darkness. At the ceiling so high that the light never reached it. At the cloud of black above their bowed heads.

Spade down. Scoop up. Lift. Pass forward.

There was a squeal of pain down the line, then the sizzle of hot ash on naked skin. A solitary sob echoed through the hall.

'Never cry,' Luke muttered. 'That's what she wants.'

'She' was Tabatha Margate, and she ruled the station. If you cried, she just blew smoke in your face. Or emptied the ash from her pipe on your hand. Or into your eye, if you didn't shut it in time. That's what she was like. She didn't care one bit about the children that worked there. For her, all that mattered was that they were cheaper than adults: they ate less food. She could fit

3

more in. And most important of all, they were easier to kidnap.

The click of her heels started again. The pace of shovelling picked up at once. It always did, when she paid them a visit.

And that was when he saw it: the girl in front could no longer keep up. Her skinny arms began spilling and flinging the coal dust. Her breaths started coming in grunts and gasps. She looked exhausted. Unsteady too. He remembered how that felt. How he'd struggled, at least until he'd met Ravi.

But it didn't matter how he felt. All that mattered was that she'd mess it all up. If Tabatha saw, the whole line would be punished. He had to do something – and do something quick – or his and Ravi's chance of an amber ticket, and a way out of this place, would go down with her.

CHAPTER 2
THE MISTAKE

Kids who couldn't keep up fell into one of two categories: fainters and flappers. Fainters paled, gave up, then fell to the floor. Flappers fought on, admirably, but ended up making an almighty mess of the coal dust. This girl was a flapper.

Click. Tap. Swish. Click.

Tabatha was close, and flappers took time. You had to talk them down from the panic, then fix their technique. Hairs prickled up on the back of Luke's neck. *Calm under pressure*, that's what his dad would have said.

Click. Tap. Swish. Click.

'Ravi, quick, pass me a stone.'

'Now? Seriously?'

'We've got a flapper in front.'

Ravi was a trader, like his dad outside. Whether it was information or goods, he was always well stocked. He didn't give things for free, even to friends like Luke, but this was an exception. If the line messed up, they could say goodbye to their amber ticket.

A pebble appeared in Luke's scoop of coal dust. He snatched it and tucked it under his arm. He had to be patient. He had to wait for a moment when they'd all be distracted. Surely it was only a matter of time?

Click. Tap. Swish. **Thwack!**

A child yelped. The smell of singed hair filled the air. A peal of laughter, like broken glass, echoed through the hall.

Luke seized his chance. It was now or never. His heart thundered. The pebble felt hot like coal in his hand. Then he flung it hard with his strong shovelling arm, across to the other side of the hall. A second passed, then . . . CLANG!

Guards began shouting. Shovellers protested. Tabatha's laughter stopped. In the corner of his eye, he saw her turn towards the noise. The click of heels faded.

'You've two minutes, max, before she comes back,' said Ravi. 'Whatever you're planning, hurry!'

Luke did not believe in hurrying. To solve something properly, you observed first and acted second. To calm the girl, he had to first understand her.

He inspected her carefully. She had short blonde hair that stuck up in places. The name 'Jess' was sewn on the back of her sackcloth. And her hands . . . they were different. They weren't callused like his, but soft and sore. They weren't pale from months spent underground, but tanned from the sun. *They were the hands of a new kid.*

Luke knew what to do. New kids brought news. It was the perfect topic: it'd remind her of home and settle her nerves. And he could trade it for rations, when all this was over.

'Psst, Jess. What's the news from the city?'

She looked up from her spade with shadowed eyes, and gave a weary smile. New kids were often lonely, and even one kind word could make their day.

'Well, I've been kidnapped, which might be news?' she said hopefully.

It wasn't news. Kids were kidnapped all the time these days. It didn't sell papers.

'Maybe . . .' Luke tried a smile. 'What about the truce with Europe?' They had no radio or televisor at Battersea. Not even a newspaper.

'Fine.' Her shoulders loosened when she talked. It helped the swing of her shovel. 'Though there are rumours they're reopening the Old Channel Tunnel.'

There were always rumours. The tunnel entrance lay deep in the ruins of London South. Haunted, toxic, out of bounds. Nobody knew what had happened: they just knew to avoid it.

'Oh, there is something,' she said, with a glimmer of enthusiasm. 'These new smog-proof riverboats. The Grand High Lord Mayor launched one the other day. They've shiny propellers to suck up the smog and glass domes to keep the fresh air in.'

Jess's breaths were less shallow. As she talked about boats, a tentative grin stole across her face. This girl was different, Luke thought. Strangely cheery, like his sister Lizzy. She'd been like that too. Most new kids didn't grin for weeks, if at all, and he'd never heard one talk so freely in the furnace hall – it wasn't wise. Yet for some reason, he looked back at Jess and found himself smiling too.

Then the click of heels started again.

'She's heading back,' Ravi hissed. 'She must have smelled a rat.'

Click. Tap. Swish. Click.

Luke looked at Jess. She'd stopped flapping, but her shovelling was still messy. 'So, about your shovelling. Try relaxing your grip. Space out your hands. And keep your eyes on the spade.'

8

Jess nodded and adjusted her hands. 'That's miles better!' she said, too loud.

Luke grimaced at the noise. At least it had worked. She was spilling less dust and almost shovelling in time.

Click. Tap. Swish. Click.

Musky perfume punctured the sticky coal-scented air. Tabatha was near. But he still had time for one more tip. If he got this right, he could be out by nightfall – that amber ticket to freedom clutched in his hand. 'Now straighten your back, and push from your legs.'

This was key. Legs were stronger than arms. His dad always said that if everyone lifted with their legs, then all backache and stooping would be gone overnight.

'Like this?' Jess said, her body rigid, as she catapulted a giant, stiff spadeful of coal dust into the air.

Luke's grey eyes widened. He watched the scoop of coal dust fly higher and higher, blending into the endless darkness above. Not only up, but back through the air. Back down the line.

He couldn't help but look. It flew fast and silent. A ball of black, straight towards Tabatha.

Tabatha couldn't have seen it coming – she was busy blowing

ash on a young girl's neck. But when the missile of coal hit her, it hit her hard, with a loud WHOOSH on the side of her head.

Black crystals burst sparkling into the air. The click of heels stopped. The shovelling stopped. The breathing stopped. The hall went silent. Except for Luke's heart, which he was sure could be heard echoing loudly.

Tabatha turned around, transformed: hair matted, cheeks caked, stylish clothes covered in a blanket of black. She looked like a shadow. A furious, white-eyed, pipe-smoking shadow, who was quite ready to kill someone.

'Who did that?' Her voice was the crackle of gravel under tyres.

'Who did that?' she said, louder this time, heels crushing coal as she stepped down the line.

'WHO DID THAT?' she bellowed. Smoke slipped from her lips, like from the mouth of the furnace itself.

Every kid's head was down. Every single one of them was still holding their breath. They all knew how bad it would be if they were caught.

Well, almost all of them.

'I did, Ms. Margate,' Jess said, only shaking a little. 'I'm awfully sorry. I'm new. It was an accident.'

Luke's heart sank. This Jess was a disaster. Messy. Noisy. Honest to boot. She wouldn't last a week in the station at this rate. But there was something about her. Something bright, like a spark, even here in the dark. It reminded him of his sister Lizzy and of happier times. He couldn't let Tabatha put that spark out.

He was a valuable shoveller. Tabatha wouldn't waste him. 'It's my fault too.' He put up his hand. 'I distracted her.'

Jess nodded.

Ravi sighed.

Tabatha smiled. 'Handing out punishments is one of my favourite things. Handing out two – well, it's my lucky day.'

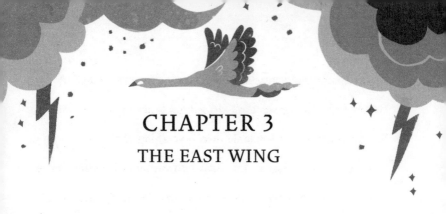

CHAPTER 3
THE EAST WING

Luke was a keep-your-head-down kind of boy: if there was a centre of attention, he tried to avoid it. But at that moment, in the hall, there was nowhere to hide. So, he stood next to Jess, paler than usual, before hundreds of gaunt and watchful faces.

And with each second that passed, his sense of dread grew. He'd never seen Tabatha quite this mad. Or the hall, for that matter, quite this still. And for what? Because some girl made him think of his sister? That amber ticket had been his way home to his sister! What had he been thinking?

Or more to the point, what was Tabatha thinking?

Rat corpse cleaning? Slug eating? Without food for a week? Or perhaps he'd be sent to the front of the line, where a single stray spark from the furnace could cost you an eye.

Tabatha didn't explain. That would have been putting them out of their misery, and misery was precisely what Tabatha loved. Instead, she reached into her pocket and pulled out her talkometer – a copper shell-shaped contraption with a wind-up handle. She turned the handle twice and whispered.

A moment later, Tabatha's manservant Terence arrived. Nobody liked Terence. Not even Tabatha. He had the body of a tall man, but his head leant in low. He had a sharp, pointy face, but a dull look in his eyes. And he was extraordinarily greasy – from the tip of his ponytail, to the ends of his shoes. Even Terence's teeth were greasy. Luke shuddered. This was a man who could do with a shower.

'Take them to the East Wing.'

'The East Wing?' Terence gulped.

Luke didn't know much about the East Wing, except that it was closed to the shovellers and always had been. He glanced around the hall: an ashen-faced Ravi mouthed 'good luck'. Only Jess smiled on. A 'tell-me-it'll-all-be-all right' kind of smile. Well, it wouldn't be all right. She would soon find out.

Then suddenly Luke found himself sliding backwards, alongside Jess: Terence had them by their collars, and dragged them towards the door. Luke squirmed. For a man covered in grease, he had a surprisingly firm grip.

They soon hurried down a very long corridor, stretching into the darkness. Lights flickered dimly, flakes of dark paint hung from the walls and black-and-white tiles zigged and zagged under their feet.

'I hate the East Wing,' Terence harrumphed, then licked his teeth.

'I can see why.' Jess nodded, squinting at the tiles.

Luke sniffed the air. A faint smell lingered, like rotten vegetables in an old wet towel. As they trudged down the corridor, the stink grew ever stronger. He tried to breathe through his mouth. The day couldn't get any worse. It literally stank.

Jess, however, was humming to herself.

'Stop humming!' Luke said as they were dragged along. 'This is terrible. This is worse than terrible.'

She bit her lip. 'Every cloud has a silver lining,' she murmured. 'I mean, at least we're not shovelling.'

Luke's spirits slumped. He'd rescued an *optimist* – they were the worst! She'd soon learn. Shovelling was the only way out of this place. Not that he could talk. After today's heroics, he wouldn't be leaving any time soon.

With a jangle, Terence retrieved a set of rusty keys from his bag. 'You must have done something especially bad. Entering the East Wing is normally forbidden. Strange things happen here.'

Luke's ears pricked up. Forbidden meant secrets and mysteries to be solved. A surge of curiosity burned away his gloom. As they entered, he scanned the hallway. Amidst the stink and decay, hung a series of photos in gilded frames, in neat intervals along the endless corridor.

'What are those pictures, Terence?'

Terence bared his yellow teeth. 'Stop snooping, you wart.'

In each photo, a smiling family stood beside the power station. Though the families changed, their features were similar. In the last photo, however, the father frowned. Instead of a wife by his side, there stood a little girl, all in black, whose amber eyes glared right back at Luke.

Luke looked at Terence. It was worth a shot.

'It's just,' Luke added, 'that the pictures are so expertly hung.'

A smile slinked across Terence's lips; he stood a little straighter. 'They're family heirlooms,' he droned. 'The Margates have owned Battersea for hundreds of years. When the war with Europe started, it was an easy target. This wing never recovered when it was over. But Tabatha has plans. Soon it will all be as good as new.'

'Maybe she could buy some air fresheners first?' said Jess, clearly trying to be helpful.

She had a point, Luke thought. By the time they were halfway down the corridor, the unpleasant pong had turned into a gut-twisting stench. A mixture of fresh vomit, bad breath and rotting eggs.

'Don't be impudent.' Terence jabbed Jess's shoulder. 'If you think this is bad, just wait for your punishment. You'll be in the sewers. There'll be a lot more of this stink.'

Luke had never cleaned a toilet, let alone a sewer. He struggled to imagine how it could smell any worse.

'But, Mr Terence, I think you'll find,' Jess continued, 'that this smell isn't sewage. My uncle's a plumber – I helped him on jobs – and sewage smells different. In fact, I don't know what this smell is.'

Terence sniffed deeply and then trembled all over. He put his hand to his mouth, as if to stifle something. Then he raised one hand and pointed ahead. His mouth dropped open, revealing the horror of his grease-covered teeth.

Luke's breath caught in his throat.

Just in front of them was a shivering, quivering, sickening mist.

It was greyish-green and glowed a little. It had grasping tendrils, like a hungry octopus, which cradled a pair of padlocked white doors. And one of the tendrils was creeping towards them.

'Open a window! Or a door, or something!' Terence cried.

Luke looked around, but there were no windows at this level of the building. And even if there had been, Tabatha would have bricked them up. She didn't like her workers to ever see sunshine.

So for a moment, he froze, unsure what to do.

And in that tiniest of moments, the miasma moved. Its eager tentacles were swiftly upon them. They snaked round Luke's feet and climbed up his legs. He scrambled backwards, but they moved too quick, slithering up his waist and surrounding his chest. Within seconds, they crawled up the skin of his neck. He gasped for air. The last thing he saw was Terence, pulling a gas mask from his bag, the stinking mist hovering above him.

Then it all went grey – to Luke's eyes at least – but his other senses immediately burst into life. The back of his mouth tasted old blood. A deep, retching odour of decay filled his nose . . . a dead rat in the garage, or something bigger. Then a howl sounded inside his skull, worming deeper with each wail, until it howled so loudly that he couldn't hear himself think. And in the howling, stinking, swirling grey, he saw something else, at the edge of the shadows. It made his heart sink. He wanted to cry. He saw his mother.

Ebony hair tied back. Eyes wet-black with tears. She looked at him: it was the first time she had.

And then it was over. The air cleared and all that was left was a loud whirring sound, and a thumping ache inside Luke's chest.

'I found the extractor vents!' Jess said, by a grate in the wall. 'They sucked that stink right out of the building. I used to repair this stuff with my uncle at weekends. Knew they'd be here – it's regulation – but some idiot had hung the pictures over them.'

Terence pulled off his gas mask and scowled at Jess. But Luke could have hugged her. She'd saved their bacon.

'What was that thing?' asked Luke.

'Some kind of smog.' Jess shrugged. 'Must have come in off the river.'

'Smog? But it had tentacles . . .' Luke stopped himself. Jess was looking at him funny.

'Tentacles? It smelt bad, I'll grant you, but it just looked foggy to me. Did you breathe any in? It can mess with your head.'

'Oh,' Luke muttered. 'Maybe that was it.'

But it wasn't it. He knew it wasn't. He had seen the thing before he'd breathed anything in, but clearly Jess had seen something different. She wasn't shaken like him. And she certainly hadn't seen his mother. Smog couldn't do that. *Could it?*

'Hold your breath next time.' Jess patted his shoulder. 'That's what I did. The smog has got pretty bad these days.'

Terence stood up, looking queasy. 'Yes. Just your bog-standard smog.' He nodded, a little too hard. He extracted a large brass key from his chain and unlocked a pair of rusty doors ahead. 'But enough talk for now. It's time for your punishment.'

CHAPTER 4
THE VOICE

Luke peered through the door into a darkened room of metal pipes. Spindly-thin pipes lined the furthest walls, medium-sized pipes crisscrossed the floor, and through the centre of the room ran a gigantic, horizontal tube – so large that Luke could have stood up inside it. With its right-angles, struts and fat metal bolts, the room exuded order and control – a welcome change from the horror of the East Wing.

Then the smell hit him: an overwhelming stink of uncleaned toilet.

Terence flicked a switch. Brass lanterns flickered into life, evaporating the darkness, and revealing the source of the unpleasant smell: there was sewage everywhere.

'Shouldn't the sewage be *inside* the pipes?'

Jess frowned. 'People always underestimate the importance of plumbers.'

'You're lucky it's so low.' Terence looked disappointed. 'It flooded up to the ceiling earlier this month – we had to double lock the doors.'

Terence shoved them forward into the room. Brown-black sewage seeped over Luke's bare feet, then trickled between his toes. A shiver of disgust rippled through him, but at least it took his mind off what he'd seen in the smog. He turned to Terence. 'What happened in here?'

'Tabatha got a new incinerator,' he grunted. 'It was meant to burn sewage, but it keeps leaking.'

'Is that it?' Jess took a step towards a blue-black, metal contraption at the end of the room – a cross between an oven and a diving bell. It had squat, black tubes going in one side, and silver cogs and funnels on the other. A polished plaque on it read: *Fornax Maxima XII*.

Terence yanked Jess back. 'Yes. Now leave it. You've got work to do.' He cleared his throat and spat some phlegm onto the floor. 'You'll wipe this place down until it's sparkling, and there'll be no food till it's done. That's if you don't drown first in rising sewage.' He pointed to a pile of bones in the corner. 'That's what happened to the last pair that came here. Dehydration, or dysentery.

I can't quite remember. It doesn't matter in the end.'

Luke wasn't sure they were human bones, but he wasn't taking any chances.

'I'll check on you tomorrow, then each day after that, until the job – or you – are completely finished.'

Luke swallowed. It was an impossible task.

Terence was already lumbering back to the door. Luke wasn't sure he'd ever seen him so happy. With a smirk, then a thunk, he locked the door behind him.

The lantern-light flickered. Luke sighed and turned to Jess. 'Without food, we'll last a couple of weeks. Without water, three days.'

'What if we need more time?'

He wasn't sure she wanted to know the answer to that, so he forced a smile. 'It'll be fine, I'm sure. My dad always says, "It's not over till it's over."'

He closed his eyes for a moment and pictured home. And although it hurt, he felt like if he believed it enough, he could almost see it: the houseboat rocking in the shade of the old Olympic Stadium. His sister and dad squabbling over burnt toast. Fishing on the bridge, looking up at the sky. Luke opened his eyes. He felt a little stronger.

He tore off two strips from his sackcloth overall and gave one to Jess. And with barely a nod, they both began wiping.

The squeak of cloth. The drip-drip of water. A squelch underfoot.

Time passed slowly. Soon, Luke's mind turned to what he'd seen in the East Wing. The smog, Jess had called it. The last time he'd seen smog had been the day of his kidnapping. It had swept across the Heath, swallowing him and his kite. He'd been calling for his dad through the grey when the kidnappers found him. He shuddered at the memory.

But it had just been mist then. Had it changed so much?

'Jess, how much do you know about the smog?'

She looked up from her cloth, grateful for the distraction. 'Plenty! I was studying it for the Plumber's Guild exam. Where shall I start?'

'At the beginning, I guess.'

So they wiped, in the stink, while Jess told the story of the Great London Smog.

'It started under Queen Victoria. The spread of factories made a sticky, grey smoke that coated the city, a bit like a duvet.' Jess gestured to the ceiling, as though the smog was right with them.

'Then in the 1950s, came a smog worse than any before: "The Killer Smog". Thousands died – it crept into their lungs, made them cough and gasp till they couldn't breathe at all.'

'Why didn't they put on their gas masks?'

'Normal people didn't have them, in those days. They had something else, it was called "prevention". There was a "Clean Air Act", they cut down pollution and hired environment inspectors. They closed factories in the city and moved them out of town. This power station, in fact, almost got made into fancy housing.'

This seemed unlikely to Luke, but he held his tongue. Jess was a good storyteller, and he wanted to hear how it ended.

She cleared her throat, wiping as she spoke. 'For a while, it seemed to work. The smog came less often, the air cleared, birds even returned to the trees. Then came the war with Europe. The imports stopped. The economy failed. The mood changed.' Jess sniffed and continued, lowering her voice. 'People said the rules were hurting business. So, the politicians came up with a new slogan. Instead of "prevention", they called it "coexistence". Pollution and people could live side by side, they said, so long as we took a few extra precautions.'

Luke's cloth squeaked loudly on one of the spindly pipes.

Coexistence, he thought, was definitely a politician word. 'When did all this happen?'

'Oh, ages ago, before we were born. And that's when we all got free gas masks. When the cars and trains got the smog-sealed doors. When ventilation systems became compulsory, and the factories were welcomed back to the city. It was a great day for plumbers.'

But not for the fish and birds, Luke thought. 'And it worked, right? I saw the mayor on the televisor. He said there hadn't been a smog death in a hundred years.'

Jess blew through her teeth. 'Kind of . . . my dad says the smog is changing. More people are getting sick – and not only in the lungs, but in the head too. It's cropping up in new places. Not following the weather.' She shook her head. 'You know, the day I was kidnapped, it came out of nowhere. It was blue skies one minute, thick grey the next. But not everyone in the Guild agrees with my dad.' She turned to Luke and winked. 'Though there have never been reports of a smog with tentacles.'

Luke tried to laugh; it came out hollow. The very thought of the thing in the East Wing gave him shivers, and after all this talking, he felt no closer to figuring it out. In fact, it was giving him a headache.

He thought back to his dad, buried deep in his case files. When he got stuck – which was often enough – he took a break. *Sleep on it*, he'd say. *What you're looking for often comes when you're not looking at all.*

He gave the smog questions a rest. They had been cleaning for three hours, by Luke's estimation. Their hands, clothes and feet were already stinking. Jess's blonde hair was coated in a layer of brown, almost dark like his. Somehow, hers still managed to stick up at the back.

'I know we might starve,' Jess said, breezily, 'but at least we can talk here. The worst thing about the furnace hall is that horrible silence.'

'And the heat,' Luke said. 'It's worse near the front. The front line kids have to throw coal in the fire with their bare hands. The flames jump out and burn off their fingernails. One kid lost an eye the other day.'

'Hmm. I kind of need my eyes and fingernails, as a plumber.' Jess's eyelids drooped, but when she spoke of plumbing, she brightened.

'Is that what you want to be, when you grow up?' Luke asked.

'Yeah. My uncle says I'm a natural. I'll be the first female plumber in the Guild!' She rubbed the back of her neck. 'Or at least I would have been.' Her face fell for a moment, then the smile fixed back on. 'I'm fine. Honestly. I just miss them, you know.'

'Missing them is good,' said Luke. 'It makes me work harder. Reminds me where I'm from, and who I am.'

They wiped for a bit longer in silence.

'And then,' Luke added, 'I think about what I'll do when I get out. And that cheers me up.'

'When I get out, the first thing I will do is give that Terence a shower,' Jess muttered.

'And a toothbrush.'

'And a haircut!'

'And that's coming from a girl with sewage in her hair.'

Soon, Jess was making more mess than she was cleaning up. She kept slipping, or wiping sewage from one pipe onto another they'd already cleaned. Luke told her to take a nap and that they'd work in shifts. She settled on the fat pipe in the middle and was soon snoring.

And it was during that first shift that it happened: in the quiet of the room, with only Jess's snores and the sound of cloth against pipe, he heard the voice. A voice so faint, it was barely a whisper. Luke stopped wiping. He stood up on his pipe and listened. *Where was it coming from?* The words came in and out of focus, swelling in time with the hiss of pipes.

Help me. Help me. Help me.

Luke put down his cloth. The words were pleading, desperate. He climbed down off the pipe and walked towards the sound. Soon, he found himself beside the great black incinerator that Terence had warned them away from. The voice was strongest there.

Help me. Help me. Help me.

Was it a trap? The machine made him nervous. It was darker, quieter, stranger than it should be. Something in the air didn't feel quite right. As he turned back, something moved.

He looked again and he saw it – something he was sure hadn't been there before. Inside the machine, behind its bulbous, glass, oven-like doors, sat a girl.

She had dark curly hair, her hands were pressed against the glass, and her big, grey eyes were staring straight at Luke.

CHAPTER 5
THE GIRL

Luke blinked. Stepped back. Then blinked twice more. Through the steamed up glass of the incinerator, there was definitely a girl. Luke couldn't help but shudder. He knew Tabatha was cruel, but this was too much. Nobody deserved a punishment like that.

And yet, he hesitated. The girl was *strange*, somehow. Her clothes, perhaps? Her wide grey eyes? Or the way she moved her hands on the glass? It was so smooth Luke couldn't say when they started or stopped. He wished he'd never set foot in this place.

Help me, please.

Her panicked voice brought Luke to his senses. She was just a kid like him. It wasn't her fault she was stuck in this creepy dark place. And who knew how long she'd been here?

He pulled at the handle of the oven-like door. It didn't budge. He ran to the side with the cogs and funnels, looking for a button, or a lever, or some catch to release, but there was nothing.

There was the occasional word engraved in the metal – instructions perhaps – but they were in a language he didn't recognise. Had it been imported? Importing anything cost a fortune these days.

The machine started to move. Cogs turned, clicked and whirred. Funnels sucked, blew and sputtered. And the voice of the girl shouted, muffled, through the glass.

Hurry! Do something!

A flurry of steam surrounded the girl. Her hands hammered against the door. Waves of damp heat burst forth from the thing, wetting Luke's pale cheeks as he tried to open it.

He wished he knew about plumbing, but there was no time to get Jess. He wished he knew what the words said, but it was too late to learn now. But there was one thing Luke was, and that was strong. Two years of shovelling his hardest each day meant he had a grip of steel and legs as strong as a horse. So he did what he could: he grabbed the handle of the door, and pushed both his legs against the side of the machine.

'1 . . . 2 . . . 3 . . .'

He pushed with all his might.

The door sprang open, throwing Luke to the floor and gushing hot steam out over the room. He squinted through the white – had he done it in time?

'Hello? Are you OK?'

There was no response. The incinerator stopped whirring and a whispering quiet filled the room. There was steam everywhere. It made the lights on the wall blur and glow. The fog was so thick, he could barely see Jess asleep on the pipe.

He got up and peered inside the machine: it was empty.

Had the girl been burned up?

Luke tasted despair. It crept up his throat, dark and bitter. He tried to swallow it, but it did no good. The shovelling, the smog and wiping away sewage – he could handle that, he was used to misery. This was different. He wasn't sad for himself, he was sad for the girl. He'd let her down.

No, it was worse. He'd let her die.

He crumpled to the floor. He had been too late.

The mist sank down, thick and opaque, and for the second time that day, he was enveloped in grey. But where the smog had been dark and stank of decay, this mist was fuzzy and had the scent of fresh rain. It tickled like a breeze or the sun on his back, and its drops on his skin were soft and calm.

Luke breathed it in and sighed.

'I'm sorry,' he said, to nobody in particular.

The mist started to clear, first from the floor then gradually higher, and as it did, he saw something: there on top of the fat, central pipe stood a pair of shoes. Inside those shoes stood a pair of legs, leading up to a fine green dress: it was the girl with the curls from inside the machine.

'My hero,' she said. 'Thank you for saving me.'

Luke didn't know how she'd got there. Or why she looked so happy after almost being cooked. But he wasn't going to complain.

'You're welcome,' Luke said.

He didn't think it was the kind of thing that heroes said, but it'd have to do.

CHAPTER 6
THE DEAL

'So tell me,' said the girl, walking a wet grey pipe like one might a tightrope. 'What on earth – or under it – are you doing down here?' It wasn't the question he'd expected. When someone bursts out of an incinerator hidden in a sewer, surely they had to be the one to explain? But he decided to be polite and give the girl the benefit of the doubt.

'I work here,' he said. 'I'm a shoveller for the furnace.'

'You're a shoveller, really? Is that an actual job?'

'It is here,' said Luke. 'But I'm not only a shoveller. I'm going to be a detective when I grow up.'

A snore from Jess cut through the air. The strange girl jumped down from the top of the pipe. It was a sizeable leap, yet she landed on the floor without so much as a sound.

'Grow up?' she said. 'Why wait? Putting things off is a dangerous habit, and a boring one too. And if something's dangerous *and* boring, it's a disaster! I mean, you might get run over by a bus tomorrow.'

The girl waited, as though for a nod of approval. It was something she had evidently said before.

'Not in here,' Luke said. 'There are no buses down here.'

'You're missing the point.'

Luke shrugged and resumed wiping. The girl took out a cloth and began to wipe too.

'You've got a cloth! Are you a cleaner?'

'No. I'm a searcher.'

'Is that an actual job?'

'I didn't say it was a job. It's who I am.'

Luke frowned, but didn't complain, for the girl was amazingly good at wiping. Every stroke left the pipe glistening.

'So what do you do? And how did you get here?'

'You're the detective, why not make some deductions?'

She was bossy, Luke thought, but in a nice kind of way. She reminded him of his grandma. She was always telling him what to do.

'OK,' he said. 'Maybe you're a chimney sweep. That would explain why you're so good at wiping, and how you came down

34

the chimney into that incinerator in the first place.'

The girl shuddered. 'Incinerator, really? Is that what that horrible thing is?' she said. 'And good guess, but no. Am I dressed like a sweep?'

Luke looked at her clothes. The flat cap and the waistcoat were chimney enough, but chimney sweeps wore black to hide the soot, not pretty green dresses.

'How about this? You're a cat burglar. That would explain why you move so smoothly. Why you jump so lightly. And how you managed to sneak out of the incinerator machine in the mist.'

'A burglar, I like it. What's my motive? Why would I steal sewage?'

Motives were important. Luke's dad always said that.

'Maybe you want Tabatha's money?'

'Better! And yet, still wrong.' The girl walked over, close to Luke. She brushed her hand against his cheek. It was cold. 'You had some sewage on it.'

She stared at Luke. It was a stare that said: *I can't believe you haven't figured this out*. It made him feel awkward. But then again, he had a hunch that she didn't mind one bit if she made him feel awkward. In fact, she probably quite liked it.

35

His brain whirred harder; the evidence didn't add up. There was too much strangeness. From her clothes, to her movement, to how she'd got into the plant. Then when she took another step closer, he noticed something. The grey of her irises swirled in the light.

'Your eyes!'

As he gasped, his breath brushed against her face, and to his surprise, its very edges blurred – like a gust of wind stirring mist on the Thames. He had an idea but the thought made him shudder.

'Are you a ghost?'

'Bravo!' she said. 'Top marks. Well, almost – I'm a ghostcloud.'

'I solved it!' Luke thwacked a pipe in triumph. The clang reverberated, then faded into an unsettling hum. *A ghost.* Was that good? Was that even possible? Shouldn't he feel scared?

But he didn't – not one bit. He just wanted to know more.

'What's a ghostcloud?'

'A sky-ghost. A mist-wraith. A wisp-wailer. You know.'

He certainly didn't, though there was no time to say it, because the girl kept talking.

'And most of them aren't all that nice, take it from me.' She looked at her fingernails intently for a moment, then back at

Luke. 'Now, detective, I've a mystery for you.' She pulled out some glasses from the folds of her skirt and put them on. They made her eyes look bigger than they already were. 'And my mystery is this: *how* did you hear me?'

Luke had never considered *how* he heard things. Surely the answer was always 'with my ears'.

'Why wouldn't I hear you?'

'That thing was airtight. There's no way the sound would have reached you. You must have heard me up here.' She tapped her forehead. 'Which means, you're *attuned*. Are you a clairvoyant?'

'No.' Luke put down his cloth. 'I'm nothing, just a shoveller.'

'You don't get it.' She rolled her eyes. 'Most people don't notice me – well, not unless I let them – they just see mist. Only a certain kind of person spots a ghostcloud: a person who knows death.' She raised an eyebrow. 'Have you killed anyone?'

'No!'

'I'm not judging. People kill all the time: it's natural. Maybe you killed someone bad?'

'I'm not a killer,' he said. And then he remembered.

The girl peered over the top of her glasses. 'You're lying.' She shrugged and resumed her wiping.

The truth of the matter was that Luke wasn't sure. It was a grey area. It wasn't something Luke liked talking about, so he started wiping too. He listened to the drip of the pipes, the faint snores of Jess, and the rhythmic squeak of cloth on metal.

It was easier to talk when you were doing something. You didn't have to look anyone in the eye.

'My mum died giving birth,' he said. 'I don't remember her, really, except from photos. But, I suppose you could say that I killed her.'

Luke remembered the East Wing. His mum staring through the smog, like the photo at home, but sadder. The eyes in the photo weren't wet-black with tears. What did it mean? Could he ask this ghost-girl? He wasn't sure he was ready.

He turned to her. Her expression had softened. 'I'm sorry, about your mum. I forget that for the living, death can seem quite . . . final.'

Luke shook his head. He didn't want anyone's pity. It was a fact, that's all. His family was just fine. 'It's not so bad. In some ways I was lucky. You see, when she had me, both our hearts stopped. Only mine restarted. Dad always said that she did an exchange. Her life to save mine.'

The girl's eyes widened to a stare. Not a stare of amusement, or sorrow, or fear, but a stare of excitement. Her eyebrows wrinkled and her mouth slid open. She walked up to Luke, put her hand to his chin and turned his face towards hers.

'Your heart stopped?' she asked, too close.

'Only for a minute. It's fine now.'

'It's better than fine. It's brilliant. It's amazing!' The girl jumped up and down. 'Of course – I knew it – I knew you were different! If your heart stopped for a moment, then you died for a moment. And if you died, well, it means . . .'

'It means what?'

'. . . you're a half-ghost!'

'A half-what?'

'Just wait till I tell the others! Who's laughing now?' The ghost-girl walked away and began searching the walls. 'Can you help me find a vent? There's got to be one, it's regulation, you know.'

'But what's a half-ghost?'

'It's rare. There hasn't been one for years. I'll explain. Once we're out.'

'Out?'

'A vent!' she cried, pointing wildly to a spot, near where

39

Jess was snoring. The girl reached out her hand. 'Just for the night, promise. It'll be my treat.'

He looked around at the barely cleaned pipes and the thick steel doors.

'I can't leave Jess here. We need to clean it by—'

The girl's grey eyes flashed electric blue, and a swathe of mist rushed from her hand and across the room. It left a section of pipes gleaming clean. She winked at him. 'I'll do the rest if you come. Now stop overthinking and wing it a little. We'll be back before she wakes.'

Luke couldn't believe what he saw. The pipes were cleaner than he and Jess would ever get them. Maybe he should follow her, after all. Crazy as it sounded, it was the only way they'd meet Terence's demands.

But what was he thinking? Following a ghost? And he'd only just met her.

'Wait . . . I don't even know your name.'

'Fair point. How rude.' The girl curtsied. 'My name is Alma. And yours is Luke – it's sewn into your sack. And now that's done, let me rephrase my question. Do you want to get out of this stinking sewer?'

Luke's jaw dropped. 'Do I want to get out? More than anything in the world.'

Alma smiled, took his hand, and everything went grey.

CHAPTER 7
THE OVERSKY

The next thing Luke saw was white. To the left, to the right, above and below. It was a special kind of white. It reminded him of paper held up to the light.

'Where am I?'

'Same place as before,' Alma said from nearby. 'Only a little higher up.'

He felt a breeze. The bright white thinned out and began to change. It mingled with yellow, red and pink until he found himself looking out over the clouds.

It was sunset. The tops of the clouds were frothy and rippled, like whisked-up cake mix. The sun had almost sunk beneath them. It cast a hot orange light across the top of the ridges, with button-black stripes of shadow in between.

'A tiger night,' said Alma, who was sitting on a ridge, further along, swinging her legs into the shadows. 'Told you it'd be better out here.'

Luke could find no words. He was outside, at last. After two years of darkness, he was above the clouds, with not a soul in view. The sun was shining just for him. If only Jess and Ravi could see this, he thought.

Then he thought to look down.

His feet appeared to be standing on a cloud. It was, he decided, both theoretically impossible and practically quite terrifying. And yet, he could feel it – wet and springy under his toes.

The cloud shimmered transparent with each passing breeze, revealing glimpses of the power station below, twinkling dimly in the gathering dusk. The station looked the size of his hand. A fall from this height would not be good.

He took a step back and it was then that he noticed his feet. They flickered at the edges, like the cloud beneath them.

'Am I—'

'—dead?' she finished for him.

She let the question rest, kicking her feet above a shadowy ravine, between ridges of clouds. A blue-grey twilight had now settled in the air and she seemed to have changed: her dress was now a dusky purple and her hair had taken on a bluish hue.

'No, not dead. I'm not that desperate for friends. You're just a ghostcloud for now. Your soul is up here, and your body's down there, unconscious.'

He held his hands up in front of him, and sure enough, he could see through them. He brought them together and with a little extra effort pushed one right through the other. It tickled.

'I thought ghosts haunted houses?'

Alma shrugged. 'Ghosts are souls that cling to this world. They bond to some matter and refuse to let go. In the stories, it's houses – but why coop yourself up in a dusty old house? There are sea-ghosts, sand-ghosts, tree-ghosts and more. And if you bond with the water in a cloud . . . voila! You're a ghostcloud.'

Luke mulled this over. It had a certain logic at least.

'But why a cloud, of all things?'

'You don't get to choose, your soul does that for you. Most of them float straight off to the End Place, but those with unfinished business cling on. Usually to something they love, and if you loved the sky, then a cloud's a good bet.' She grinned. 'I wouldn't have it any other way. Clouds can fly, for a start. Change their shape, roll thunder and make the sky pour. I can block out the sun—'

'OK, I get it. And half-ghosts?'

Alma sighed. 'Questions, questions. You lifers are boring. You say "seize the day", then spend the day discussing how – and before you know it, you're dead and you've not lived at all.' She rolled up the sleeves of her dress. 'Let's do something instead. What do you fancy?'

Luke stopped to think. In the station, they never got to choose anything. And he quite liked it up here. The sky kept changing. Ridges of clouds clumped together and grew up into pillars – connecting, contorting and colouring the sky. One even looked like a giant snake. It had a pointy snout and was drifting towards them. Alma hadn't noticed. She was adjusting her hair.

'OK, I'm presentable. What will it be?'

He pushed the snake from his mind. 'Can I see my home? It's in the east, by the Old Olympic Park.'

Alma scooped some purple cloudfluff and let the breeze catch it. It scattered downwind like a dandelion clock. 'Wind's not right. It'd take too long.'

Something tightened in Luke's chest. For the last two years, his family had been a world away, yet up here, they felt closer. Painfully close. 'But I haven't seen them for years . . .'

'I can't change the wind because you feel like it.' Alma flounced.

'I've an idea. How about I show you London instead?' And before he could answer, she winked and dived into the cloud ravine. 'Come on, jump! You can't die, you're already a ghost!'

And with that, she disappeared into the shadows below.

Luke sighed, then stepped to the edge. He'd been underground for two years, he wasn't sure he wanted to leave the oversky quite yet. It got better each second. Clusters of stars now glittered white-blue above. Rays of starlight fell down, lighting the clouds with a hazy glow.

Except for the clouds around him. The starlight wasn't falling on his patch at all. It seemed to be drenched in a long, twisty shadow.

He looked up. There, high above, was the twisting snake-cloud. Closer than before. It had an eyeless face, a wide jaw, and its nostrils flared and flickered as it moved, as though sniffing for something.

Its mouth slid open, revealing rows of dagger-sharp purple-black teeth.

Something, or someone? Either way, he didn't like it one bit.

He dived down after Alma and into the darkness.

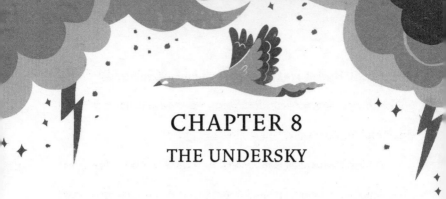

CHAPTER 8
THE UNDERSKY

Falling through a cloud-ravine was more pleasant than he'd expected.

Logically, he knew he should worry. A fall from this height, even into water, would kill him on impact. But then, logically, you couldn't stand on clouds in the first place – so he ignored reason for once and enjoyed the glide. He stretched out and brushed his hands against the sides as he fell. The clouds were like bubbles between his fingers.

A floor of charcoal-grey cloudfluff reared up towards him. He braced himself, but there was no impact, he merely sank softly into the grey. Then gradually, through the grey, faint lights appeared. Not the white light of the stars – something yellower, sharper. They clustered, came into focus and the cloud thinned out, and the glittering sprawl of London emerged.

Alma grabbed his hand and pulled him to a stop next to her,

on a swan-shaped cloud. She gestured down at the view. 'To die for, right?'

'It's something else.'

The chimneys belched smoke high into the air. The great river slurped, brown and grey. Ant-sized people marched past matchbox houses, and even the chugging riverboats looked small. But the city seemed endless, swallowing the land in all directions. To the north, it gleamed with wealth and grandeur: regal townhouses, well-kept parks and the rising green of Hampstead Heath. To the south, the slums stretched out for miles of barbed wire fences and corrugated iron, burning rubbish and crumbling walls, hollow-eyed buildings and sunken streets. His dad had never let them go south, now he saw why. Only the lights of Battersea glowed bright in the south.

She turned to him. 'And now we just need to teach you to fly.'

'Fly? Me?'

'Yep, and for you, the first step is to relax. You're far too uptight. The water drops are all pent up inside you.'

'Uptight?' Luke frowned. 'I'm not uptight.'

Alma tutted. 'That's exactly what an uptight person would

say. If you loosened up, your raindrops would too, and they'd spread into cloud, like my swan here.'

Being told to calm down, Luke thought, was like being told to forget something. The more you tried, the harder it was. And those who went around saying it usually knew better.

'I don't get it. Why do I need a swan?'

She put her hand on her chest, where her heart would have been. 'I'm only trying to help, no need to be defensive. If it's too difficult, I can drop you back at the plant. I'm sure wiping up sewage is just as much fun.'

He didn't rise to the bait. He took a breath and smiled back. 'I'm curious, that's all.'

'Well, if you must know, you need your own cloud to catch the wind. That's how you fly.'

Something stirred inside him. 'Like flying a kite?'

'A bit but, of course, it's far more difficult.' Alma shook her head. 'It takes lots of practice. And for a start you need to imagine your shape . . .'

Luke had stopped listening. He remembered flying kites on Parliament Hill with Lizzy and Dad, their tasseled diamonds soaring high in the air. The image burned in his mind. His skin seemed to tingle with the thought of it all.

'You're doing it,' Alma whispered. 'Whatever you're doing, don't stop!'

He couldn't have stopped if he'd wanted to. It was all flooding back. They'd bundle their kites up with string and catch the train, then climb the steep, muddy hill together. His dad walked in the middle, holding them each by the hand. Then when they reached the top . . .

He stopped for a moment and caught his breath. It was as though all the memories, after being buried for so long, were bursting out of him, in all directions. And there was that tingling again – from the top of his head to the tips of his toes.

Alma pulled at his hand. 'Luke, look down.'

There at his feet, a cloud was unfolding. It seemed to come from inside him, he could feel it stretching, like an endless yawn. Larger and larger, until he stood on a diamond-shaped cloud of his own.

She frowned a little. 'Beginners' luck, I guess, but it's a bit . . . edgy.'

'It's my kite, from home.'

'It's ugly. Normally, we make animals. Like my swan, you

see. It's prettier that way. But I guess, if I must, I can work with a triangle.'

'It's not a triangle. It's a diamond.'

She rolled her eyes. 'Same difference. Now, pay attention. Flying a cloud is a most technical thing . . .'

And she was talking again. Talking his ear off. A girl, he thought, who didn't know the difference between a triangle and a diamond.

'. . . and honestly, quite dangerous, if a storm gets you . . .' she prattled on.

What did Alma know about danger? She was already dead, for a start, and that morning had got herself stuck inside an incinerator.

'Are you listening, Luke? This is a regulation safety briefing. It's very—'

'But you said to seize the day, and we just seem to be—'

'Seize it, yes. Interrupt me, no.'

So he didn't interrupt again. Not when he felt the breeze brewing behind him. Nor when he realised that he could move his cloud (it was not half as technical as Alma made out).

And when the wind finally peaked, in a powerful gust, he didn't say a word to interrupt her flow. He just took a deep breath, tilted his cloud to catch the wind, and rocketed down towards the city.

Whooping, he turned back to wave at Alma. He didn't know which was sweeter: flying a cloud, or the fact that Alma, for once, looked lost for words.

CHAPTER 9
FLIGHT

Wind stung his face, his ears and eyes. It blew cold and strong, knocking him back and forth, blurring his knuckles as they gripped the edge of the cloud.

Clouds seemed so gentle from afar, Luke thought, the way they glided silently through the air. But then again, most things looked straightforward from a distance. Up close, things were always more complicated.

He bit his lip, as the wind jostled him down. It buffeted the sides of his diamond, tearing its edges, speeding him past carriages and boats far below. He clung out of instinct, though he had a feeling he didn't need to, because even when he slipped, the cloud rose to meet him. It was still part of him. It knew his intentions. Like a magic carpet, it anticipated his every thought and move.

The wind lessened, then slowed to a breeze. He risked a peek over the side. The Houses of Parliament stood not far below, their bomb-proof steel domes reflecting the starlight. At the end of the domes rose Big Ben itself, lit green and ghostly, the only part of the old building that was still intact.

In the shadow of the tower, a varnished, ebony carriage pulled up, drawn by polished robot-horses. Luke had never seen them this close. In the east of London, since the oil shortage started, everyone used coal-power for buses and boats. He'd seen the odd private car, from the industrialist's guild, but a robot-horse carriage – that was something else. Only the wealthiest denizens travelled by robot-horse carriage.

The carriage door swung open and a lion-like man dressed in ermine stepped out. Luke recognised him from the papers he'd read years ago. It was the Grand High Lord Mayor. He ruled parliament and the guilds and had worked hard to reduce kidnapping across the city. He was one of the good ones, his dad always said.

The breeze picked up. He tilted the cloud and drifted east along the embankment. East? That was odd. Alma had said the wind wasn't blowing east. And where was she, anyway?

He glanced up at the clouds. There was no sign of her. In fact, the clouds looked darker, twisted. Unease rippled through him. Surely she would have caught up with him by now? But if the wind had changed, maybe she couldn't. The truth was that he had no idea how it worked.

Then he remembered her face, He'd expected annoyance, anger even, but she'd bitten her lip. Her shoulders had slumped. It came to him at once: she was sulking, that was it. She had to be. She'd be hoping he'd panic, so she could say 'I told you so'.

Well, he wouldn't. He'd be calm under pressure. She'd soon tire and join him. It was as she had said: he was a half-ghost, what could possibly go wrong?

He forced a smile and looked ahead. The smile turned to a grin. *That was more like it: the water markets of Waterloo Pier!* There were stalls on stilts, bright-painted houseboats, black rubber dinghies, and waxed canvas rafts, with thin makeshift bridges connecting one to another. Paper lanterns and re-election posters hung from strings overhead, while sellers screamed and sang about their wares, from beetroots to badger pelts and beyond. His dad had never let him come to the markets, too dangerous he'd said, but Ravi had grown up here, in his parents' emporium. He'd told them so many stories; Luke felt he knew the place.

He lowered himself down, until his mist brushed the tarpaulin roof of a stall on stilts. Some looked up at his foggy, low-hanging kite-cloud, but they were far too busy to notice anything unusual.

'Ma.' A grubby kid pulled her mum's arm. 'That cloud looks like a kite.'

'Shut it, you half-wit. Can't you see I'm talking to Reggie?'

He had to get closer to the action somehow.

Below his cloud was a series of flagpoles, topped by damp Union Jacks. The poles protruded from the stall rooftops and strings of lanterns ran from one pole to another. Luke leapt off his cloud and reached for a pole. His hazy hand slipped at first, then instinctively, it adjusted, becoming more defined. His grip held. With a whoop, he slid down, landing gently on the tarp roof below.

He tried to slip further, through the roof to the market, but nothing happened. It made sense, when he thought about it. The tarp was waterproof, so his water couldn't pass through. That's why Alma had to leave through the vents, she couldn't walk through walls like ghosts did in the stories. And it was probably for the best – if ghosts slipped through everything, they'd fall right through the floor.

He looked out from the rooftop: he could see it all. A pickpocket here. A policeman there. All hailing, haggling and exchanging money. The smell of roast chicken and caramel-apples. The place buzzed with life.

He peered across the sea of flagpoles for Ravi's emporium – he had said it was red, and two stories tall, but even here, below the mist, he couldn't make it out.

Then for a moment, he saw Ravi. Standing on a tattered, red lifeboat, at the end of the embankment. He was selling incense – not that anyone was buying. The face turned, and it wasn't Ravi at all, just a girl with long hair who looked quite like him. She had a white streak in her ponytail and shadowed eyes.

Then she was gone, obscured by a vast, steel riverboat with a great, glass dome. It pulled up to the pier, sending heavy waves that toppled goods on the smaller stalls. It was one of the new smog-sucking riverboats that Jess had mentioned. It was a magnificent thing.

He heard a shout from above.

'Pull up! Now!' He looked up. It was Alma, hurtling down through the sky, her eyes dark and wide with concern.

What was it now? But before he could reply, a churning metal sound flooded his ears. He looked round towards it. At the back of the riverboat, huge blue-black turbines were gearing into action.

They gleamed wet under the lanterns like a hundred black knives, slicing slowly through the air.

Then from the blades, a new wind started. Slow and strong, it pulled at Luke's kite-cloud – his magic carpet – which moved towards the blades with a mind of its own. Luke tried to pull back and felt something entirely unexpected: pain. The sting of pulled hair, a papercut finger, then a burning sensation down the whole edge of his cloud.

Luke slid towards the black, whirling propellers. It didn't take a detective, Luke thought, to know that this was bad news.

CHAPTER 10
BLADES

Luke watched the blades spinning, pulling his cloud closer. He tried to breathe slower and block the pain from his mind. He had to think logically. What had Alma said? During the safety briefing he hadn't listened to . . .

'Got it!' he shouted, to nobody but himself. 'My soul has bonded with the water. The water's in the cloud. The cloud is being sucked towards razor-sharp turbines . . .'

Would his soul get sucked up? Or chopped by the turbines into a thousand pieces? Either way, he knew it would not end well if the turbines got him. There had to be something he could do.

He had made that kite-cloud by relaxing – it had come from inside him – so maybe the reverse would do the trick.

He took a deep breath and did the opposite of relaxing. He tensed every thought and cell in his body. There was a moment of excruciating nothing, then he felt it working. The mist thinned in the air and the droplets of water came back into him. His hands grew clearer and his feet stood solid on the canvas stall roof.

The relief was short-lived. The riverboat's suction grew stronger, and a moment later, his feet slid across the roof. His whole body was being pulled now. He grabbed the flagpole in the nick of time – concentrating hard so his fingers didn't slip through. Yet the wind still picked up. The flag above the pole flapped loudly. The strings attached to it bounced up and down, jangling the lanterns hanging off them.

Then the flagpole shuddered and he lost his footing entirely. The wind flipped him horizontal into the air; it was only his grip on the flagpole that stopped him from flying away.

'Hold on!' shouted Alma.

She was high above, careening towards him. At the last minute, she changed course, cutting across the wind towards a string of lanterns trailing from Luke's flagpole. She grabbed the string with such force that it snapped clean off the neighbouring tent. There were gasps from below, as the string of lanterns lifted up into the air.

'What are you doing?'

'Trust me!' She climbed along the string of lanterns towards Luke. 'Snap yours off too.'

He didn't need to be told twice. He pulled himself up to the top of the pole and yanked at where the string attached. Nothing happened. He didn't have the momentum that Alma had had. The string was thin but tough.

Then Alma was next to him, tugging at it too. He turned to her. 'Now's the moment when you remind me that ghosts can't die.'

Alma yelled over the howling wind. 'There are worst things than death. Your soul could be torn ten ways by a storm. Trapped in a pipe for a hundred years. Eaten alive by a sniffing ghoul, or worse still, the smog.'

Luke gulped and focused on the task at hand. They counted to three, and pulled in time, but it still wouldn't move. On the third attempt, the whirring grew stronger and his hands began to slip. He couldn't hold on much longer.

And then he saw it. The string was attached to the pole with a larks head knot. The same knot he used on his kite at home.

His fingers moved quickly. He pulled the string hard towards the pole, tugged at the loop, and mercifully, it loosened. He pushed it up and slipped it right off the top of the pole.

From then it was a blur. The string flew through the air, a tumble of lanterns in front, with Luke and Alma trailing behind.

'Get ready,' she shouted.

They zoomed toward the boat, clutching the string, spinning as they went, lanterns flicking and rattling over market stalls. Close up, the boat propellers were even larger than he'd thought. Closer still, and he could see their razor-sharp edges. The initials 'M.I.' engraved just above them. Where had he seen those initials before?

Then suddenly, he didn't want to look any more, for fear that the look would be his last – and it was at that very moment that Alma shouted, 'Let go!'

It all happened in an instant. String and lanterns met iron propeller, with a scream of metal, paper and wood. The propellers juddered and the string jolted, sending Alma and Luke flying high into the air over the river.

Alma's cloud filled out beneath them as they caught a breeze and flew higher. He watched the jammed propellers shrink in the distance. When they finally restarted, spitting out chunks of chewed up wood and metal, they looked so small that they barely seemed a threat.

What had he been thinking? He wanted to apologise to Alma, but she hadn't looked at him once since they'd escaped. She kept her eye on the horizon, steering the cloud, zigzagging west, back towards Battersea. Her dark hair flicked in the breeze behind her.

Down below, the north bank of the Thames passed by: Westminster, Victoria Tower Gardens, and the office blocks of Millbank. It was so light and alive there while, just across the river, stood the ruins of the south bank and the abandoned shell of St Thomas's Hospital, lit only by the fires of squatters and gangs. Somewhere behind it was the Deadzone itself and the Old Channel Tunnel. Not even the lights of squatters shone there.

Soon, Battersea Power Station reared up over the river and they drifted over the fortified walls of the compound. Alma brought them to a stop at the foot of the second chimney. She stepped off her cloud onto the roof and began pacing back and forth along a gutter. She looked up at Luke, eyes blazing. 'You . . . You . . . ignorant, ungrateful, horrid boy. I trusted you.' Her voice was hard

– a brittle kind of hard, like at any moment, it might shatter into a thousand pieces. 'If the Ghost Council find out what just happened, they might fire me!'

'I'm sorry, I just—'

'Just what? I mean, what in the skies were you thinking?'

She stared at him, daring him to speak. Luke shifted awkwardly. He had a feeling that whatever he said, she would bite his head off. 'I'm sorry. I didn't mean to fly off. I just thought you'd catch up sooner.'

She put her hands on her hips. 'So it's my fault then?'

'No! It's mine. But you asked what I was thinking, so . . .'

'It's an expression. I didn't really want to know. I wanted you to grovel.'

Luke sighed. This was the problem with people: they never said what they meant. He'd hoped dead ones might be less complicated – apparently not. She glared at him from the ledge. If he grovelled, would that help? Or had that been another expression?

A pigeon saved him. It fluttered down to the ledge below Alma, cooing gently. Her face softened. She reached down towards it. 'People call them the rats of the sky. But they're gentle really.'

Luke watched her coax the pigeon closer. It moved its neck in jerks, left and right, then hopped onto her hand. She stroked it. 'People are the real rats.'

Luke wondered if she did really think that? Life must be awfully lonely for her if she did.

He risked a step off his cloud, onto the ledge next to her. Now her anger had faded, she looked fainter, frayed.

'The truth is, I missed my family.' He waited a moment. She didn't look up. 'They feel so close out here. When you said I couldn't see them, I guess I kind of lost it.'

Alma sighed and sat down, dangling her feet over the edge.

He took a step closer. 'You mentioned the Ghost Council . . . I can apologise to them, if you want. What are they, anyway?'

'The rule-makers, obviously. Or did you think we were savages?' Her eyes flashed, but a burst of pigeon cooing softened them again. 'They guard the boundary between the living and the dead. I've just been elected. Though most of them aren't fans of half-ghosts, especially ones who trash markets.'

She gestured to Luke to sit down. He did, and she passed the pigeon to him. It was warm and soft in his hands. The breeze picked up, sending a feather dancing off to the east. East towards his home. That was strange, he thought, just like on the embankment. A horrible thought grew in his mind.

'Alma, did you lie? You said the wind wasn't blowing east.'

'Well . . .' She bit her lip. 'Technically, I wasn't lying, you see the wind was blowing west, *up there*. The direction depends on the altitude – it's a little known fact . . . 'She chanced a wink; Luke didn't smile.

'You lied.' Luke gripped the ledge till his fingers hurt. He could have seen his family after all. 'Why would you lie about something like that?'

She slumped – he had a feeling this was the closest he'd get to an apology. 'It's not the wind that's the problem, it's council rules. Ghosts can't interfere in the matters of the living. You're a half-ghost, so it's fine. But your family? No, it's out of the question.'

'But I only wanted to *see* them. I wouldn't have interfered.'

'That's what they always say, and it always goes wrong.' She shook her head. 'And if you break that rule, then it'd all be over. You'd never see your family again.'

Luke kicked the underside of the ledge in frustration. It didn't feel the same, he decided, if your foot went right through it. 'Couldn't you have given me a choice?'

Alma's cloud darkened. 'Look, that's enough. Don't try to blame me. You've been sitting underground for two years, doing nothing, and then I take you out for one night and—'

'Nothing? I've been shovelling!'

'Same difference. You've been waiting. Waiting for someone to pat you on the head, give you an amber sticker and set you free.'

'It's a ticket, not a sticker.'

'But have you even tried to escape?'

Luke looked down at the pigeon. It squirmed in his hands. He stroked it once more, then let it go. It fluttered away north, gliding between the station's chimneys. Three intact, rising high into the sky, the other emerging from the edge of the East Wing – cracked in half, charred-black and glistening.

'If I tried to escape, I'd end up like that chimney.'

'You're just scared.'

Luke stood up from the ledge. 'There's nothing wrong with being scared. Have you seen this place? It's a fortress. There are bars on the windows, guards everywhere, and if Tabatha found out . . .' He didn't dare think what she might do. 'The amber tickets are the only way out.'

'Then how, may I ask, did we get out?'

Luke paused. 'The ventilation shafts, I guess.' Luke surveyed the plant. The vents peppered its walls, high in the air. 'But there are none at ground level. It's regulation, I think. I can't just fly down like you.'

Alma smiled. She walked to the other end of the ledge, lay down and pointed down to the blackened base of the East Wing. 'Something tells me Tabatha is not a stickler for regulation.'

Luke crouched and peered down. Hidden behind a row of bushes, in the East Wing wall, were a set of monstrous, black, ground-level vents.

Alma turned to him. 'They're new, and they only open sometimes, but I bet you could wedge them open. Then make a run for it.'

Luke's throat felt dry. A vent, at ground-level? And a big one too – it'd be easy enough to squeeze through.

And yet why did he suddenly wish he'd never seen it?

Dizziness rushed over him. He pulled away from the edge, shuffling until his back rested firmly against the wall. In the distance, he saw his pigeon flying into the skyline. A yellow-gold haze rose off the buildings and into the night.

He was a shoveller, not an escapist. He wasn't cut out

for adventures. Especially not in the East Wing, after what he'd seen.

'Alma, there was something strange in the East Wing. Jess said it was smog, but it was *strange* . . .'

'Smog, inside?' Alma's eyes narrowed. 'What kind of strange?'

'It was a stinking, misty thing with tentacles. It tried to grab us.' Luke swallowed. 'And when the thing got me – I saw my mum.' Luke stopped for a moment. He didn't like to think about it. 'And as you know, she's . . .'

Alma nodded. He didn't need to explain. Her eyes took on a distant look. 'Now *that* is strange.' She looked up at the clouds moving through the sky. 'The smog is practically enemy number one, and if it's changing, that's serious. It might explain the recent disappearances. I need to get you to the Ghost Council, they'll want to know. Maybe I could strike you a deal.' She trailed off, and the colour drained from her face, her eyes fixed to the east of the plant.

What was it? Luke followed her gaze. There, drifting over the Deadzone, was the sniffing snake-cloud. Blending into the overcast sky, only its quivering tail gave it away. Its eyeless face stared right at Luke.

He shivered. 'I saw it earlier, in the oversky. Though it looks bigger now.'

'It's a cloudghoul. It must have tracked your scent.' Alma stood up and scoured the sky. 'They come from the End Place; they clean up the skies, especially of ghosts who outstay their welcome. And they love a half-ghost. You're practically a delicacy.'

A delicacy? That didn't sound good. Luke looked back at the thing. Was it him, or had its jaw widened a little?

Alma pulled him up, her lips tight. 'Right, change of plan. Let's get you back to that sewer. I'll come back in a few days with ideas on the smog.'

Luke's heart leapt. 'There's a next time?'

'Only if you promise to stop waiting for stickers.' Alma winked. 'Check out those vents. Use that detective brain of yours.'

'I told you, I'm not a detective yet. I'm twelve years old.'

'Then you're halfway to being one.' She glanced behind her at the ghoul in the distance. It was closer now, and an eerie moaning could be heard on the breeze. 'I'll come back when it's not overcast. Ghouls rarely hunt then.'

'Wait, can't you help? How will I know which vents to try?'

'After your stunt in the market, I'll be in enough trouble as it is.' She tried to ruffle his hair, but Luke pulled away. 'You'll be fine, Luke, you'll just need to *improvise* a little. You're a half-ghost, remember, so *feel* the rain.'

'*Feel* the rain? What does that even mean?'

'You'll figure it out.'

And before he could reply, Alma took his hand in hers, and everything went grey.

CHAPTER 11
THE PLAN

Luke stared up at the dripping pipes of the sewage room. Nothing seemed to have changed: the brass lanterns still flickered, the door remained shut and the fat metal pipes crisscrossed the room.

But in another way, everything had changed: he had seen the sun. The sky. And he was a half-ghost, whatever that was. But most important of all were the vents Alma had shown him.

A way out of the plant. A way home.

Something burned inside him, bright and hot. Something he hadn't felt for the longest time: a feeling of hope.

He had to tell Jess.

He leapt to his feet and stopped. The floor had squeaked, not squelched. He looked down. The layer of sewage had gone and the floor gleamed clean under his feet. It wasn't only the floor. Pipes sparkled, water dripped clear and even Jess – still snoring loudly – had regained the blonde in her now sewage-free hair.

It was Alma's doing, he knew at once.

There was a grunt to his right. Jess sat up, bleary-eyed.

'I had the worst dream,' she croaked. 'I was at the front of the line throwing coal in the fire. First my eyebrows burnt off. Then the top of my hair. And then one by one my teeth caught fire! It was—'

She stopped and looked around. She rubbed her eyes. Then grinned at Luke.

'You cleaned it!' She jumped up and gave him a hug. 'You're a hero! How did you do it? Did you get any sleep?'

Luke didn't like to lie, so he shrugged his shoulders. Jess didn't notice – she was bouncing around the room, stroking the pipes.

'It's all so *nice*,' she squealed. 'It's like morning dew. It's like summer rain. Even the air *smells* different. It's like you opened a window.'

Luke knew what she meant; there was something fresh in the air, and inside him too. Seeing Alma and the sky, if only for an hour, had changed him. He was a half-ghost now.

Now, what had Alma said about vents? He didn't know the first thing about them, though he had an idea who might. At that very moment, she was sticking her tongue out and catching drops of pipe water on it. 'Jess, do you know much about vents?'

She licked her lips. 'Vents, oh yes, they're a plumbing staple. Are you thinking about getting into plumbing? You're an excellent wiper – I could put in a good word.'

'Actually, I think I'm going to be a detective, it's just—'

'Oh, I can imagine detective Luke – standing in the rain: big pale coat and a wide brown hat. Inspector . . . Inspector what?'

'Inspector Smith-Sharma.'

Jess blinked. 'Sharma? Oh, I wouldn't have guessed you were . . .'

'Half-Indian, on my mum's side, I just came out pretty white. I'm tanned normally, but down here you wouldn't know it.' *Half-Indian. Half-detective. Half-ghost.* Sometimes, Luke wished he could be one thing properly. He wouldn't have to explain himself half as much.

'Inspector Smith-Sharma, I like it. Rolls off the tongue.' Jess nodded, emphatically. 'So will you sit the guild exams?'

'What? Down here?'

'All you need is mystery, and there are plenty of those. Like the smog in the corridor. Or how they kidnap us children and never get caught? And even plumbing mysteries – like that incinerator.'

Jess's eyes lit up. 'You know, that machine *is* a mystery. Terence said it was a burner, but the tubes look all wrong?'

Luke jumped down from the pipe with a thud – nothing like Alma's leap – but it got Jess's attention. 'There's another plumbing mystery, which I'd like to hire you for first.'

'You, hire me?' She grinned. 'Fire away.'

'I need you to find the way into the vents.'

'The ventilation shafts?' Jess pursed her lips. 'Why would we want to do that?'

'Because that's how we're going to get out.'

Jess's jaw dropped, but before she could speak, the screech of metal on metal cut through the air. The heavy steel doors slid open a fraction and Terence's greasy chuckle slithered through the crack.

'Given up yet, you warts?' His smirking face peeked through the gap, but on seeing the room, he snivelled. 'It . . . it's so clean.' His face paled under the grease, clearly shocked. 'I-I-I've never managed to get it this clean.'

'It's all in the wrist,' Luke said.

Terence frantically inspected the room: the pipes, the walls and every inch of the floor. 'But you've only been in here five hours. You're not even dirty. You should be covered in sewage. You should be full of despair. Your hands should be red raw!'

'Five hours?' Suddenly, even Jess looked perplexed. 'I thought I'd slept all night.' She scratched her head, then froze. 'My hair – it's so fluffy, so straight!' Her eyes narrowed at Luke. 'Wait a minute, you washed it?'

But before she could speak, Terence was beside them, lifting them up by their necks. 'Not a word to Tabatha,' he growled. 'Otherwise she'll have me keep it like this.'

Terence dropped them to the floor, then grabbed them by the hair. He dragged them all the way back, along the stinking, black and white zigzagged corridor, round corners and down the stairs, to the dormitory entrance, where the snores of hundreds of children could be heard.

'Not a word!' he hissed, then loped away.

Jess touched her hair where Terence had yanked it: it was oily now and stuck up again. She chewed her cheek in thought, looking at Luke.

'Four hundred pipes in five hours? That just isn't possible. Luke, what's going on?'

'Err . . . can we discuss it later? In the canteen, maybe, it's more private there.'

'I can wait.' She nodded. 'But not for too long. Especially not on the hair. I've tried every shampoo and never got it that straight.'

And with that, she skipped off to her side of the dormitory. Luke sighed, then walked back to his. Ravi lay on the bottom bunk, snoring gently. He climbed up the ladder, as quietly as he could, then squeezed onto his mattress.

His eyelids felt heavier than bags of coal. The flying, investigating, and lying had exhausted him. Seizing the day, it seemed, was more tiring than expected.

CHAPTER 12
COMING CLEAN

In the dusty darkness, bunkbeds stretched out as far as the eye could see. Blinking red lights lined the gaps between bunks, pulsing dimly through Luke's closed lids. Guttural snores from the guard, Fat Elvis, scratched through the air and into his ears. But the worst thing about the dorm was the heat. The dorm was adjacent to the furnace room: the heat seeped through the wall and hung heavy in the air. It was a miracle, really, that they slept at all. That night, however, was the worst he'd had yet. The thoughts swirled round like a storm in his head. A ghostcloud and a half-ghost? Smog in the East Wing and a ghoul in the sky? And what about the girl in the market who looked like Ravi? There were too many mysteries; he didn't know where to start. Even simple ones terrified him, like finding a way into the vents or telling Jess about the pipes. So much for sleeping on it, he thought. His courage had evaporated in the hot dark of the day.

'Stop thinking so loud,' Ravi grunted from below.

'I didn't say anything.'

'You're a wriggler. Your mattress squeaks when you worry, which is most days, but today it's so bad that I can barely hear Elvis.'

A phlegmy snort burst from where the guard slept, and Ravi's head popped up over the top of the ladder. He squinted at Luke through the darkness. 'You got off lightly from Tabatha. I thought you'd at least be missing a finger.'

Ravi loved to complain. About the heat, the food or the stink of the toilets – you name it, he didn't like it. But Luke liked him. When Luke arrived in the station, Ravi had shown him the ropes. How to hold his shovel, how to sneak extra helpings of gruel and to grease the coalsack to stop it rubbing your skin raw.

'Did blondie make it?'

'Yeah. She's smarter than she looks.'

'That's not difficult.' Ravi pointed a coal-stained fingernail at Luke. 'And you, for the record, are dumber than you look. What were you thinking sticking up for her like that? You're not a hero. You're a worker, a worrier, a survivor. You'll have lost yourself hundreds of points.'

He was right, Luke thought. Tabatha took everything into consideration when dishing out points: walking quietly was good, breathing loudly was bad. Snitching was excellent, solidarity was terrible. And throwing a shovel of coal dust right in the boss's face? That was off the chart.

'After your heroics, she ignored us altogether and gave the tickets to some kids in another line. But I'm still in the running for next week.' A rare smile crossed Ravi's face. 'Odds are 3:1 that it's me.'

'And me?'

Elvis snorted again. Ravi shook his head. 'If you keep your head down? I'd say a year, or six months if you're lucky.'

Luke's heart sank. He couldn't wait that long. Especially not without Ravi. But he didn't doubt it for a second. Ravi's intel from the guards was rarely off and he was a whizz with numbers. Though the children's points were kept secret, Ravi kept a running tab of scores in his head. Eight times out of ten, he guessed the ticket-winner right.

'Chin up, mate. You'll get there in the end. And when you're out, I'll be waiting.' He twiddled a loose strand from his sackcloth. 'My mum will cook you a proper feast, you know.

Any friend of mine is family to her.'

'Sounds nice,' said Luke. 'Though anything but gruel seems nice right now.'

'And remember, if the detective stuff doesn't work out, you can come work with me. I'd sort the numbers and you'd sort the customers. They'd trust you, I know it. And one day, we could even set up shop somewhere. A nice little one of Spitalfields Row.'

'Careful, mate, you sound almost hopeful.'

Ravi shook his head. 'It's not hope, its ambition. One gets you killed, the other gets you out.'

Luke smiled. He felt so much better having a friend here. And without Ravi's help, he'd never have made it this long. Ravi's loyalty was so fierce, it scared him sometimes.

Fat Elvis's snoring stopped, then was followed by a splutter of coughing and wheezing. Luke froze and gestured to Ravi to get down.

Ravi didn't budge. 'He's not waking up. He's like clockwork: wakes every hour, does a quick patrol, and then back to sleep.' Ravi looked at his watch. 'He's not due up for another fifteen. Which reminds me – what was it that was keeping you up?'

The events of last night flooded back to Luke's mind. He

wanted to tell, but what could he say? That he'd seen a ghost? That she'd promised a way out? It seemed ridiculous now.

'Nothing really. Amber tickets, the usual stuff.'

Ravi nodded sympathetically, then tapped his forehead. 'It's a head game, Lukey. No more dreaming or heroics. It doesn't end well. Hard work is the only way out of this place. You've got to take it one shovel at a time.'

In the distance, footsteps rumbled. Another dormitory was ending their shift. Luke lifted his head and peered around. Children were stirring. Some slipped into their overalls, covered in a thin sheen of sweat.

'And so it begins,' Ravi grumbled. 'They're lining up early. They're so *eager* – makes me positively queasy. Come on, let's get to the canteen before the best gruel is gone.'

The canteen was an ugly, sterile place. Long, white, plastic tables lined the room and squeaked horribly against plates. Low, purple strip-lighting buzzed relentlessly, casting an unpleasant glow on the whites of their eyes. The whole place stank of a minty disinfectant; it was like eating lunch in a dentist's chair. A lunch of gruel: grey, lumpy, slimy gruel.

No matter how many times Luke ate it, he never got used to it. He wondered whether it'd even be hot today, as Jess hurtled towards them.

Ravi glared at Luke. 'You invited Jess?'

'No, of course not.' Then he remembered the pipes. If he turned Jess away, she might confront him, right now, in front of all these people. 'But let's give her a chance. She's not that bad really.'

It was too late, in any case.

'So, guys –' Jess beamed, joining the line. 'I was thinking about that incinerator, and guess what?'

Luke and Ravi said nothing.

'It's not just an incinerator – it's a dehumidifier too!'

'Fascinating.' Ravi yawned.

'I know, right?'

Luke picked up three metal trays, stained with rust, and passed them down. Ravi didn't look pleased, but Luke still remembered what it was like to be new.

He turned to Jess. 'What's a dehumidifier?'

Jess prattled on about the features of dehumidifiers and incinerators. Ravi rolled his eyes and Luke's gaze wandered. At the counter, a girl with an eye-patch ladled out gruel to a bunch of kids from another dormitory. One of them – a tall, fair, curly-haired boy – caught Luke's eye. Luke quickly turned back as Jess finished her explanation.

'And that's the difference between a dehumidifier and an incinerator.'

'So enlightening.' Ravi drummed his fingers on his tray. 'Now let's talk about anything else.'

'Not yet.' Luke picked up the cutlery and passed it along. 'Terence runs facilities, he'd know the difference between an incinerator and a dehumidifier. Why would he lie about something dull like that?'

Jess almost dropped her spoon. 'It's not *dull*! It's *enlightening*. Even Ravi said so.'

She looked to Ravi, but he was looking up, to where the curly-haired boy towered over them.

Luke tightened his grip and took a step back.

Ravi took two.

Before Luke could stop her, Jess stuck out her hand. 'Pleased to meet you, I'm Jess.'

Faster than lightning, the boy whacked Jess's tray up hard into her face. There was a crunching sound, then the tray fell with a clang to the floor, leaving Jess holding her nose, gasping. The boy looked at Luke. 'It's rude to stare at your superiors, scum.' Then he walked away in plain sight of the guards.

'What a jerk!' Ravi hissed. 'He got an amber ticket yesterday. Thinks he runs the place now.'

Luke put his hand on Jess's arm. 'You OK?'

She shook his hand off, then sucked some blood off her lip. 'I'm fine. It's just my lip.' A drop of blood fell from her nose. 'Can't we do something about it?'

Luke shrugged. 'He'll be gone by tonight, it's hardly worth it. They get a fancy dinner, go to the clinic, then it's back to their family.'

'A clinic . . . what for?'

Ravi tapped his temple. 'Tabatha puts a tracker implant in, to make sure they don't talk. And if they do, BOOM! Or so they say.'

Jess swallowed. Another drop of blood landed on her tray; Ravi wiped it off. 'I'll tell you what, though,' Ravi whispered. 'When I'm out, if he ever sets foot in my emporium, I'll push him overboard.'

'That's sweet.' Jess grinned. 'Though I'm not sure he deserves to drown, quite yet.'

'He deserves worse, right, Luke?'

But Luke was only half-listening. He was remembering the girl on the raft in the market. Should he ask Ravi about it? Maybe it was a way into telling them about the ghost. 'What's it like, your emporium?'

Ravi's eyes brightened. 'Rajendra's Emporium – it's one of the biggest houseboats in the market. My dad runs the first floor, my mum the second, and my sister and sell stuff from the roof when it's busy.'

Luke smiled with relief. Ravi's boat sounded nothing like the tattered raft that he'd seen. Though the girl had looked quite a bit like Ravi. *Could* it have been his sister? But if it was, what had happened to Ravi's parents?

No, he told himself, it was just a coincidence.

They collected their gruel in silence. They found a table in the corner – Ravi and Luke's usual spot. The purple light was softer there, and it was far from the guards, so safer to speak.

Luke's heart beat faster. Now was the time to tell them, but he still didn't have a clue what say. If he mentioned the word ghost, they'd think he was crazy.

He wished he was louder, better at making himself heard.

His sister Lizzy had understood. She'd always step in when he got stuck on his words.

'What's up with you, Luke?' Ravi asked. 'Your hands are shaking.'

'And you look kind of pale,' chipped in Jess.

'I'm fine. It's nothing.'

Jess raised her finger. 'Hey, weren't you going to tell me your plan to escape?'

'Shh!' hissed Ravi. 'Never say the E word.'

Luke shook his head. 'There's no plan. It was a joke. It's nothing really.'

Ravi looked at Jess knowingly. 'He gets like this sometimes: stuck in his head.' His voice softened. 'Luke, mate, spit it out. We don't bite.'

Luke looked down at his spoon. It was easier that way. It was like Alma said, he'd just have to improvise, one word at a time.

He took a deep breath. 'I need to tell you something, about what happened last night. What really happened.'

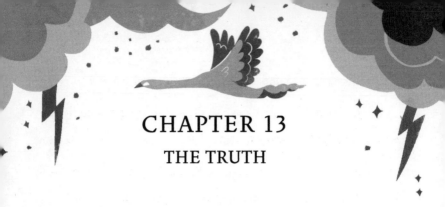

CHAPTER 13
THE TRUTH

Luke explained it as fast as he could, staring at his gruel. He missed out the girl on the raft – he didn't want to worry Ravi, when it was probably nothing – but the rest of it was there, from Alma, to the boat, and the ghoul and back. And most of all, Alma's tip-off: the vents in the East Wing and the way out of the plant.

When he'd finished, he looked up. Their faces were unreadable. The silence was unbearable. If they didn't believe him, he didn't know what he'd do.

'So what do you think?'

Ravi and Jess looked at each other, then spoke at once.

'It all makes sense,' said Jess.

'It makes no sense,' said Ravi. He looked at Jess, incredulous. 'Ghosts don't exist. Let alone half-ghosts and ghostclouds.'

'Then how did Luke wipe the whole room clean in hours?'

'There has to be a million other possible explanations.'

'Think of one,' said Jess, staring him down.

Ravi relished a challenge. 'OK, maybe he rerouted a water pipe and hosed the place down.'

Jess shifted in her seat. 'OK, that's not bad. I probably should have tried that. But Luke's not a plumber. He wouldn't know how.'

There was another problem, Luke realised. One his dad would have spotted. 'What about *motive*, Ravi? Why on earth would I lie? You know me, I don't make things up. I keep my head down. Exploring vents is hardly my cup of tea.'

Ravi leant back in his chair, and sighed, defeated. 'I know. That's the problem. It doesn't make any sense.' He leant in and inspected Luke. 'Your eyes are bloodshot. Did you breathe that smog in? Maybe you hallucinated . . .' He looked at the two of them and shrugged. 'OK. I don't know. But let's assume you're right, for a moment, why would I even care? What difference does it make?'

Luke leant forward. 'Because we've found a way to escape!'

Ravi's gritted his teeth and looked behind him. 'I told you. Never, ever, use the E word.'

But just saying the word made Luke feel braver. He had

tasted freedom, up there in sky. He couldn't let it slip away from him again.

Luke cleared his tray and on it, in gruel, drew an outline of the building. 'The ventilation goes everywhere. We need to follow it to the East Wing and check the rooms on this side. When we find those big vents, we make a break for it at midnight, when the guards change over.'

Ravi shook his head. 'I can't believe we're even talking about this. This is real life, Luke. We're not playing detectives. If they find you trying to escape, you're dead. Does your ghost-girl even get that? How do you know she doesn't want you dead?'

'If she wanted me dead, she wouldn't have saved my life. I trust her, all right.'

Ravi fiddled with his cutlery. 'Can the vents even carry your weight?'

'Yep.' Jess nodded. 'Maybe not that curly-haired giant over there, but none of us are that big. I'll warn you, though, it's slow work and there are miles of shafts. It could take months.'

Luke sat back. 'But we'll find them in the end, if we keep at it.'

'You need to find a way in first,' said Ravi. 'Every room has a guard. They'd spot you the moment you went near a vent.'

Luke's stomach felt heavy. This was the problem he'd grappled with all night. The sewage room had been unguarded, but they wouldn't get back there anytime soon.

Ravi folded his arms, evidently pleased that he'd found an obstacle.

Jess waved her hands over Luke's gruel map. 'There must be somewhere unguarded.'

'Nope,' said Ravi. 'It's one of Tabatha's rules. A guard for each room.'

There had to be a way. Luke tried to think. But with both of them staring, it was impossible to concentrate.

Ravi picked up his tray. 'Well, that solves it. We stick to plan A: amber tickets. It's tried and tested . . . and much less likely to get you killed.'

'He needs time, Ravi,' Jess said. 'His dad's a detective. He'll solve it.'

They both looked at Luke, who looked in turn at the gruel-streaked map. Jess stifled a yawn.

'Look,' Ravi said. 'Even Miss Sunshine's bored now. Come on Luke, let's go.'

Jess bridled. 'I'm not bored. It's that stupid guard in the dorm.

He snores non-stop. I hardly slept at all.'

That's it, Luke thought. He looked up from his tray. 'There is a guard in every room, but they're not all awake.' He had their attention again, except this time he didn't mind. 'Fat Elvis naps like clockwork, right, Ravi? We'll sneak past him to the toilets, and make sure we're back before he wakes.'

Ravi scowled, then he shook his head, resigned. 'I'll help you with the prep, but I'm not coming with you.' He gestured to a tiny speck of gruel on the table. 'I'm *that* far away from an amber ticket, I can't risk it all on some crackpot idea.' He stood and walked off, calling back. 'And, for the record, I still don't believe in ghosts.'

Luke's sackcloth collar felt tight around his neck. He did everything with Ravi. Ravi was sharp, wary and knew the plant like the back of his hand. Could he do it without him?

Jess interrupted his thoughts. 'We'll win him round. Give him time.' She smiled, then pointed at the gruel map. 'We'll tackle a section each week. That's about two hundred metres. Pretty standard for ventilation work.'

And Luke knew, suddenly, that he'd be fine. Jess knew her stuff, and not only that – he felt hopeful with Jess, bolder too.

If he was going to crawl through vents, in the dead of night, a little courage was worth more than all Ravi's cleverness put together.

CHAPTER 14
VENTS

Luke lay on the hard mattress, listening to the drag of Fat Elvis's feet around the room. He'd spent the whole day dreaming of exploring the vents, but now it was upon him, all he could think about was getting caught.

Elvis's laboured breathing wheezed close and Luke felt a sudden urge to sit up and confess. Then the sound faded. Soon, the footsteps slowed, the guard's chair creaked, and the snoring began.

It was now or never. He pictured home: his grandma's visits in winter and her hot chicken curry; the flags on the waterways fluttering white, blue and red; his dad and Lizzy at the winch on the lock. This was his chance to see them again.

He slipped off the mattress and crept down the ladder.

Ravi's eyes were wide open. 'You're crazy.'

'Aren't we all?' Luke sat on the edge of Ravi's bed. 'You sure you won't come?'

'I'm getting my ticket any day now. I can't throw that away for some half-baked ghost-plan.' He paused and looked up. 'Sure you won't stay? You've shovelled for two years, what's another six months?'

'I'm still shovelling, I'm just keeping my options open.' Across the gloom of the dormitory, he saw a flash of blonde hair. Jess must be making her way to the meeting point. 'And let's face it, Jess is never going to get out by shovelling.'

'It's not your job to get her out.'

Something hot rose up in Luke's chest. Ravi could be so hard, sometimes. 'It's not my job to shovel either.' Luke stood up to leave. 'They force us do it. At least this is something I have choice about.'

'Wait.' Ravi reached into his pillowcase. 'I got you these.' He pulled out a screwdriver and a wristwatch. 'The watch lights up. It'll be dark in the vents.'

Luke touched the items in wonder, quietly humbled. 'These must have cost you a fortune.'

'I won't need my credit once I'm out. Now get lost – you've only got an hour, remember.'

Luke tucked the objects into his inside pocket and nodded

goodbye. Ravi turned away to sleep. 'Remember, if you're caught, you're on your own. I can't help you then.'

The dormitory was thick with darkness. A chink of light crept out from the toilet block, at the end of a long avenue of creaking beds. He stopped at the end of the line and watched the guard. Up close, Fat Elvis resembled a sea creature: there was something jelly-like about him. Sunk into his chair, he bulged outwards, each snore sending ripples across his body.

The only way was right past him. Luke stepped forward, then froze. One of Elvis's eyes was half-open. He stood for a moment, in full view of the eye, his heart racing.

Elvis didn't move.

Jess stuck her head out the door to the toilet block. 'I don't think he can see us,' Jess whispered. 'I knocked into his chair and he didn't even blink.'

Luke wasn't entirely reassured by this, but he followed her anyway.

The toilet block was dimly lit, with putrid green tiles from floor to ceiling. Tea-coloured damp stains dripped in the corners and black mould flecked the cubicle doors. Luke opened the third one. The toilet seat was up, the enamel discoloured and covered in hairline cracks. In the corner lived a colony of cockroaches, scurrying back and forth through a hole in the paint. It was the grimmest of the cubicles, and nobody ever went it. In other words, it was perfect.

Luke pointed at a wall panel with Ravi's screwdriver. 'I thought we'd start here.'

'You could.' Jess frowned. 'But it'd be messy. That's the septic tank. The ventilation shaft is here.'

'I told you I needed you.'

She grinned, took the screwdriver, and began to undo the rusty bolts.

Luke watched Jess with fascination. So clumsy in the furnace room, with a screwdriver she looked different. Poised, confident, even graceful. She unscrewed bolts rapidly and without sound. Even the ones caked in rust posed little resistance – whether an expert tap, shake or wriggle – she had them loose in moments. Within a minute, she lowered the panel carefully to the floor.

'Roll your sleeves over your hands,' she said. 'There might be sharp edges. The last thing you want down here is tetanus.'

She gave him a leg up and he squeezed into the vent. Jess followed and put the panel back in place, plunging them into darkness. A wave of nerves washed over Luke. He flicked on the watch, lighting the shaft with pale green light. 'Well, here goes nothing.'

They shuffled forward, on hands and knees, over smooth, warm sheets of metal. The sheets held their weight, as Jess had promised, though flexed more than he'd like. The issue was the noise: a slight flick of the elbow sent clangs reverberating down the shafts, to who knew what room. So, with utter concentration, they inched forward, at an excruciating pace. After a handful of minutes, Luke's whole body ached with the strain.

'I'll leave a scratch at each junction, so we know our way back.'

'How do know which turn to take?'

'We don't. But we'll learn.'

Fork after fork, junction after junction, vent after vent. Knee-stabbing, elbow-burning, back-cricking vents. The journey seemed endless. After an age, they saw slats of faint red light: they'd reached the first grate.

Luke pushed his eye to the metal and looked through the gaps. 'We're still above the dormitory.'

Jess sighed. 'Can we take a break? My back is killing me.'

'No, we push through. It always gets worse before it gets better.'

And it did, because finally, they found their rhythm. The pain subsided into a dull ache, and each time they peeked through a grate, their spirits rallied. Soon, they'd reached the canteen corridor and a fork in the shaft.

Luke checked Ravi's watch. 'Twenty-five minutes left.'

'Should we head back?'

'Let's go another five minutes, we're quicker now than before.'

'OK, boss,' said Jess. 'Left or right?'

He listened to the sounds of the plant in the dark. Mechanical whirrs. The skitter of hot water pipes. The distant laugh or snore of a guard. It all felt connected, like the nervous system of some giant animal, made of living, breathing parts.

'Wait. Did you hear that?'

'Hear what?'

'The rain.'

Luke couldn't quite explain it. He thought he'd heard it, but it was more than that. It was in his bones. Somewhere down the shaft he could feel it raining. Rain bouncing off a concrete floor. But how could it be raining inside the plant?

It had to mean there was an opening.

'Turn left.'

'I don't know, it's late.'

'We'll be quick.'

They crawled faster. Luke's knees stung and blood pooled in his face from the effort. He pushed aside the pain and focused on the rain. He could smell it now. It had to be a half-ghost thing, like Alma had said.

At the end of the shaft, they turned left, then right, getting closer each time. He ignored the urge to look at the watch.

'Look, over there!'

A grille lay ahead, spilling out blueish light. He heard the patter of rain. He tasted cool, evening air. The same air he'd tasted just the night before.

Jess unscrewed the bolts. 'Cross your fingers,' she whispered, as she removed the last screw. 'We could be out of here tonight.' She lowered herself down.

'What is it?'

Luke dropped down after her. The room was a cone with the top chopped off: wide and circular at the bottom, sloping up to a tiny opening, high above. Moonlight and rain fell through the opening, painting a glowing, wet circle in the room's centre.

But it was the room's edges that grabbed him. 'What on earth?'

The walls swarmed with cats. Cats of every colour, shape and size. Meowing, purring, pouncing and prowling, or draping themselves along steaming copper pipes.

Jess's eyes were wide. 'It's probably the hot water. Or shelter from the rain. There has to be a reason. Nobody comes to Battersea unless they have to.' Jess scanned the walls. 'And if the cats came in, there's got to be a way out.'

The rain stopped and the cats started moving, like a writhing fur carpet, towards the corner of the room – it had to be the opening. Then something rubbed at Luke's leg. A brown and white tomcat had its tattered collar caught on a nail. Luke unfastened it gently. 'There you go, buddy, you're a free man now.'

The cat gazed at Luke, then licked his hand with a rough-tickle tongue. Its ear was torn and its fur swirled in patterns.

'He's half-brown, half-white.' Luke grinned. 'Just like me.'

'He's gorgeous, that's what.' Jess stroked the cat's neck. It nuzzled her in return, then ran noiselessly off to join the others.

Jess looked after him, to the corner where the cats filed out, and her face crumpled. It was a pipe, painted green and covered in cat hair. A pipe barely the width of two fists.

'Well,' he said, 'it's a way out of sorts, but not one for us.'

Jess watched the last cats leave. Long seconds passed. Then she walked up to the pipe and kicked it. The clang reverberated round the room. Jess winced a little.

'Jess, are you OK?'

'No. Not yet.' This time, she ran up, and kicked harder. 'Ouch!' She cried, over an even louder clang, then began hopping about, muttering words he wouldn't have dreamt she'd have known.

She slumped to the floor, nursing her foot. 'Well, that feels better.'

'It doesn't look it.'

'Well, it does. This, at least, is a pain I can handle.' She looked at the pipe, with bitter eyes. 'That pipe. It's like ... It's like the opposite of a silver lining. Something that looks good, that's actually disappointing.'

'You know,' Luke said. 'I think that's quite common. Someone needs to invent a saying for that too.'

Luke sat down beside her. Rainwater seeped up through his sackcloth. They were quiet a moment.

'Well for a nice girl, you know a lot of bad words.'

'Plumber curses.' She tried to smile. 'They're even filthier than the sewer.' She rubbed at her foot. 'Luke?'

'Yeah?'

'No one's rescuing me, are they?'

Luke had to assume she meant her parents, but the way she asked it wasn't really a question.

'Why not?' she whispered. 'Why aren't they looking harder?'

'They're looking hard, I know it, but we're too well hidden. They'll never find us down here.'

'And we'll never find a way out. Not with pipes like that.'

He stood up, took her hand and pulled her to her feet. 'We will. It'll just take time. The vents in the East Wing were big enough, remember?'

Jess nodded. He looked at his watch. 'We'd really better get going.'

She glanced up at the opening. Now the rain had stopped, there was a twinkle of starlight. 'At least we found the sky. That's hopeful somehow.'

Luke knew what she meant, only too well. And without another word, they squeezed back into the shaft and crawled back to the dormitory.

CHAPTER 15
CHORES DAY

Tuesday was 'chores day'. It was an unlucky dip: you never knew what you'd get, but you knew it'd be bad. Like peeling potatoes till your fingers bled or bleaching the floors till fumes whitened your hair. Luke had done it all, and then he'd done it again, but today was different. After the long night in the vents, he'd hoped for a slow one, but Terence had something else in mind. He had woken the three of them early and, now with drowsy eyes, he, Jess and Ravi trailed Terence through the West Wing.

'The other kids will be rat-baiting,' said Terence. 'But after that stunt in the sewage room, I'm keeping an eye on you three. If any of you snitch, you'll end up in a ditch.'

'But sir,' Ravi said. 'I wasn't in the sewage room. I was shovelling, remember?'

'Quiet, Lalwani,' Terence spat. 'Smith-Sharma and you are joined at the hip. You'll have played your part.'

Ravi glared daggers at Terence, then turned to Jess. 'This is your fault,' he hissed. 'I'm being tarred with your brush. Luke and I were fine before you got here.'

'Ravi, come on. It's hardly her fault.'

But Jess hadn't heard. She was sniffing the air. 'Do you smell lavender, guys?' She looked around. 'It's quite popular these days in high-end toilets—'

'Stop talking about plumbing!' burst Ravi. 'You're a broken radiophone – plumbing's all we hear. And I'm sorry to break it to you, but I really don't care.'

Jess fell quiet and stared at a wall. An unremarkable one, Luke thought, all plaster, red-brick and rusted iron fittings. He'd been watching the walls the whole time they'd been walking – counting the vents, in case it helped with their search – but now he found himself watching Jess.

'You all right?' he asked. 'He doesn't mean it, you know. He's just worrying about his amber ticket.'

Her hands were in her sackcloth. 'No, it's not that. He just doesn't like me.'

'No. You're fine.' Ravi searched for words. 'But in moderation. Like broccoli, you know? Nice on occasion, but not every day.'

'Broccoli?' Jess said. 'What's wrong with broccoli? It's delicious. And good for you.'

'Guys,' Luke said. 'Look ahead.'

A maroon carpeted stairway rose before them, leading up to the fabled ground floor. He'd never been above ground in the station. They weren't normally allowed for fear of being spotted by the public or a passing inspector. Yet Terence climbed the stairs, and they followed behind, hushed and hopeful. Would he see daylight again? Would someone see *them* and save them?

'Don't worry,' Terence chuckled. 'We've drawn all the blinds and the doors don't open for a good few hours. You won't see nothing, and nothing will see you.'

He ushered them out onto a plush velvet landing, with high ceilings, wood panels and tall shuttered windows. From the shutter edges, a little dawn-glow seeped through. Muted as it was, it lightened Luke's thoughts.

He might be out there soon and back with his family. If they found the right vent, they'd be free like the light. Then he remembered. There had been hundreds of vents. It could take months, or years. He squashed his hopes down and shut the box tight.

Terence led them down a corridor to a black wooden door,

inlaid with amber. Perfume and tobacco hung heavy in the air.

'Tabatha's office.' He pushed open the door, revealing an immaculate study with marble walls, chandeliers and a huge black fireplace. 'It has all the trimmings: private bathroom; underfloor heating; a maharaja's desk; and of course, a fireplace that leads straight to the furnace. It's a long way down.' He gave a greasy wink, then droned on. 'You'll be replacing the bulbs with LED lights. More efficient, says Tabatha.'

Luke looked up at the chandeliers: hideous, hundred-bulb-headed monstrosities, dribbling gold and crystal, like leaky showers. In the corner lay a stepladder and boxes of bulbs. Luke stared.

'The ladder,' he said. 'It's nowhere near tall enough.'

Terence smiled. 'I know. What a shame. I suppose you'll have to make a human pyramid, or something. And if you fall, don't worry, I certainly won't catch you.'

And with that, Terence slumped into a chaise-longue to watch, chewing his filthy nails like one might chew popcorn.

Luke grabbed the splintering wooden ladder then moved it to the centre, under the largest chandelier. He climbed to the top. 'I'll be the base, and Ravi, you can stand on my shoulders. Jess, grab a bulb, and climb to the top.'

'I'm not having her climb me. Have you seen these sackcloths? It's indecent, and anyway, we're in the middle of an argument.'

'I don't know,' said Jess. 'It might be just what we need. Like a teamwork exercise, to build trust and all that.'

'Build trust? Or break legs?'

'Ravi,' Luke said. 'We don't have a choice.'

Muttering, Ravi climbed the ladder, followed by Luke. His weight sent Luke teetering, and the ladder groaned underneath him. Or was it Terence, groaning with glee? He couldn't be sure. He bent his legs deeper, steadying himself, even though it burned his thighs. He wouldn't give Terence the pleasure of seeing them fall.

'Jess, your turn.'

She flashed him a smile and quick as a mouse, she clambered up. Unlike Ravi, he barely felt her weight. She wasn't just light, she was nimble and balanced. Before he knew it, she was down again, opening another box.

'I've done this before,' she said mid-scramble, in the tone you might take between sips of tea. 'But I won't go on, in case I sound like broccoli.'

Within half an hour, they'd finished the first chandelier, and Jess dropped to the ground, tired but smiling. Luke's legs ached, Ravi looked sheepish, but Terence looked the worst. Disappointment snarled across his pointed face. His nails looked well and truly chewed.

'There are two more chandeliers,' he spat, getting to his feet, and walking over to the bathroom.

Ravi turned to Jess. 'I'm sorry about earlier. It's just that things were easier before. When it was only me and Luke.'

'I get it. I know.'

'And you really can't shovel, even after Luke's tips. That's a problem, you know. This bulb stuff is great, but it's not every day. It won't get us points.'

'Then you're lucky that I've got some tricks up my sleeve.'

'Tricks?' Luke asked. 'What tricks?'

'Shh!' Jess watched the door to the private bathroom with hawk-like attention. 'Wait for it.'

'Wait for what?'

A flush sounded from within, followed by a vicious sucking sound, and an ear-splitting howl. 'The toilet! It's got me!' Terence yelled from within.

Jess turned and winked. 'Hydraulic toilets – that's some serious suction. I fiddled with the settings while he waffled about furniture earlier.' She glanced to Tabatha's desk, with its folders of papers. 'That's information, right? Could we trade any of it, Ravi?'

Ravi's eyes greedily took in the desk. 'This is a goldmine.'

Terence whimpered and yowled from behind the door. 'It hurts! Oh it hurts!'

'I can help,' Jess shouted back. 'I'm a trained plumber. I'll break the lock!'

'But I'm not decent!' Terence fell into self-pitying sobs.

Luke looked at the desk. 'How long do we have?'

'I can release it whenever,' Jess said. 'Five minutes, maybe? Longer than that, and it might do some damage.'

Ravi rubbed his hands together. 'Then make it six.'

CHAPTER 16
CLAWS

It had been a productive few days.

While Terence had been stuck in the loo, Ravi had found (and memorised) the supply cupboard codes – he was now better stocked than ever and trading up a storm. As a result, he and Jess had become firm friends, and any mention of broccoli had long been forgotten. Terence, for his part, had been so grateful for his eventual release that he'd given the three of them the afternoon off.

Most important, however, was what Luke had found in the desk: an old maintenance map of the plant's ventilation. It was incomplete, but all the same, it would save them weeks, if not months, of exploring the vents.

They soon established a new routine. They ate their gruel, shovelled wearily, then lay awake listening for Fat Elvis's snores. They always went back to the cat room first – Jess insisted on it – she said the glimpse of the sky kept her going. Luke liked it too.

He liked to imagine his sister Lizzy was looking up at it, from their boat, in the east of the city. And then he'd think of Alma. He hadn't seen her since the night they first met. Was she up there right now? How did she spend her days? And when, if at all, would she come back to see him?

Then one day, in the cat room, the brown and white tomcat he'd rescued popped up. It scampered right up to him and purred at his feet. It even followed him back into the vent.

'Shoo!' Luke said. 'The guards will hear you.'

But he didn't make a sound. Not a meow, purr, or tap of his claws. It was as though he understood.

'We should call it Stealth,' said Jess.

So they did.

Each day they entered the vents, Luke's hope grew. They wouldn't solve it overnight, but if they kept ticking off rooms, they knew they'd find the East Wing eventually and the room with the vents – and the way out of the plant. He didn't mind waiting, so long as he saw his family at the end.

Luckily, thanks to the map, progress came faster than he'd hoped. The first day, they found the canteen, and peered at pots of fly-ridden gruel. With the canteen located, they mapped the corridors leading to it, the dormitories and finally the great furnace room. The latter looked creepier than ever by night, but proved useful, as its vents climbed high into the air, giving them access to the upper floors. The shafts even had climbing rungs inside.

'It's like they've left ladders for us,' Luke whispered, half expecting a trap.

'It's for the maintenance sweeps. We're lucky we're so small.'

On the day after finding the furnace room, they found themselves on a long, wide shaft – newly built. When they reached a grate, Luke peered through the slats onto black and white zigzags. 'It's the East Wing. I'd recognise those tiles a mile off.'

'That's weird,' said Jess. 'They've changed the ventilation. It ran behind the pictures before, not along the top of the corridor. This stuff is expensive.'

'Maybe they did it to get rid of the smog.'

At least, Luke hoped so, because Jess had already started unscrewing the grate. He leant back and prepared to hold his breath. He suddenly wondered if this was entirely wise.

Jess peeked down into the corridor.

'No sign of the stink!' Jess whispered, and Luke breathed again.

They proceeded down the new ventilation. It wasn't what Luke would spend money on, but it was much nicer to crawl in: it was sturdier, quieter and spacious by comparison. It was also perfect for exploring, because a branch ran off the main shaft into each room of the East Wing.

'There must be at least fifty rooms,' he said, a little daunted. 'I guess we go one at a time.'

The first were all storerooms: one for coal dust, food and unused sackcloths. One for light bulbs, gruel powder and cleaning products. By the ninth storeroom, which was full of shovels, Luke's head was aching, but something inside him spurred him on. For all he knew, the vents to the outside could be in the next room.

'Do you think I could switch mine for this?' Jess asked, holding a bright brass shovel. Stealth jumped up and down trying to grab it, without so much as a sound. 'I've always wanted a shiny one.'

Luke shook his head. 'Come on, Jess. We don't have much time.'

Jess yawned. 'Are you sure you saw these vents? Ground-level vents are pretty illegal.'

'100% sure. But they weren't on all the rooms.' He went down to the end of the storeroom. Maybe he'd sense rain through the outer wall? He placed his hand against it and felt nothing.

'Nothing, again. I guess the whole place is sealed.'

Jess put the spade carefully back on a rack. Nothing was out of place. Tabatha, it seemed, was frightfully organised.

'Okey-doke,' Jess said. 'If there's nothing here, let's move on.'

Stealth jumped up into the vent and Luke climbed after him. He flicked the watch light on, and noticed Stealth licking something. The letters M.I. were engraved in the vent, the same initials he'd seen on the boat.

'I think we better head back.' Jess called up, screwing the vent behind them. 'Elvis wakes up in twenty minutes.'

Luke nodded, but didn't turn. Stealth had stopped at the next fork along, his tail raised. Was he telling him something? Luke began crawling towards the cat.

'Seriously, Luke, Elvis will wake soon.'

A few more feet, that was all. He'd check what the room was, and then he'd come back. 'Hold on, Jess, just a peek.'

He reached the cat, and suddenly, he felt it: the sensation of rain. But a fuzzier, darker rain than in the cat room. Rain against glass? Or was it steam? He couldn't quite picture it, but it was definitely coming from the next room along.

'Jess – I can feel it! The vents must be in here.'

Jess scrabbled behind him, cursing under her breath. He peered through the grate: a white-doored room lay below, glistening new amidst the decay of the East Wing. The door sign read 'Sick Bay'. But why would they need those huge vents in a sick bay?

There was only way to find out. They'd have to go inside. He looked down the shaft that led down into the room.

'Jess, come on, one more room, that's all.'

'No, we're going back. Stealth, you too.'

Stealth laid a paw towards Jess, then froze. His ears pricked up. The door below opened.

Click. Tap. Swish. Click.

Through the grate, Luke watched Tabatha step into the corridor. Her black-nailed hand clutched the talkometer.

'Yes, of course.' Her voice was dark glass. 'It's practically perfect for the effort with Europe.'

As Luke watched, he felt the blood drain from his face. If he could see her, surely she could see him? He shuffled back a few inches, as quiet as he could.

'Mm. Yes. But this smog is different. I've tested it thoroughly. But first I need your approval, for the third chimney repairs.'

Tabatha testing the smog? He looked to Jess – she gestured frantically at the watch. Were they out of time already? They couldn't move now. Tabatha was too close. He could make out the hairs on her black fur stole. And was that Terence behind her? One false move and she'd hear them.

'I promise you, when I'm done, your next campaign will be most generously funded.'

The pipe creaked under Luke. He pulled back to the shadows, just as Tabatha's head whipped up towards the grate.

'Mr Mayor, let me call you back.'

Luke stayed back out of sight, as quiet as he could, but his thoughts echoed loud. The mayor and Tabatha? It didn't make any sense. The mayor had cut down kidnapping. Or had he been working with her all along?

Tabatha broke the silence. 'Did you hear that, Terence?'

'It was the shaft, ma'am. They creak sometimes.'

'I saw something move. Inside the vent.'

'Ma'am, I think you'll find—'

Three sharp, black nails shot through the grille, stabbing and scraping viciously. They missed Luke's hand by a hair's breadth. Sweat dripped down his brow, but he didn't move.

'Screwdriver, Terence.'

'I'll go fetch one, ma'am.'

'You manage facilities. You should have one to hand, you half-wit!' She slapped him hard across his face. 'As always, I'll have to do this myself.'

Black nails reappeared beneath the grate, this time twisting instead of jabbing. Metallic squeaks reached Luke's ear. *Surely she couldn't be?* But she was. The screw nearest Luke was already moving anti-clockwise. She was unscrewing the grate with her nails! What were they made of – metal?

His sweat began dripping onto the metal of the shaft. He had an urge to wipe it. He looked to Jess – her mouth hung open. Only Stealth seemed relaxed. The cat moved closer to the vent, intrigued by the squeaks. His tail brushed Luke's arm.

'Throw me the screwdriver,' Luke mouthed.

Jess swallowed, then shook her head.

The first screw came out, and a moment later, the next screw began twisting. Once two screws were out, Tabatha could easily pull back the grate and look inside. Luke gestured again to Jess. She grimaced, took it in her right hand, then threw it towards him. He caught it an inch before it hit the side, then wedged it against the turning screw.

His heart thumped his ribs. He held the screwdriver firm. The screw tugged insistently but didn't budge.

Tabatha cursed from below. 'It's stuck.'

'It might be rusty, ma'am.'

'These are new. There's no rust yet. There's something there, I can feel it.'

A second later, a thin steel blade shot through the grate at an angle, an inch from where Stealth had stood. A dent, then another, appeared just shy of Luke's hand. He bit his lip to stop himself crying out.

'Ma'am – it's reinforced steel. A blade won't cut it.'

'Then fetch me my musket.'

'But this is brand new ventilation—'

'Fetch it now!'

The door creaked. Terence's footsteps faded into the neighbouring room. A plume of tobacco smoke seeped into the vent, stinging Luke's eyes and the back of his throat.

Click. Tap. Click. Tap.

Tabatha paced below. Far too close. With the smoke, Luke found it hard to breathe. He looked up at Jess.

'What do we do?' she mouthed.

Luke wasn't sure. Whatever Tabatha wanted with a musket, it couldn't be good. He tried to shoo Stealth away, but the cat insisted on nuzzling Luke's arm. It was the last thing he needed when he was trying to think.

If they moved, she'd hear them, and they could hardly outrun her, crawling in the shaft. Could they go back to the stockroom and lock themselves in? They wouldn't last long.

Then Terence was back.

'Here's your musket, ma'am. Let me load it for you.'

Luke's brain whirred ferociously. Could he attack first? Maybe the screwdriver would do it, then he'd grab the musket. No, that wouldn't work. They'd never open it in time. He wasn't thinking straight – and it didn't help that Stealth was now licking his fingers. Below, Tabatha and Terence bickered.

'Don't know how to load a musket?' Tabatha hissed. Terence was silent. 'Speak up, man, or has the cat got your tongue?'

The cat! Luke knew at once what to do. He looked at Stealth, and mouthed, 'I'm sorry.' Then he grabbed a whisker and pulled.

Stealth yowled, then ran away down the shaft, clattering claws along the metal.

There was a silence below.

'It was a cat, ma'am.'

'How insightful of you, Terence.'

'Thank you, Ms Tabatha.'

They heard the tap of nails, then a door opening below. 'Terence, I want these vents vermin free. Pump this shaft full of carbon monoxide. That should kill them off. In fact, do it daily, for the rest of this week. And double the perimeter guards, just in case.' There were two whirrs and a click. 'Mr Mayor, yes. Now, where were we?'

They heard the door slam shut and Tabatha's voice disappeared inside the sick bay. Terence grumbled. The drag of his feet faded down the corridor, deeper into the East Wing.

Luke breathed for the first time in an age. 'Doubling the guards? We'll never get past them.'

Jess's face was pale. 'It's the carbon monoxide that I'm worried about. We better start crawling.'

'What's carbon monoxide?'

'Bad news,' said Jess. 'Very bad news.'

CHAPTER 17
AN UNEXPECTED GUEST

They crawled in the darkness, as fast as they could, with the dim glow of the watch lighting the way. There wasn't time to crawl carefully, and soon his knees rubbed raw against the shafts' metal plates.

Luke sniffed the air. 'I can't smell any gas, so that's got to be a good sign?'

'Not really. You can't smell it. Or see it. But it kills you all the same.'

'It kills you?'

'Yep. Not even gas masks can stop it. Don't worry, though. You'll feel sleepy first. That's how it starts.'

'But I'm always sleepy.'

'Not like this.'

Jess stopped suddenly to check the way, and Luke crashed right into her. He noticed, even now, that her legs were still shaking. He checked his hands – steady as ever. The eye of the storm, his sister had called him. When things got bad, he just kept going.

The watch began flashing. 'We're done for, Luke.' That's Elvis's wake up.'

Luke shook his head. 'It's not over till it's over.'

He squeezed past Jess and led the way. They'd got so close to the East Wing vents, to the way back home, he couldn't give up now. Then he remembered.

'Jess – I forgot about Stealth! He ran the other way. Does the gas affect cats?'

'Don't know,' Jess said, though something in her voice made him think that she did. 'But one thing I do know is that cats are clever. They've nine lives and all that. He'll figure something out.'

An uneasiness settled in the pit of his stomach. If Stealth was gone, who would be next? There was no point finding an exit if it cost them their lives.

Then before he knew it, his aching hands touched the grate of cubicle three. He felt a rush of relief. Journeys always felt quicker on the way back.

He put his ear to the metal and listened for Elvis. Nothing obvious.

'He'll be patrolling, but he might not have seen our bunks. If we stagger our exit, we can say we'd been to the loo.' His voice sounded calm, but his heart thumped.

He lowered himself down. His foot touched the damp tiles, sending a startled cockroach scuttling. Jess landed next and screwed the vent shut. Opening the cubicle door, he stepped out into the block.

Something was wrong. It was far too quiet.

When Elvis walked, he wheezed, dragged his feet and tapped his club. But there was not a sound. Luke signalled to Jess to wait, then tiptoed round the corner. He peeked into the dormitory.

A thick, pearly mist hung in the air. It hovered over the crumpled form of Elvis, who lay on the floor not far from his chair.

Elvis wasn't snoring. He wasn't moving at all.

Luke stepped back into the toilet block, but to his horror, the mist followed him. It crept silently along the floor, wisping past his feet. Had the smog come to finish him off? Should he call out to warn Jess?

But the mist didn't surround him, it slipped right ahead, skimming over the floor towards cubicle three, where Jess was hiding. It stopped by the door and rose up to form a quivering pillar.

Then the mist did something strange: it chuckled. A muffled, though not unfriendly sound. One that sounded familiar. Then the pillar shimmered, cleared, and standing before him was none other than Alma. Luke laughed in relief.

She pulled a face. 'I've been waiting an hour – and I'm not used to waiting! A little scare was the least you deserved.'

'We must have just missed you. We've been busy investigating.'

Alma nodded with approval, then the cubicle door burst open and Jess stumbled out, stepping right through Alma. She waved her hand in front of her face. 'Why's it so foggy?' She looked around. 'And who are you talking to?'

Alma had returned to a plume of mist.

'Alma, can you show yourself? I've told her about you.'

Nothing happened. Jess raised an eyebrow.

'Alma, come on, you're making me look like an idiot!'

'Good!' came a voice. Finally the mist cleared. Alma stood there, hands on hips. 'I could get in trouble for this, you know. Only 'attuned' people, who know death, are meant to see us. Us ghosts like a little mystery.' She turned to Jess and, with a sigh, held out her hand. She seemed to think she was doing everyone a favour. 'Pleased to meet you, I'm sure. I'm glad to see you can speak. For a while, in the sewage room, I worried that all you did was snore.'

The jibe slipped off Jess like water off rubber and her face lit up with a giddy grin. 'I *knew* it! I always knew there were ghosts. Can I ask, is there a heaven?'

'Can it wait?' Luke asked. He was acutely aware that they were out of their bunks, having narrowly escaped Tabatha. It didn't seem the right time to discuss the afterlife. He turned to Alma. 'What's happened to Elvis? He isn't moving.'

Alma shrugged. 'Don't worry, he's only sleeping. I just cleared his sinuses; his snoring was terrible. No wonder he kept waking up every hour.' She cocked her head as if listening. 'There's a boy coming. Running in fact. I can feel it in the mist. Dark skin, glasses, straight black hair.'

'Does he look grumpy?' Luke asked.

'Yes, but kind of cute.'

'He is, isn't he?' Jess sighed. 'But he's not into girls.'

'The cute ones never are. Shall I knock him out then?'

Luke shook his head. 'No, he's one of us.'

Ravi rushed round the corner, clutching some gas masks. He saw Alma and stopped. 'What's going on? I thought the smog had got in.' He looked at his masks, a little sheepish. 'Temporary trade with a kid in another dorm. Thought they might come in handy.'

Luke smiled. Gas masks weren't cheap, even for Ravi. 'Ravi, this is Alma. The ghost I mentioned.'

Ravi's face soured. 'Ghosts *actually* exist?' He looked ready to kick a cubicle, then thought better of it. He walked up to Alma, with some trepidation, and stuck out his hand. 'I'm Ravi. Though I can't say I'm pleased to meet you. You've lost me a bet and almost got my friend killed, and he only met you the other day.'

Alma didn't reach out her hand. 'He's quite the charmer. Are you sure I can't zap him?'

'Yes, quite sure.'

'*Boring*.'

Ravi shuffled awkwardly. 'Where were you guys, anyway? I never can sleep when you're out. And when you didn't come back . . .'

'It's a long story,' started Jess. 'We saw Tabatha. And she had knife. And a musket. And nails like screwdrivers. And then there was carbon monoxide—'

'Knives *and* a musket?' Alma's face fell. 'You're meant to be sensible, Luke. I wouldn't have shown you the vents if I'd known you'd be reckless.'

'He wasn't.' Jess beamed. 'He was as cool as a cucumber. He jammed the vent shut and pulled out a whisker . . .'

'A whisker?' said Ravi, looking lost.

Luke felt a little sick thinking of Stealth. 'We handled it, Alma. And we found the vents, which means we're almost home.'

Home. Just saying the word was enough. He could see it in his mind. The houseboat creaking in the water. His dad's arms outstretched. And a hug that didn't end till his arms ached. But then he remembered.

'There's a problem, though – the perimeter guards. Tabatha said she's doubling them. We'll never get past them alone.'

'Doubling, really?' Alma's gaze drifted to the corner, where a pair of cockroaches watched, antennae twitching. 'Then we'll need *their* help.' Her mist darkened. 'I can't interfere without the Ghost Council on board. Though it might come at a price.'

Luke thought for a moment. 'It won't hurt to meet them. If we don't like their offer, then we don't have to take it.'

Jess leant in. 'It'll be an adventure.'

'But adventures are fun,' Alma said. 'This is more like a quest. I feel almost responsible.'

'You *are* responsible,' Ravi said. 'Luke's my friend. You'd better keep him safe.'

Alma sniffed. 'Nobody's safe, Ravi. Not down here, or up

there.' She straightened her sleeves. 'But I promise you I'll try. All right, let's do this.'

And with that, Alma marched off towards the dorm, dragging Luke behind her. A moment later, they stood at the foot of the bunk. 'I'll zap you in bed, then it'll look like you're sleeping.'

Luke climbed the ladder. He wasn't sure he liked the sound of zapping. 'Can't I try it myself?'

'Well, you're a half-ghost, so technically yes.' She frowned. 'When you die, a hole opens in your soul – a hole to the ghostrealm.' She touched his chest, just above his heart. 'Most people fill it with love, but down here there's so little that the bonds have weakened. The wound's reopened.' She shrugged. 'That's why you could hear me, and travel with me.'

Luke didn't like the idea of a wound in his soul, but it explained a lot. 'My dad said I was always looking at the sky. Like I was searching for something.'

'That makes sense,' Alma said. 'That's the pull of the End Place. Or heaven, as you call it. If you die, even for a moment, it knows. And now a strand of the End Place is pulling you up. It wants you back.' She looked at him. 'To travel solo, you'd need to follow that pull.'

'Follow it? How?'

She bit her lip. 'Open the wound further. Push the living from your mind, think of the sky, and death, and let the End Place pull your soul from your body.' She shook her head. 'But it's risky. It can pull you too far, if you let it. And then, there's the problem of getting you back.'

Opening the wound? It didn't sound pleasant. But in his experience, important things rarely were. 'So how do you get back?'

Alma looked at her watch. 'Look, how about I show you next time? It's tricky, and I don't want to miss the council.'

She was right, he thought. If the Ghost Council could get them out past the guards, then he couldn't risk missing them.

'Sure, next time.' He felt a little relieved. 'Just zap me gently.'

Alma gave a mock salute. He squeezed into his bed. There was a crackle of blue, the smell of rain, and then everything went white.

CHAPTER 18
THE HEATH

Feathers. White, wet and soft. He seemed to be lying face down in feathers.

He sank in his hands, pushed up and looked around: he was lying on the back of Alma's swancloud. Alma stood on its neck, her black curls blowing in the breeze. He got to his feet and peered over the edge. Not far below, the black Thames shimmered. Its surface rippled with Battersea's lights, like some swirling, liquid, stained glass window.

'Why are we flying so low?'

'Because of that.' Alma nodded upwards.

Above them, strewn across the sky, were mottled ghostclouds of all shapes and sizes: shimmering fish and ghostly cavalry; monstrous insects and miniscule monsters; jagged clouds, fluffy clouds, dark clouds and light clouds. They moved back and forth in an elaborate dance.

'There are no ghouls, at least, but the sky's too frisky. Frolicking, merging, that kind of thing. You could start off a swan and end up a snapdragon.' She brushed down her waistcoat. 'I'd be worried about getting you back in your body.'

Luke nodded. That ranked relatively high on his priorities. He looked up and frowned. A horsecloud and fishcloud combined into a merhorse.

'Isn't that confusing?'

'Not really. You lifers have a phrase for it too. When you hang out with someone, they "rub off on you", right? We're just a bit more literal.'

'Oh, I see.' Though he wasn't sure that he did.

'Don't worry. It'll make sense when you've met a few of us.'

Alma tilted the swan and caught a slow breeze north. They flew low over the wedding cake mansions of Pimlico, home to politicians and wealthy city workers.

'So where are the Ghost Council anyway?'

'They sit on Parliament Hill, that's where they make the rules. It's on the Heath, you know it?'

Luke knew it well. It was the biggest park in London and overlooked the city. He'd flown his kites there on the weekend with his dad. If tonight went well, maybe he'd fly them there again soon.

Alma turned back to Luke. 'They'll want to hear first-hand about the smog in the East Wing, and in return, they should help you get out of the plant.' She frowned at him clinging onto her swan. 'Now get your own cloud, you're cramping my style.'

It was easier the second time. He relaxed, and thought of his home and family. With a tingling breath, his kitecloud unfurled beneath him, next to Alma's swan. He rode his kite alongside her, peering down at the buildings. Soon the grey of the city gave way to splashes of green. The houses grew taller and the gardens longer. Trees sprouted on both sides of the road, their dark green boughs neatly trimmed, casting angled shadows on the street below.

'There are an awful lot of cafés here.'

'There's an awful lot of money. It's the north of the city, what do you expect?'

Below him walked a well-dressed couple in furs.

It was all so wasteful. He shovelled all day to power the city and they squandered it on streetlights for their evening strolls.

'I don't get it. There's an energy crisis, don't they feel bad?'

'Good question.' Alma grinned. 'There's only one way to find out.'

'What, ask them?'

'No, silly. Rain on them, of course. Come on, it's the best!'

Luke raised an eyebrow. He couldn't see how raining would make any difference, but before he could speak – as was often the case – Alma had already started. 'So the principle is this. People are mostly made of water, and so are clouds. When those waters connect, so do our thoughts.'

'Our thoughts connect? So I'll know what they're thinking?'

Alma nodded. 'We call it "reading", though it's more like painting, really. You'll see. Now think of rain. Imagine great big drops of it.'

Luke did as she said. Normally, he remembered London on a sunny day. Now, he thought of the wet ones. The days stuck inside, face pressed against the window, watching droplets trickle down the pane. He thought of the day they'd got drenched on the way to the park, and his dad had insisted he sit by the fire once they got home to warm up. And of the day they kidnapped him, in the pouring rain and blinding smog.

And sure enough Luke felt it coming. The droplets tingled

inside him. They clumped into fat, round drops that splattered and splashed and bounced within his kitecloud. Then all of a sudden, they started to fall.

It was the strangest feeling. He was everywhere at once, as if he'd split himself into a thousand pieces. As his raindrops fell to the street, he felt every one of them. He felt the moonlight refracting inside them, and the finely dressed lady zooming towards him. And then, when the drops hit her skin, an extraordinary thing happened: parts of his cloud glimmered with light.

'What on earth?'

'Just watch.'

Fine sprays of mist burst up all around him, on top of his cloud, shimmering and dancing with silver-white light. Then the white light refracted into a rainbow of colours. He looked closer. It wasn't a rainbow, but images, drifting in and out of focus. Images of the woman.

Of her rushing round Harrods, trying to pick the right dress. Stopping in a hallway and faking a smile. Standing in a party but looking at the door.

'They're her thoughts, her memories,' Alma said. 'At least the ones front of mind.'

Luke watched, captivated. Her life was so different: expensive shops, houses, and glittering dresses. He hadn't realised that people really lived like that. Her feelings, however, were more than familiar.

'She feels trapped,' he said. 'But why? She has everything.'

'We make our own traps,' said Alma. 'People, possessions, they hem you in. That's why I keep to myself. I'm freer that way.'

Luke knew what she meant, he thought, but it was only half-true. The right kind of people could free you from yourself. Jess made him feel braver. Ravi helped him stay focused. But as he searched for the words, the images faded.

Luke looked down at the street. It was empty, she was gone. 'What happened to that lady?'

'Oh, she's fine. Probably drying off in a café somewhere. It only lasts for as long as the water touches the skin.' She looked to the horizon. 'And it's good timing, anyway, because we're almost there.'

Luke looked ahead. The streetlights stopped abruptly a few streets away, before iron railings and a set of huge, black gates, topped by curling spikes with gold tipped points. Behind the gate, shrouded in mist and shadows, rose the ancient hills of Hampstead Heath.

CHAPTER 19
THE GHOST COUNCIL

Alma lowered her cloud to the ground and, with a deep intake of breath, absorbed it back into her. She gestured for Luke to follow suit, before hastening down a path into the park.

The Heath after dark was not the one he knew. His footsteps fell silent on the gravel below. Earth, trees and leaves were shades of ink upon shadow. The benches glistened wet and black and empty. And there was not a soul there: no kids playing tag, no lovers on the green; no picnics, ice creams or barking dogs. Even the pigeons were absent. It was quiet, still and entirely strange.

But it still brought back memories. 'Lizzy and I built a den over there, and I cut my hand here.' They passed an upturned oak tree, its branches stretched on the grass like fingers. 'I remember that too. We used to sit there and eat our sandwiches.'

Luke looked up towards Alma. She'd almost turned the corner.

'Alma, wait up!'

'Nope, can't be late. These guys are important.'

Luke just hoped what he'd seen in the East Wing was worth the council's time.

'So what does the council do anyway?'

'All sorts, really. We keep watch for the smog, storms, pollution, and so on. Ensure the waters are safe and the rules are observed. We keep the balance with the End Place, so the ghouls stay away and us ghosts can roam free, for the time that we're here.'

They walked down path after path, past thorn-dark thickets and dark-soil clearings, before the view opened up onto a vast, black lake. A tiny wooden pier crept out into the middle, with a cabin on the bank. Alma kicked some leaves. 'People swim here in the day, even in winter, but at night it's ours.'

Alma crouched down by the lake and thrust her hand under the surface. She nodded to Luke to do the same.

'He never rushes. We might as well grab a drink while we're waiting.'

'A drink?' Luke looked at the black water. It wasn't the kind of thing he'd drink normally. Then again, nothing was normal these days. He crouched down and copied Alma, dipping his hands in the lake.

His hands dissolved into strands of mist. They tingled all over, then spread out across the surface of the lake like roots. And all at once, he sensed the water. He tasted its ripples, pondweed and foam. And he could feel something else – droplets from the lake streaming up his arm.

His arm, half submerged, grew more opaque. He could feel the pressure of the water growing inside him, pushing outwards to fill more space. He felt stronger – bolder, even.

'Not so fast,' she said, 'that's enough for now.'

'But it feels good.'

'Sure, it feels good, but do you feel yourself?'

What kind of question was that? Then his arm jerked and bulged of its own accord. He pulled it out of the water.

'Clouds aren't steady,' said Alma. 'People are more fixed – you're a tall or short person, dark or pale, old or young. Ghostclouds aren't like that. We change all the time. The water you've taken – do you know where it's from? Do you trust it? Do you want it to outweigh your own?'

Luke looked at the ripples in the water below. They seemed darker than before.

A clapping interrupted his thoughts. It came from within

the mist.

'Wise words,' spoke a deep, sing-song voice, 'from a foolhardy ghost.'

Alma opened her mouth, then closed it, lips pursed.

The voice continued. 'Who rushes without thinking and gets stuck in human machines.'

Alma bridled. 'Sal, I told you. It was that strange new metal with a watertight seal. There was no way I could have known—'

'– a ghost who should know better than to travel down pipes. Or to let a half-ghost loose on a market.'

Alma blushed pink-grey as the lake mist cleared. There, lying on the water, was a man with sunken cheeks and a rotting top hat. His arms were emaciated, skin pearly-grey, and eyes open and white. His mouth moved, 'Don't think we didn't notice, Alma. We see everything.'

'Not underground you don't.' Alma stared down into the lifeless eyes. 'You're lucky I found him. You can't see inside the plant, or where the ghosts are going missing. Now please, stop trying to spook him and introduce yourself properly.'

The whole lake seemed to sigh, then the head of the man lifted out of the water, at an unnatural angle. The body followed, rising to a lopsided standing position on the lake's surface. The image shimmered, transforming into that of a thin-faced, old man in a brown top hat and tails. He smiled genteelly and offered Luke his hand. 'Is this better?' he asked in his sing-song voice. 'My name is Methuselah. But you can call me Sal.'

Luke took the hand. The man shook it weakly but didn't let go. 'Alma tells me you have something to show me?' His hand squeezed tighter. 'May I see?'

Luke looked to Alma.

Alma nodded. 'Sal's a reader. One of the best in the realm. And he can show the others what you saw.'

'What others?'

The water bubbled, and rising from it came a handful of figures, some faded, some bright, in a circle around them. Luke made out a few in the gloom: a priest with fierce, electric-blue eyes; a smiling old-lady in a thick winter coat, and a black-beaked plague doctor with a cloak and top hat.

Alma gestured around. 'We've stormbreakers and mistmakers, healers and hailers, blizzardhearts and blue-skies. They're all here to see you.'

'May I?' Sal asked again, gripping Luke's hand.

Luke nodded.

The old man smiled, his eyes glowed and a crackle of sparks jumped from his hand. A burning pain shot up Luke's arm. He bit his tongue so as not to cry out.

Sal smiled wider, till the tips of his grin almost met his eyes. Then all at once, the surface of the lake burst into life. The black erupted in a haze of colours and, in the mist rising off it, the East Wing appeared. He saw the zigzag tiles moving under his feet, a hazy Terence loping ahead, and then there, further along, as though it was right there with them, was the shivering, sickening mist, glowing green-grey and hungry. Luke's heart beat fast, and he took a step back, but Sal held tight, even though the mist's hungry tentacles were already creeping towards him, wrapping around his leg. The stench of death filled his nose and then . . .

The old man let go, and the image vanished.

Luke's chest heaved. Alma rushed to his side and helped him sit on the water's surface. 'It was only an image. It can't hurt you, not really.'

It had felt so real. He looked at the surface of the lake again – it was a black mirror now. No trace remained of what he'd seen.

Sal stroked the breast of his suit, nodding in thought, while the other ghosts watched. 'Interesting, indeed.' He turned to them all and flashed his hard, white teeth. 'It looks to me like a tortured soul.'

Others in the group nodded.

'A what?' Luke asked.

He tapped his temple. 'A ghost who's half-dead, who has suffered so much that they've lost themselves, even their shape.' He adjusted his top hat. 'If the house a ghost haunts is burnt down, for example, that might do it.'

'What about my mother?'

Sal laughed darkly. 'It's only an image of her. These things are hungry – they latch onto the darkness they can find in your soul. Whatever makes you feel the pain like they do.'

Alma stepped closer. 'He heard Tabatha say she was testing the smog. It's obvious she's trying to meddle in the peace treaty with Europe. She could cause a war.'

'Meddling indeed, but how?' said the old man, his eyes glassy. 'Remind me, what is it that you want in return for all this?'

'Permission to interfere. They've found a vent out of the plant. I need to mist up the compound and knock out a few guards so they can make a break for it.'

Half a smile crossed Sal's lips. 'That's your plan?'

'Well, I might help them across the Southern Slums too, but then they'll be home.'

A murmur passed around the ring of councillors. Snaps of blue leapt back and forth on the water. Sal nodded twice, then gestured for silence. He looked directly at Luke.

'So you're running away.'

Alma pouted. 'I saw it more as a *daring escape*. But in any case, there's nothing wrong with them running away.'

'Of course not, if it works.' A fly landed on the old man's jacket. He flicked it away and turned to Luke. 'Does Tabatha strike you as someone who leaves loose ends? If she lets you escape, what would the other children think?'

'I don't know.' Luke bit his thumb. 'She's so busy all the time and there are thousands of kids. Why would she bother to track me down? I'm not even sure she knows my name.'

Sal raised an eyebrow. 'I'd wager she knows a lot more than that. People like her are thorough. They have to be.'

Luke remembered the store rooms. Everything had a place; everything was counted. 'Even if she did try to find me, my dad's a detective – we could go into hiding.'

'I thought you wanted to be free?' Sal leant closer. 'You've spent two years underground, don't you deserve better?'

Luke wanted things to be like before. To be back in his boat, safe with his sister and dad, not watching his back like a fugitive. 'Of course I do, but I don't see how it's possible.'

The old man looked down. The fly had returned and settled on his collar. He watched it for a moment, then crushed it between his fingers. 'To be truly free, you'll need to stop her.'

'Stop her? How? I'm just a kid.'

'I've suspected the power station for some time. The smog is thickest there and too many ghosts have gone missing. But having conferred with my colleagues, we cannot interfere on a hunch, nor a snippet of conversation.' He flicked the remains of the fly into the water. 'We need more evidence.'

'What kind of evidence?'

'Conclusive evidence linking Tabatha Margate to the smog. Now, all you have is hearsay. We need to catch her red-handed.' He drummed his bony fingers against his chin. 'So my offer is this: be my eye-witness. Get into her lab and see exactly what she's doing with the smog, and you'll have your freedom.'

Luke's throat felt dry. 'Nobody even knows where her lab is.'

Sal shrugged. 'I never said it'd be easy. But if you find it, the council will stop her permanently.' The old man smiled. *'Find the lab, find your freedom* – it's as simple as that.'

Alma shook her head. 'It's too dangerous. Getting that kind of evidence could get him killed. Surely there's another way?'

Sal shivered. His image blurred and diverged into two separate figures: a younger version of himself and a pale-faced woman. She was faint but there. She took his hand with sorrowful eyes, then whispered into his ear.

He paused, shook his head, and the woman vanished. He turned back to Alma, his eyes narrowed.

'No. That's my final offer.'

'But he'd be better off shovelling for an amber ticket!'

'Tell me, will his friend Jess be able to shovel her way out?' The old man waved a hand dismissively. 'Half-ghost, you can visit the places we can't. You have a chance to stop the smog that's killing our city. Would you walk away?' He looked down at his nails. 'And may I remind you that there are far worse things than dying. Like living with regret. Betraying your friends. Disappointing your father.'

Alma's eyes blazed. 'Stop it, Sal, with your weasel words. They work on the others, but they won't work on me.' She took Luke's hand. 'We're leaving, we'll think of something else.'

'Half-ghost. Half-coward. Wholly disappointing.' Sal shrugged and turned away. 'The offer still stands. Find the lab, find your freedom.' He walked back across the lake, though his voice seemed to come from its very surface. 'But I suppose you'll go and chase your "amber tickets". Tickets to where, I wonder . . .'

Alma and Luke stood on the bank and watched him slip into the darkness, and the other councillors fade. Alma threw a pebble into the water. 'He wants you to do all the dirty work. It's safer that way – he's afraid of losing his grip on the council.' She threw another pebble, harder this time. 'He's a creepy, old coward. Ghost politicians always are.'

Living ones weren't any better, Luke thought, but the councillor's words echoed in his head. 'Can they really stop her?'

'Of course they *can*. A lightning bolt normally does the trick. The question is *will* they?' Alma bit at a nail. 'He's clever, you see. It doesn't matter to him if you die trying, because he'll get the intel from you anyway, once you're a ghost.'

Luke kicked a stone; it sank into the water. It wasn't fair. He just wanted to get home.

'Alma, you know, he was right about one thing. Jess will never get out from shovelling alone.'

Alma stepped onto her swan-cloud. 'At the end of the day, Luke, there's only one life you can save, and that's your own.'

The wings of her swan fanned out and a gust carried her up higher over the lake. Luke gazed into the water; his reflection rippled dark on its surface. He stepped onto his kite-cloud and drifted up after Alma.

CHAPTER 20
HALFWAY TO HEAVEN

They rose from the lake on a current of hot air, past insects and beetles flitting by the bushes, squirrels and pigeons sleeping in the treetops, and the rooftops and steeples at the edge of the Heath, until they reached the cloud line.

The words of the councillor swilled in Luke's head. Finding the lab was crazy. Surely there had to be another way? They'd almost found the vent – he had felt the rain through the walls of the sick bay. He just needed to go back, wedge it open and run for his life. But with Tabatha on his tail, would he ever stop running?

'Keep going higher,' Alma said. 'There's a strong south wind further up.'

He pushed his thoughts aside and tugged at the rough-fluff fabric of his kite. He tilted upwards and followed Alma higher, to where the air became thin, cold and light. Though the sky seemed busy from the ground, at this height it cleared and Luke made out new clouds high above – flatter clouds which moved white, grey and bluish through the starlit sky.

'Altostratus,' said Alma. 'There are three layers of clouds – that's the middle one. Above you get cirrus.' The sheet-clouds were close now. Alma scanned the sky. 'And a little bit higher and we should have our—'

The wind caught them both at once, shoving them south and not letting up. His cloud plunged at first, but with an effort, he wrenched it back in line with Alma's. It was only then he noticed his hands. 'What's going on? My hands are sparkling.'

'Ice crystals. It's always colder up high.' She gestured to the sky. 'I love it up here. It's so empty and calm. It's halfway to heaven. No grumpy old weasel ghosts telling me what to do.'

Luke felt small. There was so much space. Even the clouds kept their distance. The thin bright air snapped at his edges, trying to stretch him out flat like an altostratus.

'What happens if you go higher?'

'After a point, nobody returns. The air's so thin, you get stretched out for miles and your water becomes ice. It's the way to the End Place, they say.'

He peered up at the shimmer of cirrus clouds, so far from

the smoke and hustle of the city. 'You know what I keep thinking?' He tore off some cloudfluff and scrunched it wet in his hands. 'That I wish the smog-thing *had* been my mum. Then at least she would have seen me. She never did when she was alive.'

'How do you know she's not watching you, from up there, right now?'

Luke looked up at the cirrus clouds high above. Could she be watching? He felt a pang of envy. It'd be simpler up there. No more danger or struggle, and definitely no shovelling. But it wasn't the same. He wanted her here by his side. It reminded him of something.

'Alma, who was that lady on the lake? The one watching Sal. She was only there for a moment.'

'His sister, I think. They died together in the war and their spirits mixed.' Alma sighed. 'It's a pity he ignored her – she's the kind one.'

'They mixed?' Luke scratched his head. 'So is he a guy, or a girl?'

'Does it matter?' She shrugged. 'Things aren't black and white for us ghosts, they're usually more grey. You're half your mum, half your dad. You've a bit of Jess, and a bit of Ravi. We're all mixed, in the end, if you don't overthink it.'

Luke frowned. Sometimes ghost matters made his head hurt.

A burst of birdsong interrupted his thoughts, and Luke looked over the edge of his cloud. Far beneath them stood the dark green lawns of Regent's Park. At this time of night, they hung still and silent, except for the creep of wandering cats. At the top of the park stood a complex, filled with wires and nets.

Alma had leapt to the edge of her cloud. 'It's the bird enclosure of London Zoo. I love it down there. Aside from pigeons, they're the only birds left in the city.' She cupped her hands over her mouth and cooed. It echoed through the sky. A moment later, another burst of song erupted skywards. 'If you go low, the parakeets fly right through you. It tickles. The only thing better is Battersea Dog and Cats home.' Alma smiled. 'Maybe next time.'

Next time? Luke's spirits rose. Now he'd tasted the sky, he wasn't sure how he'd cope without it.

In the distance, the four chimneys of Battersea Power station reared up. Alma turned back, pleased with herself. 'We've made good time. Not a ghoul in sight.'

The sky around Battersea swelled purple and bright, the air fresh, despite the plumes of smoke rising from the chimneys.

The streetlights glowed dimly, the roads were quiet. A little slum boy sat at the riverboat stop, his fishing rod dangling into the misty Thames.

Alma looked around. 'You know, at times, this place is quite picturesque.' She lowered her cloud and stepped off onto the outer wall of the plant. Luke joined her and they sat watching the river: the little boy fishing, the billowing, pale chimney-smoke rising over them, and into the sky.

'Alma, what on earth am I going to do now?'

'It's obvious, isn't it? You ignore that meddling councillor and start shovelling your heart out.'

'But we've almost found the vents, couldn't you help us a bit, knock out a few guards and all that?'

'Without permission? No way. They wouldn't just fire me, they'd drag me straight to the End Place for breaking the rules. I'd end up as ice crystals.' Alma shook her head. 'It's too dangerous, Luke.' She patted his hand. 'I'll visit you, sure, but it's back to plan A: you shovel, and that's it.'

They sat there, at a stalemate. The smoke from the chimneys had crisscrossed above them. The little boy by the river waited patiently for that elusive fish. He'd be waiting a long time, Luke thought, with a river that dirty.

'If it's that's dangerous, Alma, why were you in the plant in the first place?'

She blushed. 'It was an accident. I was floating along, and I got sucked—'

'Rubbish. I've seen you fly, you're in complete control.'

She fiddled with the top button of her waistcoat. 'OK. It sounds stupid, really, but I was looking for my death.'

'Your death?'

'Yeah. I died around here, it's my "haunt", so to speak. I never gave much thought to it, but then, one by one, my friends found out their deaths, and ran off to the End Place.' She took out her glasses from her pocket and held them in her hand. 'I guess I got curious.'

'I don't get it. You don't remember how you died?'

'Ridiculous, right? But it's common, actually. If your death was sudden, or unpleasant, the soul blocks it out to protect you. And over time, memories fade.' She folded and unfolded the glasses in her hand. 'But it's no big deal. It was just a phase. I'm over it now.'

'Then what *do* you remember?'

'Nothing, really. I've just a sense that my life wasn't much fun. Lots of rules, I think. That's why I'm so desperate for adventure,' Alma said, her voice quiet. 'But I'm over it, remember? Who cares where you come from, what matters is now.'

'I guess.' Luke found himself watching the river. It didn't look right, but he couldn't put his finger on why. 'But still, you must have found something. Some kind of clue.'

Alma shrugged. 'Well, I checked all the buildings round here – the dogs and cats home, town hall, slums and so on – but there are barely any records. They all got destroyed in the war.'

Luke was only half-listening. It wasn't only the river that seemed strange. The smoke from the plant's chimney hung still in the air. Smoke normally rose, fading, but today it just sat there, criss-crossing the air.

'The only place I hadn't checked was the power station – it's so sealed up that I kept putting it off. Then one day, I got this feeling that it had to be it, and you know me, I dived in. I told myself the pipes had to lead somewhere.' She clapped her hands together. 'And obviously, they did – right into a horrible, ghost-proof incinerator.' She turned to Luke. 'Are you even listening?'

The truth was, he wasn't. His eyes were fixed on the little

boy fishing. 'Do you notice anything odd about that boy?'

'No, funnily enough, because I was busy pouring my heart out.'

Like the smoke above them, the boy was still too. It didn't feel right. Boys his age weren't like that: they fidgeted and moved. This boy barely breathed.

Alma waved her hand in front of his face. 'Come on then, tell me, what's on your mind?'

'How do you spot a ghoul?'

Alma puffed up. 'Well, they're crafty, and often difficult to spot. They shift their shape to trick you, though the giveaway is the eyes. They never have eyes. They smell their prey . . .'

The fisher boy stood up. His movement was slippery, like jelly. Luke shivered. What was wrong with him?

A thick wall of mist rose off the river, next to where the boy stood.

'Alma, look at the river.'

The moonlight faltered. Luke looked up. The criss-crossing chimney-smoke was not still any more. It was a net, and sinking fast towards them from above, squares getting tighter by the second. Then from the river, came a slow, moaning sound.

The boy turned to face them. He smiled and waved. His eyeless face stared straight at Luke.

CHAPTER 21
GHOUL

As the eyeless boy waved, the moonlight disappeared. The whole of Battersea plunged into darkness. Even the lights in the windows seemed dimmed and shadowed.

The cloud-net above them writhed like a python, a forked tail slipped down, wrapping tight round a chimney. From the banks of the river, behind the boy, rose the grinning face of a monstrous snake-cloud. It stared at Luke, licking its lips.

Luke swallowed. 'I assume this is bad news.'

'No.' Alma stared at the net above. 'I'd say it was terrible. Any ideas?'

'Well, if we can't go up, we have to go down.'

They jumped to the pavement and began running west, staying as far from the riverside as possible.

The snake rose from the bank and the eyeless boy climbed on its back. The snake-jaw opened wide, then wider still, revealing fangs in every shade of dark, until the whole sky thrashed with teeth and tail.

'A manhole!' Luke shouted, pointing to a rusty panel near Battersea's wall. 'We head down into the sewer. It can't rain on us there.'

They sprinted across. The rain lashed down behind them. The wind caught some and gusted it over Luke – it burned on his back – but then they had reached it. He heaved the manhole open and slipped inside.

Darkness. Dripping. The scuttle of rats. How were they meant to escape down here? Luke couldn't see a thing. Then, as if reading his mind, Alma's hand glowed blue, lighting a network of glistening tunnels.

Thud. Thud. Thud. Thud.

Alma looked up. The manhole shook with each thud. 'I fused it shut, but it won't hold that ghoul long.'

'Then let's get moving.'

They ran east down the tunnel across the surface of the water. The ceiling curved overhead and discoloured bricks dripped thin, brown fluid. It smelt of the Thames.

Thud. Crack. Thud. Crack.

He looked back and saw a handful of bricks fall by the manhole, throwing dust and sewage into the air. Luke swallowed and ran faster. He'd hoped running might be easier as a ghost, without a heart and lungs, but his throat felt tight and fear thumped in his head.

'Remind me,' he said, without missing a step. 'Why does it hate us so much?'

'Not us, just you. You upset the balance. You're a hole to the End Place that needs patching.' She winked, running ahead. 'Though he's bound to swallow me too.'

Luke wondered if it hurt. He assumed as much. He looked at the weaving brick patterns overhead, it would almost be pretty, if he wasn't running for his life.

Thud. Crack. Thud. CRASH.

Alma's eyes widened. 'It's broken through. Run faster!'

Then came the sound. A horrible, hungry, wailing moan.

'Couldn't the End Place use something a little less terrifying?' Luke said. 'Like angels? Or puppies?'

'That would hardly put you off. I'd break all the rules if they sent me puppies.'

Then ahead Luke saw it: chinks of light and, above, a ladder leading up to a manhole. 'That's the one!' he said. 'We'll just have to chance it.'

At that moment, the moan morphed into an ear-piercing howl. Luke couldn't stop himself: he looked back. The huge, eyeless snake slithered round a bend and into view, scales slapping hard against slick, black bricks. The boy rode on its back. He seemed to stare at Luke and gave a guttural growl.

The snake's jaw opened and thousands of skittering mist-snakes leapt out.

They shot along the water, churning it into a hissing froth.

Alma rolled up her sleeves. 'You open the manhole, I'll slow him down!'

Her eyes fired blue and a crackle of electricity shot from her hand towards the approaching mass of snakes. The sewer shrieked and the water snakes dissolved. A mineral tang cut the air, and the ghoul hissed and shrieked in pain. Now it was angry.

Luke climbed the ladder. A plaque by the manhole read: Vauxhall Pier. He reached out and pushed: the manhole didn't budge. Then he noticed the arrows on the metal. A screw-top manhole? It was the last thing he needed.

'Just open it, Luke!' Alma shouted, running towards him.

The snake was gaining. A hundred feet. Eighty feet. Sixty-feet. Forty.

A deep rumbling sound. Atop the snake, the eyeless boy smiled.

A swathe of grey water erupted from the snakemouth, filling the tunnel with teeth-like waves.

'He's flooding us out!' Alma shouted. 'Now, now, now!'

'Calm under pressure. Calm under pressure.' Luke repeated it, as though saying it might make the manhole open faster. And maybe it did, because a moment later – CLANG! The manhole popped out and they leapt onto the street.

The jagged grey water rushed past beneath them.

'Luke, you did it!' Alma squealed.

But what they saw ahead cut any celebration short. There, at the pier, bobbed a glass-domed riverboat, its blue-black turbines gleaming in the lamplight. The turbines were spinning, and the dreaded wind had already started. Luke could feel its pull.

The light faded from Alma's eyes. 'There's nowhere to hide.'

Luke felt a rumble beneath them: the snake was almost there. Above was its net, to the right, the Deadzone. There was nowhere to go. Then he had an idea so crazy it might just work.

'Follow me!' He ran towards the riverboat.

'Wait, the turbines!' shouted Alma then, cursing loudly, followed him anyway.

Luke ran up the pier, as the last few passengers disembarked. The propeller wind grew stronger, pulling at his mist, but it was not yet strong enough to lift him off the ground. With a final burst of effort, he ran through the last couple of passengers and into the boat, with Alma right behind.

The boat's door slid shut with a hydraulic hiss.

'*Inside* the boat?'

'You're always telling me to improvise,' Luke said. 'So I did.'

And to Luke's relief, nobody even blinked. Factory workers, policemen, fishwives and nurses, all squeezed into their berths, happy but weary at the end of the shifts.

'Luke, look!' Alma whispered. 'It's coming. That dome had better hold up.'

Through the glass, they watched the vast snake squeeze out of the manhole, the eyeless boy on its back. It rushed forward towards them, smacking its teeth against the glass and clutching the boat with creeping tendrils.

Luke breathed in relief. The glass didn't move. The other passengers didn't even look up, they just carried on talking and munching their snacks. To them, it was just another foggy day.

Beyond the glass, the ghoul's face changed. In an instant, it switched from fury to fear, as it turned to look at the boat's turbines. It thrashed in the air, trying to pull away, before sliding slowly across the dome, towards the dark whirling blades. It glanced back at Luke with hatred, then vanished into the propellers.

Alma punched Luke's arm. 'Only a half-ghost would have thought of this – it's bonkers, but brilliant.'

Luke felt giddy. 'It's pretty genius, isn't it?'

The air around the boat cleared.

'I almost feel sorry for it,' Luke said.

'Don't,' Alma said. 'It wouldn't have felt sorry for you.'

They watched out of the glass, as the boat moved west down the river. They passed the quiet streets of Chelsea, Fulham and New Putney, where the boat stopped. Then, as the last passengers left, and the turbines had finally stopped, they slipped out of the boat and caught a stiff breeze back east. Soon, they approached the chimneys of Battersea.

'You know what,' Luke said, 'it's less picturesque without the little boy fishing.'

'Not funny, Luke. That was too close for comfort.'

They stopped at the foot of the second chimney and Alma turned to him. 'Now here's the plan. You leave that lab well alone and shovel your heart out. We'll have adventures in the sky until you get that amber ticket.'

Luke stepped down onto the ledge. 'But what if Sal's right? We have a chance to stop her.'

'If he cares that much, he can stop Tabatha Margate himself.'

'And Jess? She's never going to shovel her way out.'

Alma flounced. 'Luke, this is the problem with quests. Instead of seizing the day, and having adventures with me, you're worrying about the future.'

Luke shook his head. She just didn't get it. 'But Alma, I can't just leave Jess there. She's my friend.'

'But I'm a friend too!' Alma jabbed her finger at Luke. 'Look, finding that lab will get you killed — and I'm the reason you're looking for it. Just imagine, if you die, how guilty I'll feel!'

'If I'm dead, that'll be the least of my worries!' Luke's fists clenched. Did she ever think about anyone else? 'You started this, Alma. You showed me those vents.' Luke was speaking too fast, but he couldn't slow down. 'I can't go back to how I was. I can't just pretend.' He sighed. 'I was taken from my family, I was kidnapped! I just want to get out and find them, more than anything in the world.'

Alma opened her mouth, then stopped. She turned away and spoke quietly. 'Do you want to die, Luke? Do you want to end up like me, haunting some slum, searching for your death? Because that's what will happen!' She paced on the ledge. 'No. You listen to me. If you don't promise to avoid that lab, I'll . . . I'll . . .'

'You'll what?'

She turned to him. 'I'll never come back.'

Luke froze. *No more visits? No more trips to the sky? Would she do that?* He looked at her: her jaw was set, her eyes burned blue. But something inside him burned hotter still. 'It's my life, Alma. You can't make me promise.'

'I can, and I will.'

Luke swallowed. 'No. I won't lie to you. I'm going to look for Tabatha's lab. If we find it, we could stop this thing once and for all.'

'I wasn't lying either.' Alma stepped forward. 'Goodbye, Luke.' Then she touched his shoulder, and everything went black.

CHAPTER 22
THE ANNOUNCEMENT

Luke yawned in the line to the washroom. He had returned to his body late and hardly slept. Had Alma really meant what she'd said? Would he never fly again? Even considering it made him feel a little sick.

Either way, Jess and Ravi's questions were the last thing he wanted.

'So, let me get this right.' Jess scratched the back of her neck. 'The Ghost Council guy was a dead body floating in the water, then he stood up all fine, messed around with your head, then disappeared into nothing?'

'And then,' Ravi added, 'another bad ghostcloud – a snakey one – tried to eat you, but got gobbled up by a boat?'

'And then somehow, after all that, you fell out with Alma?'

Luke sighed. The conversation wasn't going quite the way he'd hoped. He wished the guard would hurry and let them in for their wash. 'The point is, the council will only help us stop Tabatha if we get more evidence. *Find the lab, find our freedom*, that's what they said.'

'*Stop* Tabatha?' Ravi blinked. 'You hate conflict. You don't even like arguing. What on earth makes you think you could stop Tabatha?'

'The Ghost Council will do that. They'll zap her or something. But it's a crazy idea, I know. Especially when we've basically found the vents.'

Jess's eyes were wide. 'They can zap people? That's cool.'

'Delightful, Jess. They sound like real team players.' Ravi looked ahead for movement in the queue. 'Look, I hate to admit it, but I'm with Alma. This all sounds too risky. Shovelling's the only sensible option.'

'For you,' said Jess. 'I've got no chance just shovelling. I vote we escape through the vents in the sick bay. We almost got there last time. We don't need the council. We'll just check for carbon monoxide then make a break for it.'

Ravi rolled his eyes. 'And single-handedly take out all the guards?'

'I've two hands, actually. And with Luke, that's four.'

'Stop it, you two.' Luke waved his hands between them. 'Listen, we can do both. We'll continue shovelling by day and look for the vents at night, once Tabatha stops pumping them with carbon monoxide. And if we find Tabatha's lab while exploring – it's a bonus. We tell the Ghost Council and everyone's a winner.'

The two were silent, then Ravi shrugged. 'Conflict avoided. But really you're just putting off the decision.'

'No, he's *hedging our bets*. I've got a question though. If Alma doesn't come back, how can we tell the council?'

It was a good point. Luke had lain awake worrying about it all night. 'She'll come back, don't worry, she just needs to sulk for a while.' He hoped he sounded surer than he felt.

The whistle blew and ended their conversation. A uniformed guard strode down the line, a sour look on his face, ushering them into the washroom.

After quickly showering, they were the first ones to arrive in the canteen. The purple lights flickered over empty white tables while the serving girl with the eye-patch ladled gruel at the counter. In the depths of the kitchen, the scowling cook, Bertha, wound an enormous meat grinder, in a crunching blur of serrated steel, gristle and cracked bone. A pyramid of foil-wrapped packets sat next to her. She looked like she'd slept even less than Luke.

They grabbed trays and went to the counter, where the girl filled their bowls with gruel. Luke wondered how she could work for someone as angry as Bertha while remaining so calm. He smiled, but she didn't look up. A queue of children had grown behind them; she had her work cut out.

They took their cutlery, and turned towards their table, when Bertha howled. She'd knocked over her pyramid of foil packets. In frustration, she thwacked the table, upending it, and sending the meat grinder flying to the ground.

It happened in slow motion. The grinder fell and hit the floor, sending a serrated steel blade spinning towards the counter.

All the children in the line ducked, but not the serving girl. She was used to Bertha's howls. She didn't think anything of it; her eyes were fixed on the ladle.

Luke watched open-mouthed. She was in the blade's path. This would not end well.

He dived across, knocking her to the ground; something wet splattered across his face and chest, followed by screams and the screech of metal. Had he been too late?

He looked around from the floor. To his right lay the girl, pale but breathing, and splattered with the gruel from the bowl in his hand. Behind her lay a white table, ripped almost in two by the serrated blade.

'Are you all right?' Ravi was already at his side, helping him up.

Luke nodded, then turned to the girl. 'You?'

She nodded then, ashen, walked to the counter and began ladling again. Luke pulled himself up. Shards of wood littered the ground. That could have been him. He didn't feel hungry any more.

He sat with Jess and Ravi at their usual table.

'That was close,' Jess said, prodding her gruel. 'Are you sure you're OK?'

'Is Bertha OK?' said Ravi. 'Looks like she's losing it. I bet it's linked to those foil packets. What are they for? Some special occasion, maybe?'

'It's not just Bertha,' Luke said. 'It's the guards too. They're smarter than usual, shoe polish and everything. Something's up.'

Luke felt a tap on his shoulder. It was the girl from the counter.

'Can I wipe your table?' Her voice was barely a whisper.

'Of course. Go ahead.'

As she wiped, her expression turned serious. Her uncovered eye remained on the cloth, and under her breath, she whispered to him. 'There's going to be an announcement in the furnace hall. Make sure you wait in the front row, far left.'

He looked round. She had spoken so quietly, Ravi and Jess hadn't even noticed, they were too busy speculating about the little foil packets. Luke nodded to the girl.

She smiled faintly. 'And thank you for earlier.' Then she walked to the next table and resumed her wiping.

Ravi turned to Luke. 'We've decided that those foil packets are either roast chicken wraps or freeze-dried rats.'

Jess nodded. 'They're about the right size. I hear they eat them in the slums.'

Luke felt a little queasy. 'Guys, eat up. We need to get to the furnace room.'

The first thing Luke noticed was the lack of shovels. Normally, you took your shovel from a trolley by the door. This morning, however, there were no trolleys, only a raised platform at the front of the hall, near the flames. Guards stood round it, pulling uncomfortably at their sweaty uniforms.

Against his better instincts, Luke led his friends right up to the platform. Front, far left, that's what the girl had said. He didn't know why, but he trusted her.

Ravi tapped Luke's shoulder. 'It's roasting. Can't we move to the back?'

Luke shook his head.

Jess smiled. 'At least my hair is drying.'

Children entered from the canteen, in dribs and drabs, mostly staying near the back of the hall. Over the crackling flames grew a murmur of voices, as children wondered what on earth was happening. Luke couldn't remember a day when they hadn't had to shovel. He soaked it all in. All the guards' boots shone. Even the floor was polished. Tabatha had to be coming.

Next came the kids from the other dorms, with a certain swagger, and finally, the children from the second chimney, rubbing their eyes. Soon the hall was teeming with bodies. Even Bertha, Luke saw, squeezed in near the back, sweaty and scowling.

Out of the darkness stepped Tabatha. She stood on the platform, the flames casting her shadow long across the children. It must be sweltering up there, thought Luke, but if it was, she didn't show it. She wore a full black lab coat and a black fur stole, holding her pipe in one hand and clipboard in the other. She placed the pipe in her mouth and blew a cloud of smoke over the audience. A hush fell on the hall.

'Everything burns at the right temperature.' She flashed her white teeth in the darkness. 'Coal. Wood. Metal. Stone. Even children. All of them become fuel, under the right conditions. In the right furnace.' She breathed out, letting the smoke seep from the corners of her mouth. 'The third chimney will be that furnace. It will revolutionise energy, it will bring light to all of London and revive the economy.' She paused, inhaled from her pipe, then spoke.

'Over the next ten days, we will build this chimney. You'll work double shifts, receiving meals at your stations. Sleep will be limited to four hours a night.' A wave of whispers rolled up the hall. Tabatha clapped her hands, and silence fell. 'The top ten per cent of workers will earn their freedom. Those who can't be useful will receive some of this.' She held up a conical glass flask, filled with black liquid.

What was it? The guards looked equally confused. Some children even began to whisper again. Luke knew to keep quiet.

'You.' Tabatha pointed, from her platform. The crowd of children cleared around a blonde broad boy from another dorm. 'You have a lot to say for yourself. Come here.'

The boy shook his head and stepped back. Two guards appeared either side of him and shoved him forward. He swallowed, then began walking, his head held high, his hands shaking as he made his way to the stage.

Tabatha extracted black liquid with a thin glass pipette. She smiled. 'Open wide.' She leant in, with a whisper that the whole room heard. 'Or there's always the furnace.'

The boy opened his mouth and stuck out his tongue.

'Just one drop.' She squeezed the pipette.

Silence fell on the hall, but nothing happened. After a few seconds passed, the boy shrugged, turned around and began walking back to his place, through a sea of watchful faces. The silence grew thick; his steps echoed like thunder. When the boy was halfway there, Luke heard something. A faint hiss, like hot kindling. At first, he assumed it was the furnace, but as the boy moved, the sound moved with him, and grew into a crackling, grating wheeze.

Next came the smell: a distant scent of coal-smoke and rain. It started mild, almost pleasant, then grew sharp in the air around the boy. The crowd parted, but the boy doggedly trod on. He was dripping with sweat and walking fast now. The wheezing grew louder with each step.

Luke didn't want to watch, but he couldn't look away.

When the boy had nearly reached his spot, his step faltered. A second later and he stopped altogether. He patted his chest, then cleared his throat, and the strangest thing happened: a puff of smoke escaped from his mouth.

The children gasped. The boy's eyes grew wide, then he doubled over and began coughing, sending bursts of grey-yellow smoke into the air. He clutched at his throat, as though trying to stop it, but the coughs kept coming. Then, with an inhuman effort, he forced himself upright to look at the crowd. His mouth moved, but no sound came. What was he trying to say?

Then the boy fell to the floor, in convulsions of smoky, rasping coughs.

A moment later, and he had stopped moving altogether. He lay there, eyes closed, chest rising and falling, pumping great plumes of smoke into the dark furnace hall air.

Luke felt sick. If she did this for talking, what would she do if she caught them trying to escape? Maybe Ravi was right. Maybe shovelling was the only sensible option. Yet part of him resisted. What she was doing was wrong. Someone, somewhere, had to stop her. Luke sighed; did it really have to be him?

Tabatha spoke from the platform. 'Don't worry, he'll be fine. One drop never killed anyone. But if he talks again, I'll make sure he gets two.' She put the stopper back in the bottle. 'So please, children, *do* try your hardest.' Then she left the room.

Terence appeared on the stand and bared his teeth. 'Listen up. We're now handing out roles. Front row, far left, you're in the kitchen, delivering food. Front row middle, room 221, boiler repairs . . .' The list went on.

'We're in the kitchen, with Bertha?' Jess said, uncertain. 'Is that a good thing?'

Luke frowned. 'I guess we'll find out.'

CHAPTER 23
BERTHA

There were ten of them in all. They stood in silence in the sterile white of the canteen, watching Bertha stir a monstrous, copper pot of steaming gruel. At one point, a girl with long red hair had whispered something, but Bertha had given her such venomous look, they'd all held their breath since.

Why had the serving girl wanted him to work here? Bertha seemed even meaner than Terence. The serving girl, conveniently, was nowhere in sight.

Grunting, Bertha bent and picked up a grey hunk of meat, swatting away a few, but not all, of the flies that were on it. Swinging her cleaver down effortlessly, she sliced through the joint, splitting bone, flesh and fly alike. 'That's you,' she uttered, in a throaty drawl. 'If I have to tell you anything twice.' Her voice made a clicking sound when she paused for breath.

She picked up a silver foil package. 'Take these to each

workshop. Don't drop 'em. Or open 'em. It's unhygienic.' She squashed a fly in her left hand, scraped it up with her thumbnail, and sucked it. Then she lumbered over to a tin box in the corner and lifted its lid. A meaty aroma filled the air, as she pulled out a roast chicken drumstick.

Luke held his breath. He'd not seen food like it for over two years. Crisp-skinned, golden-brown, dripping with gravy, just like his grandma would have cooked it. He felt a pang of worry. Would his grandma still be there, if he ever got out?

'For those who work hard, there will be rewards.' She licked the drumstick twice, like a lollipop, then chucked the whole thing in her mouth and chewed. She looked up at Luke, gravy smeared across a set of surprisingly white teeth. 'You, boy, take these to the basement. Rooms A to C.' She handed him a wire basket, filled with foil packets. 'And do it sharp!'

Luke nodded, took the basket, and ran from the room down the corridor, almost crashing into an open storeroom door. The serving girl poked her head out from the storeroom, gestured him in and closed the door.

The shelves were stacked high with labelled jars: vitamins of every shape and colour. The girl's voice was a whisper. 'I'm Violet.'

She checked the corridor through the keyhole, then turned back to Luke. 'Bertha's not as bad as she looks. If you do a good job, she'll make sure you're looked after.' He nodded and made to move, but she tugged at his sackcloth. 'But whatever you do, don't deliver to the third chimney, whatever they say.'

And with that, she opened the door and scurried out, back to the canteen. Luke picked up his basket and set off to the basement.

The basement, it turned out, was not really a basement. It was the sewers below the plant, blocked off and refurbished by Tabatha, as her own industrial complex – a maze of arched brick tunnels and workshops. Using the map from his basket, Luke found his way to room A. It dawned on Luke that Violet had unwittingly found them the perfect job. It took them all around the plant. *Find the lab, find your freedom*, Luke told himself. With this job, surely, it was only be a matter of time.

Room A was bustling. Children sat in neat lines on the floor with blowtorches and different shaped metal plates. At the head of the line stood a supervisor in a black boiler suit, the words *Margate Industries* sewn on his front in amber thread. He strode up and down, flanked by guards, shouting at any child who made a mistake, giving the occasional kick with a studded boot.

They were only a few hours into these new tasks and some of the children already looked tired. Luke laid the foil packets on a table, avoiding eye contact with the glowering guards, and left right away.

Though he longed to explore more, he remembered Violet's words and sprinted off back to the canteen. Turning the corner, he knocked into some kids from another dorm carrying a heavy metal cylinder. They snarled, but were too weighed down to chase him, and he sprinted upstairs. What was the cylinder for? Luke's mind buzzed with the possibilities.

He arrived back at the canteen to find Bertha adding powder to the gruel. She tasted it, glanced back at a well-thumbed book on the table, then added more. He'd never imagined that she followed recipes. Luke made a mental note to never use that cookbook.

'Back already?' she grunted, looking at her watch. 'Violet said you'd be quick. Well, you might as well help while we wait for the others. Fetch me more vitamin C from the cupboard.'

He found it easily enough – a square, green glass jar with a wooden stopper. Bertha wheezed and measured out several scoops, smiling to herself. 'Not one case of scurvy or rickets since I started.

That's why Tabatha keeps me. I'm efficient.' She turned to Luke. 'It seems you are too.'

She gave him a drumstick from her pot and turned back to her gruel. Luke looked at it in absolute wonder. It'd be the first mouthful of real food he'd eaten for two years. He raised it to his mouth and sniffed the buttery aroma.

'Stop, right there,' a greasy voice growled. Terence stood in the doorway, sneering. 'Luke Smith-Sharma, what a surprise. Hiding in here, pilfering supplies. Highly inefficient. I'll have to report that drumstick to—'

A spoon of scalding gruel narrowly missed Terence's head. Bertha glowered from the counter. 'If you're going to report us, get a shower while you're at it.'

Terence's eyes narrowed. He opened his mouth, but Bertha picked up her meat cleaver, and he closed it promptly. He turned to Luke. 'You, I want a word with you about the sewage room.'

Bertha marched forward, sweating fury. 'If I were you, Terrikins, I'd worry about your own staff. I hear the third chimney kids are dropping like flies. That's hardly efficient. What would Tabatha say?'

Terence spat on the floor, then walked away, muttering.

Bertha returned to her gruel pot and began stirring, a little out of breath. There was a hint of a grin beneath her scowl. 'Now eat that bloomin' drumstick, before someone else comes in.'

Luke grinned; Violet was right. Bertha wasn't quite as bad as she looked.

That night he compared notes with Jess and Ravi in the toilet cubicle, while trying his best to ignore the cockroaches.

'It's been fascinating, don't get me wrong, but I'm always sent to the same rooms – all welding and hammering. Nothing smoggy in sight.'

Ravi sighed. 'Tell me about it. Mine are all molten metal, poured casts and that kind of thing – a lot of kids have burns. They've got no protective clothing. Most kids don't even have socks.'

'But the drumsticks are nice, right?' Jess fished one from her pocket.

'Jess,' Ravi said. 'Just for one second, can you stop being so happy?'

'Will it cheer you up?'

'No. Probably not.'

'I thought as much.'

'Guys, focus,' Luke said. 'Drumsticks aside, we do have a problem. If we keep delivering to the same spots, we won't get any nearer to a way out, whether it's finding the lab, or those East Wing vents.' He looked at them both. 'Any ideas?'

Jess stared at her drumstick. Ravi fiddled with his watch.

'I'll take that as no.' Luke said. 'Well, it's late. Let's sleep on it, I guess.'

They slipped back to the dormitory. Luke sighed as he climbed the ladder to his bunk. They were stuck, and he knew it. He had a feeling it would be yet another sleepless night.

CHAPTER 24
SPECIAL DELIVERY

Luke wouldn't have gone as far as to say that he hadn't slept a wink – that would have been inaccurate – but if he had been counting winks, he could have done it on one hand.

They were so close to finding the lab, and their freedom. It felt just around the corner. And yet for some reason, when he'd slept, his dreams had been horrid. Of vivid, eyeless ghouls, kids coughing up smoke, and of Alma. She'd been flying through the skies, searching for him, but when he called out to her, she didn't seem to hear him.

If he was honest, he missed her. He had been sure she would cool down and come back to patch things over. That's what friends did. Surely, she understood that he had to at least try to find the lab and the vents. And he missed flying! Now he'd tasted the freedom of sky, he couldn't just sit back and wait, and shovel like before. And there was Jess, too. She'd never earn a ticket the way she shovelled.

Yawning, he pushed the thoughts from his mind and crawled out of bed. Everyone else was still sleeping, but a guard walked him down to the canteen anyway. He found Violet prepping for the day.

He coughed and she looked up. 'Do you mind if I help?'

She smiled and gestured for him to join her at the chopping board. He watched her chop for a minute or so, then did his best to imitate. Violet nodded appreciatively, though her hands moved much quicker. Normally so shy when she served up the gruel, she had a quiet authority about her in the kitchen. It made him wonder.

'Violet, how long have you been here?'

'Nine years.'

Luke did a double take. Nine years? It was unheard of. 'And you never got an amber ticket?'

Violet shrugged. 'I'm from the south, originally. I didn't particularly want to go back. My parents couldn't really afford to keep me, anyway.'

Luke's eyes widened. He'd not met anyone from the south before.

Violet carried on. 'Terence said it was an accident. I was begging north of the river. They probably meant to get some north London girl, but mixed us up in the smog.'

The slums, Luke thought. He'd seen them from the clouds –
all corrugated iron and soot-stained canvas. Could it really be
worse than here? He thought of his own home, the little yellow boat
in the eastern waterways. He hoped his dad was OK.

'I got kidnapped in the smog too. It came out of nowhere.'

'Nothing comes from nowhere.' Violet looked at him. 'We saw
the smog often enough in the slums. And you know what's weird?
They say it always starts on the hour. Never a few minutes past, but
bang on the dot.' She stopped chopping. 'Weather doesn't do that.'

'Are you sure?' It didn't make sense, Luke thought, but then
rumours often didn't. 'Wouldn't the officials have noticed?'

'Not if they're all paid off.' She looked behind her. 'They
say she's doing weird experiments in a secret lab in the East
Wing. And there's another rumour, too, about the amber tickets.
They say –' Violet stopped. Her face paled. 'Did you hear that?
I heard footsteps.'

But Luke heard nothing, ony a pair of words echoing in his
head: Tabatha's Laboratory. It was in the East Wing! He turned back
to Violet – he had to ask more – only to find her chopping onions,
looking squarely away. It was as though they'd never even talked
at all.

A puce-faced Bertha burst through the door.

'I've had a call.' She quivered in fury. 'Janey's in the sick bay. Something happened when she was delivering food to the third chimney. That poor girl.' Bertha slammed her cleaver into the wood. 'That bloomin' Terence. Well he can deliver his own food to the East Wing in future.'

Luke's ears pricked up. The East Wing? The chance was too good to be true, even if his throat felt dry at the thought of bumping into Terence.

He stepped forward. 'I'm fast. If you want, I can deliver there before my other jobs start.'

Violet stopped chopping. Bertha looked at him funny. 'Nobody *wants* to deliver to the East Wing, especially when the last girl ended up unconscious . . .'

Unconscious? Luke swallowed his fear. He had to do it. Their only two routes of escape were in the East Wing – Tabatha's hidden lab, and the sick bay, with its guarded ground-level vents. It was that or go back to shovelling. 'I'm not worried,' he lied then, to make it less suspicious, he added, 'but I'll need an extra hour in bed for me, Jess and Ravi.'

Bertha's eyes narrowed. 'Half an hour, max. OK, fine, leave

those wraps at the chimney door.' She packed the silver packets onto a trolley. 'Oh, I forgot.' She spat inside one of them. 'That one's for Terence.'

A few moments later, Luke trundled the trolley out of the service lift and onto the zig zagging tiles of East Wing, already wondering if he'd made the right decision. The whole place had been redecorated: pristine, black wallpaper covered the walls and the ventilation dripped with fresh, black lacquer, the coal-coloured marble sparkled underfoot. It was like walking into midnight. Had they redecorated it for visitors, for the third chimney's big launch? The place gave him the creeps: the first time he'd been there, he'd met that smog-thing. The next time, Tabatha had almost caught him in the vents. He wished he could have taken Jess or Ravi with him.

He shook his head and looked at his list. The rooms were numbered. The first few were storerooms – coal dust, food, and unused sackcloths – he knew them already from his searches with Jess. The only difference was now, in each room, a guard was counting stock. They each looked bored out of their mind. Luke delivered the wraps and moved on.

Soon, he reached the sick bay, a white door in a sea of dark brick. He sensed the rain at once – in his bones, in his soul. The vents had to be in there, he was sure of it. But to his disappointment, the sick bay was not on his list. Surely if Janey was in there, she'd need something to eat? He paused a moment. Maybe he could pop in and say he'd made a mistake? If he could just see how heavily the vents were guarded.

A door slammed somewhere down the hall, and fear dampened his curiosity. He'd do his deliveries then try on the way back. In any case, he still needed to find the lab.

After the sickbay and sewage room came a series of offices, each with a quota of wraps. Guards sat in every room, behind rickety desks, filling in sheets of coal-stained paper. But still no sign of the lab. Before he knew it, he'd reached the last room on his list.

He held his breath. It had to be there. He opened the door.

It was just another office. Longer, empty and better furnished perhaps, but otherwise unremarkable. It smelt slightly of cold fish and chips.

Luke's shoulders slumped. He didn't know where he'd gone wrong! He walked over to the desk at the end and plonked two wraps down, but as he turned to leave, he heard an odd little sound. A sort of strange, muffled, barking squeak.

There it was again. It seemed to come from a box on the desk.

It was around the size of a melon and had holes in the side. Luke peered closer; a tiny nose peeked out. It belonged to a thin, greasy, sad-eyed rat. It sniffed towards the gruel wrap on the desk.

'You hungry, little thing?

The rat, of course, didn't reply, but Luke pushed some gruel-wrap through a hole anyway. It squeaked and began nibbling, furiously, sending specks of gruel flying across the papers on the desk.

Great, Luke thought. He reached for a tissue to wipe up the mess.

But as he leaned down to dab, he noticed, at the top of a gruel-splodged paper, the word 'Laboratory'.

He picked the sheet up. It was a floorplan labelled with sections A to K. There were gangways, offices, several levels. The map stretched over five pages. But it didn't make sense. How could a lab that big even fit in the East Wing?

Clump. Clump. Clump. Clump.

Footsteps in the corridor. Just around the corner. Luke dropped the papers and spun round, just in time to see Terence and a guard walk in.

Terence stopped in the doorway and stared at Luke through

bagged, yellowed eyes. 'You,' he hissed. 'What are *you* doing in here?'

'Gruel delivery, sir.' Luke patted the trolley, trying to look calm, but it squeaked, and he couldn't help but jump a little.

Terence eyed him suspiciously; he took a step closer. 'The other day, Smith-Sharma, Tabatha asked me about the sewage room, about why it was so clean? So *unnaturally* clean.' Terence licked his teeth and began walking nearer. 'Of course, I said I'd done it, but do you know what? She wasn't convinced. And then, of all things, she asked about *you*.' He stood so close now that when he spoke, flecks of spittle landed by Luke's feet. 'Now, why would she do that? Have you been snitching?'

Luke shook his head. He hoped that Terence couldn't hear his heart thumping.

'He's lying.' The guard sniggered. 'You should put him in the cage. Or the front of the line. Or better still, give him a golden ticket!'

And then a strange thing happened. Terence's eyes flashed and his anger changed target. He turned and grabbed the guard by the collar, unhinged. 'What I have told you? Zip it! Or *you'll be the one eating French food instead.*'

The guard gasped. 'Sorry, sir! I-I-I didn't mean it, sir.'

Luke didn't understand what had just happened. What he

did know, however, was that he'd gained a moment's grace. He had to use it. So he grabbed Terence's wrap and held it up, not unlike a shield.

'Sir, here's your wrap. It's still nice and warm.'

Terence swivelled back. His stomach rumbled. 'Fine. You're lucky I'm hungry.' He let go of the guard and snatched the wrap. As he peeled the foil back, Luke saw a glob of Bertha's spit ooze from its side.

Luke held his breath. Terence hadn't noticed. He just bit right in, without taking his eyes off Luke.

'Well, sir, I'll be going now. Deliveries, you know.'

Terence nodded and Luke pushed the trolley past him. He still hadn't breathed, but he felt a glimmer of hope.

'Wait.' It was Terence, his eyes narrowed. 'This wrap, it tastes . . . different.'

'Err . . . New sauce, I think. Bertha made it herself.'

Terence wiped gruel from his chin. 'Well, I hate to say it, but it's good. Moister. Saltier too. They're normally like rubber.'

Luke gave a strained, chimpanzee kind of smile. 'Well, I'll tell Bertha. I'm sure she'll be thrilled.' He pushed the trolley again, past the guard, past the walls, and right up to the door. He was pulling it open, when something squeaked sharply.

But it wasn't the door. Or the trolley. It had come from behind him.

He glanced back: it was the rat and it was munching through the map of the lab.

'Snuffles!' Terence snatched the papers off the rodent. 'I've told you before: don't eat my stuff!' Then he froze, staring at the sheets in his hands. 'But how'd you get these? And why is there gruel on it?' His eyes shot up towards Luke by the door. 'You! You were looking at my papers, weren't you?'

'No. The gruel splattered when I fed the—'

But Terence was on him already and grabbed him by the ear. 'You were snooping, that's what! Top secret documents.' Terence leant in close; his breath damp and stale. 'And I bet you snitched to Tabatha too!'

'Please, Terence!' Luke's ear stung in his grip. 'I never spoke to her, honest.'

'That's *Mr* Terence to you.' And suddenly he was pulling Luke, by his ear, out into the corridor. The zig zag floor blurred. A guard chuckled from behind. Luke's ear felt like it might fall right off.

But it was Luke who then fell, hitting the black and white

tiles hard. He was at the end of the corridor. Before him stood a door. A huge steel door with a wheel in the middle. A brass sign above it read: 'The Third Chimney'.

Terence turned the wheel.

'Mr Terence, please, I didn't snitch, I promise.'

The door opened, with a hiss. The light blinded after the darkness of the corridor.

Terence laughed. 'We'll soon find out.'

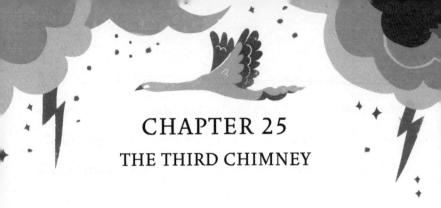

CHAPTER 25
THE THIRD CHIMNEY

Luke had never been inside a chimney, but he had a good idea of what they were like: dark, hot, pokey places, made of brick and covered in soot. The third chimney, however, was none of those things. It was huge, cold and bright. The walls were pure poured concrete. They curved flawlessly round, narrowing up towards a circle of sky, from which rain and light fell in equal measure.

It was like he'd fallen down a well. One where there was no chance of ever being rescued.

Then his eyes adjusted and he took a step back. The furthest half of the room was dark and strange, dripping and oozing. White ivy and mottled fungus clutched to its walls. Piles of weedy rubble littered the floor, alongside rippling ponds of inky liquid.

What on earth happened here?

Terence shoved him forward. 'The Europeans bombed the station to cut off our power. Experimental weapons, they say, nasty stuff. It worked. This chimney's remained damp ever since – never been able to light so much as a candle in here.'

Nasty indeed, thought Luke. The whole place felt unnatural. The oozing damp seemed almost alive. If he could tell the Ghost Council, maybe they'd know what had happened, though that required him to survive whatever Terence had planned.

A greasy palm rested on Luke's shoulder. 'Luckily for us, Tabatha's just developed a way to clear this place up.'

Terence held out a vial of red liquid. 'A few vials of this and the place is halfway dry already. You see that?' Terence pointed to a charred pile. 'There was a black pool there. One drop of this was all it took. Too much, and you'll probably blow off your hand.'

Luke looked at the tube. The liquid in it glowed crimson and danced in the light. A pipette was built in to measure out drops, it reminded him of the black liquid that had made the boy cough smoke. Where did Tabatha get this stuff from?

But before he could ask, Terence prodded him forward, towards a cluster of workers – boys from another dorm – wearing gas masks and yellow, plastic, full-body suits. Each had a red vial which they held at arms-length, through black rubber gloves.

'It's still under development.' Terence shrugged. 'So it's not

100 per cent safe, but I'm sure an expert cleaner like you will manage.' A sly grin crossed his face. He pointed a yellowed fingernail at a pool of dark liquid. 'Why don't you start with that pool. Unless you want to confess?'

Luke tried to think logically. He hadn't snitched, and he'd only seen those documents by accident. Was it worth explaining? He had a feeling that whatever he said to Terence, he'd end up in trouble.

He looked at the vial of red in Terence's hand.

'Is there protective clothing?'

Terence scoffed. 'The whole point is to scare you. It's not scary if it's safe.' Terence tapped his head as though he'd solved a complex problem. 'And if you don't make it, at least you won't snitch in future.'

Luke grabbed the vial. It was warm to the touch, but not in a comforting way. He approached the dark pool: it was the biggest by far. None of the other children stood near it.

Terence watched, enjoying himself. 'We don't have all day!'

Luke closed his eyes. He had to be calm. It was like fishing, that was all. Like he did off the boat, in the summer at home. It was just the water was darker here. And the air colder. And there was a hopeless, dank smell in the air.

He opened his eyes. He'd have to get it over with. He pulled off the stopper and squeezed the pipette.

A drop of crimson fell down. It hissed as it fell, like the quiet wail of a burning branch. When it reached the pool surface, it rested there, red on black, then a fiery glow surged out from it. Luke jumped back, as sparks flew in all directions, followed by grasping, vermillion flames.

Scratch that, he thought. It wasn't like fishing at all.

'Get back!' shouted a yellow-suited boy.

Luke stepped back, stumbling over rubble as he did; he couldn't look away. The pool bubbled and seethed as though fighting the flames. It erupted in spurts of flaring black slime. A splash missed Luke's foot. What was he doing watching? He had to run, and quick.

He turned to sprint to the others, but he tripped over a rock covered in sticky, dark goo. Tumbling to the floor, he glanced back at the pool. The dark liquid and the flames were battling now. Spiralling, twining, hissing and howling. Steam billowed up and ash drifted down.

And that was one drop? What would a vial of it do?

The vial . . . where was it? It must have slipped from his hand when he'd fallen. He peered through the smoke and saw it at once:

it was rolling away. Rolling right towards the pool of black.

He ducked down behind a boulder, just as the vial rolled into the pool. There was a second of silence, then a wave of heat, a deafening roar and a monstrous, bright, blinding flash. Clumps of flaming black liquid rocketed into the air, then splattered – still burning – to the ground all around him.

'Help!' he shouted.

The flames encircled him in a fiery wall, surging skyward.

'Get some water!' he cried.

Through the flames, he saw the yellow-suited boys back away – had they even heard him? Even if they had, he thought, there was little they could do for him now.

He'd never seen anything like it. The flames blazed a hundred feet up, to the lip of the chimney. Waves of heat blasted him, dripping him in sweat. Yet for some reason, the flames crept no nearer. In the furnace room, the flames grasped for anything they could, but these only reached heavenwards, like pillars of fire.

He should be dead by now. It didn't make sense.

Then he saw the faces in the flames. Faint, flickering and watching him: faces etched in orange, black and crimson. They rose up the columns, towards the sky.

A final surge of heat. Eye-stinging, skin-flaying, hair-raising heat. Then a crash of thunder and the rush of rain.

A downpour of water drenched Luke to the bone, cooling his skin and sizzling the air with steam. And when the mist cleared, he looked up from the floor. The other children cowered in the far corner, trembling.

Even Terence was shaking.

Then everything went black.

CHAPTER 26
THE SICK BAY

Luke opened his eyes. The lights shone dazzlingly bright, sending waves of pain through his skull. He closed his eyelids and waited for it to subside.

It wasn't the dormitory – he could tell that much even through closed lids – the lights were dimmer in the dormitory. But where was he? The air smelt clean. Not the fresh, bright clean of the sky outside, but a hard-won cleanliness, of scrubbing and scouring with bleach. Over the buzz of lights, he heard clicks and whirring: the sound of machines. Under his fingers he felt crisp, starched fabric.

His head stopped throbbing and he opened his eyes a fraction. It still stung but, through his lashes, the room came into focus. It was large and white, with a life size diagram of the human body on the opposite wall. Half the body stood skinless, arrows pointing to various muscles and organs; the other half was fleshless, with labels pointing to the skeleton's bones. Above it, a printed sign read '*Sick Bay*'.

Luke smiled despite the pain. This was where the vents would be! He couldn't have planned it better.

He forced himself up, even though his head burned hot from the effort. There was a tube going into his arm, attached to a machine with fluid to his right. His foot was freshly bandaged, burned in the flames, no doubt. The rest of him looked unharmed.

'Ouch,' he said, and felt a little better.

He scanned the room. Against one wall stood white shelves and an immaculate white desk. Against the other lay machines: monitors and screens, drips and pulleys, canisters of oxygen and other gases. In the space between, pristine linen beds and white wooden cabinets were arranged in rows.

But the vents to the outside were nowhere to be seen.

It didn't make sense. He'd sensed the rain from right outside this room. And he'd seen the vents from outside, they'd been huge, black things, not the kind that could be hidden behind cabinets and shelves. Where had his logic gone wrong? There had to be something he was missing.

He lowered himself down, keeping the weight off his bandaged foot, then limped over to the shelves. In theory, the vents should be right there, but there was nothing. All he saw were white folders arranged in alphabetical order: Aaron to Andrew, Annabel to Benjamin, all the way up to Zephaniah. The labels neatly typed, spotless and centred. This was an organised person.

He was reaching for a folder when a noise made him freeze.

Click. Tap. Swish. Click.

He rushed back, jumped into bed and closed his eyes.

Hisssss.

A door had opened. A current of air passed over his face and the heels clicked closer.

Something sharp jabbed into his shoulder; he cried out in pain, opening his eyes. Tabatha looked down at him, a long, black-painted fingernail hovering by his shoulder.

He'd never seen her up close. Her face was pale and pretty, but her eyes, like amber, glowed bright and hard. So unfeeling. Luke found himself avoiding her gaze.

'I'm glad you recovered,' she said, though Luke doubted this very much. She checked his readings on the monitor. 'You know, Luke, I can make almost everyone I meet do exactly what I want. Do you know why? Because I make it my business to understand what motivates them. Mostly it's fear: they're afraid for themselves. But you, Luke, don't fear for yourself, do you?' She stared at him, unblinking.

'You fear for *others*. In that way, you're like your father.'

The mention of his father threw Luke off completely. She knew his dad? His heart beat faster.

She smiled – a thin, bored smile. 'He loves you very much, you know. After I kidnapped you, he dropped his case against me at once. He'd do anything to protect you.' She picked up a white folder from beside the monitor. The letter 'L' was printed on its spine. 'And when the third chimney rises, and I've brought light to London, you'll be able to go home to him, in that little yellow houseboat of yours.'

How did she know all of this? A shiver ran up Luke's spine. Then again, she knew everything that went on in the plant. Why was this any different?

He tried to focus, even though his head spun. This could be his only chance to talk with Tabatha. He had to find out something about the lab.

Her voice hardened. 'And that's why you must tell me the truth.'

'W-What do you mean?'

'You're a smart boy, Luke, can't you work it out?' She sighed. 'A good bedside manner is overrated – all that chitchat and pleasantry is quite inefficient.' She put the folder down. 'I'm telling you all this to remind you what's at stake: you don't want anything *bad* to happen to your family, do you? Before you have the chance to return to them?'

Did she know about the escape plan? Her face was unreadable. He felt sick inside but stalled for time. 'Tell you the truth about what?'

Her eyes narrowed and she folded her arms. 'I like things to be neat. And right now, too many things don't stack up.' She clasped her hands together. 'Number one: why was the sewage room so clean? The two of you couldn't possibly have wiped it that fast.'

Luke was ready for this; he'd prepped it with Jess. 'We rerouted the pipes, to wash it down. Jess's dad is a plumber, so she knew how.'

Tabatha sucked air through her teeth. Her expression remained blank. 'Number two: why didn't the flames burn you in the third chimney?'

'I don't know, I really don't,' he blurted out honestly. 'They shot straight up. They were strange . . .'

She cocked her head. 'What do you mean by *strange*? Did you notice anything unusual?'

Something told Luke not to mention the faces in the flames, but he struggled to think of something else. Her stare was unbearable. He stuttered, 'I-I-I don't remember. It's all black now.'

She leant forward and yanked the tube from his arm. He cried out with pain.

'Liar,' she hissed. 'Your eyes moved to the right. It's a giveaway, unless you've had practice, like me.'

'But it's true! I don't know.'

'Then it's a half-truth, and half-truth is no better than a lie.' She leant in. 'But why? What did you see worth lying about?' She drummed her nails on the side of the bed.

Her watch beeped. She cursed under her breath.

'I've run out of time. All this talk has taken me away from my research. Let me see if I can incentivise you.' She picked up the white folder and opened it on a page with a photo he knew well. A photo that stood on the mantelpiece at home. It showed him and Lizzy as kids, clutching each other, in the door of their boat.

He'd not seen her for so long. His eyes welled with tears. She was grinning, like he remembered her, like she always did, her hair tied back in a ponytail.

Tabatha ran a nail over Lizzy's face. 'I could kidnap her . . . or make her disappear?'

Luke swallowed. His voice was barely a whisper. 'You wouldn't.'

'You know I can and I would.' She looked at her watch. 'But not tonight – I don't have time with the chimney opening this week. You've got three days, then you'll tell me everything. Won't you?'

Luke nodded, but inside something hardened in him. Sal had been right. Even if he escaped out the vents, they'd never be safe. Tabatha would find him, and his family too. Stopping Tabatha was the only way.

Tabatha spoke softly. 'I know that look in your eyes: it's hope, and I don't like it one bit.' She shoved him off the bed. He winced as his bandaged foot hit the floor. 'Now get out. And shut the door behind you.'

He limped to the door. Had he learned anything at all? Except, perhaps, that the Ghost Council had been right: he needed their help to be truly free.

He pushed the door shut. It closed with a quiet click.

A click! That was it! It was the clue he'd been waiting for – the whereabouts of Tabatha's secret laboratory.

He had to tell Jess and Ravi. Three days wasn't long, but it was long enough. *Find the lab, find your freedom*, Sal had said. If they could get in there, even for an hour, he knew he'd find the evidence of the smog that the Ghost Council needed, and he could be free of Tabatha – and this whole place – for good.

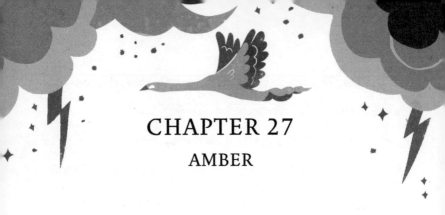

CHAPTER 27
AMBER

Luke rushed as fast as he could, through the East Wing and back to the dormitories. Guards flanked the corridor, under glowing purple lights. Purple lights meant night-time – had he been unconscious all day? He quickened his step.

By the end of the corridor, his foot burned beneath the bandage. He slowed to a hobble, to take weight off the wound. The last thing he wanted was to get an infection. Bertha wouldn't want a limping delivery boy.

He entered the dormitory as quietly as he could and made his way to his bunkbed. He put his hand on the ladder and Ravi's eyes opened.

'You know,' Luke said. 'We should swap bunks. You'd stand a better chance of getting some sleep.'

Ravi shrugged. 'Sleep is for the weak. And at least this way, I don't miss anything.' He stood up and did something he'd never done before: he hugged Luke. It was an awkward hug, but it felt good all the same.

'I'm fine,' Luke said. 'Don't go soppy on me.'

'Sorry. It's just good to see your stupid face.' Ravi stuck his hands in his sackcloth pockets. 'I was sure you were a goner. They said the flames were a hundred feet high. I felt terrible – I should've stopped you. But somehow, even I got carried away with this crazy idea of escaping. That's the problem with hope.' He shook his head. 'I don't sleep well at the best of times, but these last few nights, I've not slept at all.'

Luke reeled. *Last few nights?* 'Wait, what day is it?'

Ravi raised an eyebrow. 'It's Sunday. Didn't they tell you? You were out for three days.'

Luke couldn't believe it. What if Alma had visited while he'd been unconscious? He didn't have much time. 'Ravi, when's the next time Tabatha's out?'

'It's tonight. She always takes the amber ticket kids out herself.'

'Amazing,' Luke said. 'Then we'll go tonight.' He smiled at Ravi. 'You won't believe it, but I think I've found Tabatha's lab. And we have to go there, it's the only way. Well get the evidence for the Ghost Council and . . .'

Luke trailed off. Ravi stared at the floor.

'What's up?' Luke waved his hand in his face. 'I'm the worrier, not you. And come to think of it, where's Jess?'

'She's getting ready.'

'For what?'

Ravi sighed. He opened his left palm. Inside was a crumpled amber ticket. 'She got one too. We're leaving tonight.'

Luke's chest tightened. He looked at Ravi, waiting for a wink, or some sign he was joking. There was none. Luke's mouth opened, but no words came.

Ravi shook his head. 'I'm sorry, Luke. I mean, it doesn't make sense, maybe they missed you because you were ill? Or maybe Terence rigged it?'

Luke forced himself to breathe, but he didn't feel any better. He kicked the floor. 'I should have guessed something was wrong when you hugged me.' He tried to laugh; it came out bitter.

Ravi folded then unfolded the ticket in his hand. 'They gave out loads the day you went down, to lift morale. So, I guess we've got you to thank, if that makes you feel better?'

It didn't. In fact, all Luke could feel was a churning in the pit of his stomach, rising to his chest. It wasn't fair. Not fair at all. He clenched his jaw and tried to hold the feelings down. 'But I've been here two years, and Jess can barely shovel! Why her and not me?'

Ravi's ticket was now crumpled beyond recognition. 'I don't know.' He thumped the mattress. 'It was only the sections that excelled. Lots of us kitchen-workers got one.'

That was some consolation, he thought, although it still felt raw.

'Luke!' A cheery voice from behind interrupted his thoughts. He turned. Jess bounded towards him, her amber ticket pinned to her lapel, grinning. Despite himself, he smiled, a little.

She stopped before him and held out a paper bag. 'It's so awfully unfair, this whole thing. And I hate saying goodbye. So, rather than talk about it, I thought we could skip straight to the presents.'

'Presents?'

Jess nodded. 'Farewell presents! I'd left them in the canteen, in case you didn't wake up in time, so apologies if they smell a bit of gruel. Anyway, this is from Ravi.' She handed him a ring, with a light on the top. Ravi leant in, excited.

'It's a carbon monoxide detector. It lights up if the level gets too high.'

Luke looked at it in wonder. It had to have cost him a fortune. Ravi grinned. 'A kid nicked it off Terence; I traded it for a drumstick.'

'And this,' Jess continued, 'is from me.' She gave Luke the biggest hug and didn't let go for quite a long time. When she did, her eyes were wet. 'I've been told I give good hugs.'

'It was a very good hug. A lot better than Ravi's.'

Ravi scowled. 'A hug is not a real present.'

'Anyway,' she continued. 'Last one. It's from Violet and Bertha.' She pulled out a large foil packet and a waft of butter and onions hit him. She unwrapped it to reveal a mouthwatering plate of food: steak, thin cut chips, peppery sauce, and even salad. 'Violet said it was for Tabatha's guests.'

Luke frowned. *French food*. Terence had mentioned French food – why?

'Don't you like it?' Jess was practically drooling. 'I'll eat if you don't.'

'No, I do.' He picked up the steak and tore into it, then offered the chips round. 'It just reminded me of something. Before the chimney incident, Terence mentioned amber tickets and not liking French food.'

Ravi wrinkled his nose and held up a chip. 'Weird, why wouldn't you like this?'

'Too much garlic?' Jess said.

Luke shook his head. 'No, Terence said it like a threat. Like the tickets were bad. Don't you think that's strange?'

Ravi shifted on the bed. 'Look, you've been unconscious for a few days . . .'

'No, it's not that. Violet said something too. And Sal, the head of the Ghost Council, now I think of it.' He put the plate of food down. 'It doesn't add up. And why so many kids being freed all of a sudden? Even people who can't shovel, like Jess.'

Jess looked at him, a little hurt.

Ravi sighed. 'Stop it, Luke. I know you're not well, but it's not OK. You should be happy for us, not putting us off. My family is waiting for me. I'm not throwing that away on some half-baked plan.'

Yet the more Luke thought, the more worried he felt. There was something off, he knew it. Hearing Ravi talk about his family only made it worse. He couldn't help himself. He had to tell him what he'd known all along. 'They're not there waiting for you, Ravi. I saw your stall on the river. It's not what you think.'

Ravi's face darkened. 'What do you mean? Of course they're

waiting. They've the biggest stall on the water market. It's—'

'No they don't. It's just a red, tattered raft. There's nothing left of it. Just a girl selling incense, knocked about by the waves. She's got a sad look in her eyes and a streak of white hair here—'

Ravi faltered. 'Radhika? How do you know what she looks like . . .' he trailed off, then stood up, his eyes wet. 'You're lying, Luke. I don't know how you know that, but you've got to be lying.'

'I'm not, Ravi. I wish I was. I saw her that first night when I was flying with Alma.' *Alma*. Luke felt a pang of sadness. She was keeping her promise not to return.

'Then why didn't you say? You're jealous, that's it.' Ravi's eyes darted around. 'After all I did for you. I practically raised you in here.'

'It's true! I promise, but we can still make it right, if we can just find the lab and see what Tabatha's doing—'

'Stop it! Just stop it!' Ravi pushed Luke away. 'I've heard enough. The old Luke would have been happy for me, but all this ghost stuff has changed you. You're selfish now. You've risked all our lives, over and over again, so you could act the hero.' He shook his head. 'Well, I'm not playing any more.'

Ravi turned away and began walking.

'Wait, Ravi please. Just listen for a minute.'

'Don't talk to me again.' He called back behind him. 'Not here, or on the other side.'

Luke stood up to follow, but pain shot up his foot, knocking him back to the bed. He watched his friend leave. What had he done?

A hand touched his shoulder. It was Jess. She sat down next to him. 'You really saw his sister?'

Luke nodded.

'And you've got a bad feeling about the tickets?'

'A very bad feeling.'

She unpinned her amber ticket, took a deep breath, then tore it in half.

'Wait!' he cried, but it was already too late.

Jess shrugged. 'I had a bad feeling too. I just wanted to believe.' She handed him half her ticket. 'You deserved it more than me anyway.'

He smiled at Jess, taking the ripped piece of amber paper. He'd wanted a ticket for so long, and now he had half. Like so many things these days, it seemed 'half' suited him just fine.

'So, Lukey, what happens next?'

A wave of doubt hit him. He'd be risking her life, just like

Ravi had said. 'You sure about this? It'll be dangerous, Jess. There might not be any silver linings.'

'I know,' she said 'This is the thunder and rain. But we'll be prepared. We'll pack our umbrellas.'

She winked at Luke. And despite everything, he smiled.

Jess stood up. 'So boss, what's the plan?'

'Find the lab, tell the Ghost Council, take down Tabatha and live happily ever after.'

'Sounds like my kind of plan,' Jess said. 'I'll try to persuade Ravi, but either way, I'll see you by the vents at midnight.'

She walked away leaving Luke to his thoughts.

CHAPTER 28
LAST CHANCE

Elvis's snores cleaved the dusty dorm air. Luke crept down his ladder, quiet out of habit, and tried not to glance at Ravi's empty bed. He tiptoed towards the toilet block, taking care with his bandaged foot. He paused as Elvis's chest rose and fell, then forced himself on. No matter how many times he did it, it never got any easier. Heroes in books dashed fearlessly into danger, but that would never be him. He was just someone who stuck at things; he hoped it was enough.

Anyway, he thought, if he found Tabatha's lab, and the evidence for the Ghost Council, he'd never have to fake being brave again. *Find the lab, find your freedom*, he thought *and get the freak out of here*.

He unscrewed the vent in the toilet cubicle and waited. Cockroaches scuttled by his feet, nervous, like he was. He wondered if Jess had managed to convince Ravi.

Footsteps neared and the door opened. Jess's face said it all.

'He's still mad.' She sighed. 'But I could tell he's going to miss you.' Luke wasn't sure he believed her, but it made him feel better to hear it.

They crawled through the darkness of the vents. Luke's foot throbbed. He didn't feel like talking but Jess, as always, had plenty to say.

'Can't we visit the cat room? It'd cheer you up.'

'We don't have time.'

'What if Stealth's there?'

What if he wasn't? Luke couldn't handle more bad news right then – there was too much at stake. 'We need the time in the lab. It might be our only chance.'

His foot knocked against the shaft; he gasped with pain. Jess flicked on the watch, lighting the tunnel in a dim red glow. She inspected his foot.

'It's bleeding through the bandage. Let's slow down. We don't want you leaving bloody footprints everywhere.'

'I'll be fine,' said Luke, and picked up the pace.

They reached the ventilation of the East Wing, and he checked Ravi's carbon monoxide detector: it was safe. It was also silent. Where were the guards? Had something happened? Everything bad happened in the East Wing. He shivered, then crawled on, counting off storerooms until they reached room ten: the sick bay.

He lowered himself into the empty, bleached white room. The bed he'd lain in had been remade and the monitor put away. There was no sign he'd ever been there.

Jess landed on the floor behind him. 'You said we were going to the lab, not the sick bay.'

'We are,' Luke said. He opened the sick bay door a fraction, then closed it with a click. 'Hear that? When Tabatha came in, the door *hissed* . . . which means there's another door: the door to the lab. That would explain why she's always down here. Why I felt the rain.'

Jess's eyes lit up. 'If it hissed, it's hydraulic. Dead expensive. We installed them in rich people's houses. They keep polluted air out.'

Or the fumes in? Luke noticed a cabinet with gas masks. He opened it, took two and gave one to Jess. 'Who knows, we might need one later.'

Jess walked around the room, running her hand against the

walls. 'No matter how well they're installed, hydraulic doors always have a seam, where door meets wall. The button to open it is usually nearby.'

Something told Luke the button wouldn't be that obvious. Tabatha was thorough; everything had a place. But where to start?

Luke scanned the room. Lining the walls were hundreds of cabinets, stacked with gas masks, painkillers, bandages and creams. Most of them looked barely used. If he were hiding something, he'd choose one of those: he'd hide the button behind a stack of goods.

He moved the pile of gas masks and peered behind: nothing. Checking each cabinet would take too long, there must be a quicker way . . .

Then he noticed the handles. They gleamed clean, save for the one he'd opened, which had a grease mark from his fingers. That was it! Tabatha went to the lab daily, so if the button was in a cabinet, the handle would have a mark too. Serves her right, he thought, for being so tidy.

'I found the door,' Jess called, pointing at diagram of the human body on the wall. 'It's creepy. They hid it in the skeleton half.'

'Any sign of the button?'

'None. I'll keep looking.'

Luke scoured the rows of cabinets for handprints. After dozens of spotless handles, he noticed one with a hand-mark. A particularly greasy hand-mark. It had to be Terence. Was the button in there?

Inside it were vials of green liquid and cotton wool pads. The cabinet wasn't as full as the others; it must have been used recently. He picked up a vial. It was transparent, thin and emerald in colour. What was it, antiseptic?

He pulled out the stopper and sniffed. It was peculiar scent, a mix of alcohol, bleach and something sweet.

Blood rushed to his head. His sight blurred and he staggered back, woozy, almost falling to the floor. He grabbed the cabinet to steady himself.

'Are you OK?' Jess rushed over.

Luke pulled himself up and inspected the tube. 'What is this stuff?'

Jess sniffed gingerly; her face darkened. 'It's Chlor. Two drops on your tongue and it knocks you out. We'd use it on hornet nests, but I imagine it's what they use for kidnapping kids. Knocks you unconscious.'

That was it, Luke knew it. 'I remember it now. They held it over my face, on this horrible rag.' The memories swam into his mind. His father shouting through the smog, then a hand over his mouth, and the same sickly scent as he smelt now.

He put the vial in his pocket and pushed the memories away. *Stay focused, Luke*. He had to solve this. 'Jess, look for handprints on cabinets or any of the furniture. There's got to be one.'

Luke reached the end of his row and saw the desk. He could see the white, leather folder Tabatha had showed him on the shelf, the letter 'L' printed neatly on it. He couldn't resist. He took it off the shelf and looked inside.

There were rows of names. It was a list of all the children who'd been in the plant. The dates went back a hundred years; it must have all started before Tabatha's time. There were notes in the margin. A code of sorts. What did they mean? The same letters came up: 'Fr', 'Es' and 'De'. Almost all the children had the initials by their name.

'Any luck?' Jess called.

He closed the folder and shoved it back on the shelf. It knocked the other folders out of whack. *Focus, Luke*. He lined them up carefully and patted them flush with the wall – except one wouldn't. The 'W' folder stuck out. Had he knocked it? Unless . . .

He pulled it out. Behind the folder was a white button, almost imperceptible against the wall. He pressed it.

Hisssss.

Luke looked round. The skinless half of the skeleton man on the wall split in two, revealing a narrow opening into darkness.

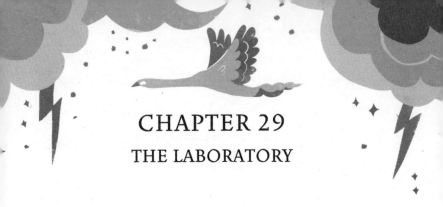

CHAPTER 29
THE LABORATORY

His chest tightened. What was Tabatha hiding? Jess hovered by the door. He had to go in – he knew he had to – he just wasn't sure he'd like what he'd find inside.

He stepped through the opening into the darkness. At first, there was nothing, except the clang of metal under his feet. Then a light flickered on. A strange teardrop lantern that dangled on a chain from high above. The bulb glowed grey, painting the surroundings in a calm monochrome. He'd never seen anything like it.

A black, metal walkway stretched out ahead of him, with railings either side. Beyond the railings lay more darkness, though far below he made out lights: greys, dirty yellows and green glows.

But strangest of all was the feeling of rain. It filled the room. It seeped through the very walls above and below, and yet, to his eyes, there was no rain in sight.

He stepped forward again. A handful of the same grey lanterns flickered into life, lighting the length of the walkway. *Some kind of motion sensor, perhaps?* He peered into the bulb nearest him: there was no heat coming from it. As he touched the glass, the grey gas inside it swirled by his hand.

'That's weird,' Jess said. 'There are no wires going in. What's powering it?'

'I don't know. But I don't like it. Let's keep moving.'

His eyes adjusted. The raised walkway was fixed into the rocky walls of a huge underground cavern. Stalactites hung from the roof and, a good twenty feet down, was the cavern floor, shrouded in darkness, save for the odd lantern. A metal staircase connected the walkway to the lower level.

Jess called from behind. 'Can we stick together? I don't fancy getting lost in here.'

He knew what she meant. They followed the walkway along the edge of the cavern wall, and soon a set of huge black vents appeared above them, set into the wall.

'They're the ones I saw from outside,' Luke said. 'Not that they're any use to us now.'

'Are you sure?' Jess asked. 'Couldn't we just make a run for it?'

Luke thought of the threat Tabatha had made: *you don't want anything bad to happen to your family, do you?* He shivered. 'Even if we made it past the guards, she'd catch us, and you know it.' Luke shook his head. 'We've got be patient. We need to find out what she's doing with the smog, then we get the Ghost Council to stop her, like they promised. It's the only way.'

'And you're sure we can trust them?'

'We don't have much choice.'

His gaze lingered on the vents, all the same. What he'd give for just a night of freedom, in the arms of family. He forced himself to look away and hoped his trust in the Ghost Council wasn't misplaced.

Ahead, along the walkway, an office was embedded in the rockface, with meticulously stacked shelves of books and white binders. In the centre of the office was a large white table, with a monitor, microscope and a spiral notebook.

'There's got to be something in here. Some record of her smog-testing.'

'Well, let's find it quick. I've got a feeling if she catches us, she'll skin us alive.'

A white ring binder rested on a table near the shelves, next to a glass cabinet of what looked like fingernails: some long, some thin, some with serrated edges. Luke shivered again, then opened a white file, filled with spidery handwriting.

'*Optimal ignition conditions remain elusive. Product is either unstable and explosive, or has too low a lumen for commercial use.*'

'What's a lumen, Jess?'

Jess was busy examining a control panel of sorts, with a bewildering array of buttons and dials and screens. 'A lumen? It's an electrical thing. Something to do with light.'

An amber paperweight lay on the table, a spider preserved perfectly within the stone. It almost looked alive. How long had it been trapped? Longer than him, that was for sure. Gingerly, he removed it and leafed through the papers underneath: an architect's drawing of a refurbished third chimney and a large map of London covered in pins. Overlaying the map was another made of intersecting lines. It couldn't be a train map; there were too many lines.

Then it hit him: they were sewers.

He read a note pinned to Oxford Street.

Target: Sarah Banks

Context: Father is a politician – opposes opening of the third chimney

Grab point: Sewer exit E11-23

Smog window: Wednesday, 15th Jan, 15:00-16:30 (Walk home from school)

He knew at once what it was. 'Jess, come here! It's a kidnapping map.'

She rushed over. Her face fell. 'Can we stop it? Can we take the targets off the map?'

'Tabatha would notice. And it wouldn't work anyway, she'll have backups somewhere.'

Jess inspected the other pins. 'What's a "smog window"? How can they know when it's coming?'

But before Luke could answer, they froze dead.

Thud. Thud. Thud. Thud.

Luke looked at Jess. The sound came from the lower cavern level.

'What is it?'

'I don't know,' Jess whispered. 'Maybe we should leave.'

Luke swallowed. 'But we haven't found anything. At least nothing proving that Tabatha's meddling with the smog.' He looked down towards the noise. 'We have to investigate.'

'Can I stay here?' Jess pointed to the monitor. 'I reckon I'm more use here than with dark, thudding noises.'

Luke nodded. He didn't blame her. In a way, he felt happier with her away from the scary noise too.

He limped back along the gangway to the spiral staircase that led to the lower level. He stepped carefully, to stop his bandage getting caught, and watched the lower level light up before him. It was vast, dark and split into two distinct sections. The left side held rows of wire cages, filled with small animals. The right side, however, was shrouded in shadows. The thudding came from there.

Just his luck, Luke thought.

He stepped towards the noise.

Thud. Thud. Thud. Thud.

The rain-feeling grew stronger. It didn't make sense. It couldn't rain underground. But there was another feeling too. Hairs prickled on the back of his neck and a shiver of fear ran down his spine.

He stopped and slowed his breathing. The evidence he needed for the Ghost Council might be just around the corner. Some sign of the smog in the lab. Or perhaps someone trapped in there. What if it was Janey?

He had to go on. He took another step forward.

Thud. Thud. Thud. Ssssss.

A new sound had started. A hissing, moaning, high-pitched wail. Luke wasn't sure why, but it sounded familiar.

Then suddenly, he saw them, peering at him through the darkness. Hundreds of them, like an army of squat, blue-black metal shadows. The incinerators. They were larger and more robust than the one in the sewage room, he could have stood up easily inside one. He shuddered, remembering how Alma had struggled inside one. He didn't know what Tabatha was doing, but it wasn't going to be good.

Thud. Thud. Thud. Ssssss.

The thuds came from the nearest incinerator. Unlike the others, which looked empty, its glass chamber swirled with steam. Through the grey, he glimpsed a fist beat against the glass. Luke rushed forward and pressed his face to it. Slumped in the mist sat a figure, but it was hard to see.

Could it be Alma? Was that why she hadn't visited? His heart thumped loudly.

Luke tapped on the glass. 'Are you OK?'

The figure sat perfectly still, then its head swivelled to reveal a familiar face: an eyeless boy with a sharp-toothed smile.

The ghoul. How was that possible? The boat had swallowed it.

He took a step back. The last time he'd seen that thing it had tried to kill him, but it looked different now. Smaller, wearier. It stumbled towards Luke. A long, snake-like tongue shot out and licked the window of the chamber, at the exact spot Luke's face had been.

Luke recoiled. Still just as creepy, he thought, grateful for the glass.

The ghoul grinned and pointed to the incinerator's control panel. Words glowed on the screen:

Specimen source: Vauxhall Pier

Countdown: 10 seconds

Property: Margate industries (M.I.)

Luke froze. M.I. stood for Margate Industries. They were the initials he'd seen on the riverboat turbines. It could only mean one thing: Tabatha manufactured the smog-proof riverboats!

It began to make sense. If she made the boats, she could keep whatever they sucked up. And it wasn't just smog, it was ghosts too. But why did she want ghosts? Luke looked at the ghoul. 'What's she doing to you here?'

The ghoul pointed frantically towards a large green button. On the screen, the countdown was almost over.

5 . . . 4 . . . 3 . . . 2 . . .

Luke hesitated. He didn't know what the green button did. He couldn't just press it. It might set the ghoul free.

Then the countdown hit zero. Metal screeched from the chamber ceiling. A panel slid open, revealing blue-black, metal blades. The ghoul snarled and hammered desperately against the glass. Luke didn't want to watch. He moved his hand away.

The eyeless boy's face twisted into a sneer. Baring its teeth, it rammed its face into the glass. The whole chamber shook. Then the propeller switched on.

Whirring metal drowned out its cries. Within seconds, the blades tore it to wisps, which spun round the chamber and through the propeller over and over again, until all that remained was grey steam. The propeller stopped, and from the bottom of the machine, cogs and valves began to move and hiss, culminating in a set of gentle thunks, as a series of glass vials and flasks popped out into a tray.

Luke inspected them. They were all too familiar: the red 'liquid fire' from the third chimney, the black syrup that made that shoveller cough smoke, and a teardrop bulb of glowing grey mist, like from the walkway above. They were all made from ghosts. Refined and repurposed into products that Tabatha could use.

All of a sudden he missed shovelling. And sewage wiping. And sprouts. All of those things were better than this. This was a whole other level of evil. No ghost, or even ghoul, deserved a fate like this. They were souls, like him – you couldn't shred them and bottle them up.

The Ghost Council couldn't ignore this. It broke every rule. They would have to intervene and help him escape. But first he had to get out of this toe-curling lab.

A beep sounded from the control panel, making him jump. The countdown on the screen had started again, at ten minutes. The ghoul's wisps began to coalesce. How many times had that ghoul been ripped apart like that? How long would it take before he was entirely spent?

He turned away from the chamber. He had what he needed. He rushed up to the stairs, to find Jess at a monitor, examining diagrams.

'What do you want first, Jess? Bad news or good?'

Jess puffed. 'Can't I just hear the good?'

'Good news: we've got the evidence we need to persuade the Ghost Council. Bad news, Tabatha's manufacturing things from ghosts with those horrible incinerators.'

'I see.' Her face darkened. 'That's why they looked like

dehumidifiers. They must condense the ghostcloud into liquid, before heating it up and separating the parts.' She looked uneasily at the wireless, hanging grey bulbs. 'I guess souls burn bright, even without electricity.'

'It's efficient,' Luke said. 'I'll give her that. With bulbs like that, there'd be no energy crisis. And it explains the feeling of rain. There are ghostclouds – or what's left of them – in every one of these bulbs.'

Jess pointed at a map. 'There's another thing too. She pumps the waste from here around the city. The pipes run through the sewers. It's a mean piece of plumbing.'

Even at times like this, Luke thought, Jess was talking plumbing. He wished he could tell Ravi, he'd roll his eyes for sure. But then that wasn't likely to happen now, not in this lifetime at least.

'Let's talk plumbing later. We better head back, before someone finds us.'

They rushed along the gangway, but in his haste, the bandage on his foot caught the railing. He winced in pain.

'Let me sort that. I'll be quick.' Jess crouched down and began unwrapping. She stopped dead.

Luke looked down. 'What's wrong? I know should have cut my toenails—'

'No, it's not that.' Jess pointed at his foot. There was no burn mark, only a neat incision, sewn up with stitches. In the darkness of the lab, a faint red light pulsed from under the skin. 'It's a tracker, Luke.'

A tracker? He felt sick to his stomach. 'She'll know I came here. When she's back . . .' He trailed off. He could see it only too clearly.

Tabatha would return in an hour, maybe two, and as soon as she did, she'd know what had happened. That he'd broken into her lab. He wouldn't stand a chance. Not only that, she'd get Lizzy too. He knew, he just knew, that she'd make them both pay.

He sat down on the floor. He had the evidence he needed to persuade the Ghost Council, but he'd run out of time.

'Luke, get up.' Jess shook his arm. 'We need to keep moving.'

But Luke couldn't. His legs, normally so strong, wouldn't move an inch. He felt heavy and cold. Discovering the tracker had drained the very last of his energy.

He found himself being dragged up.

'It's not over till it's over.' Jess had her arm under his and was heaving him to his feet. Then she began half-dragging, half-walking him back towards the sickbay. 'Now use that big brain of yours and think of something.'

Luke looked at Jess's face. It was paler than usual, but her eyes were set with a fierce determination. She wasn't giving up.

He swallowed down his fear.

'OK. First, we get you back to the dormitory. I'm the one with the tracker. She doesn't know you've been here.'

Jess nodded. 'And second?'

Luke's brow furrowed in thought, as they slipped through the opening back to the sickbay. After the grey light of the lab, the bright white hurt his eyes.

'I have to speak to Alma before Tabatha gets back. That gives us a few hours at best.'

'And if Alma doesn't come in time?' Jess asked. Luke had hoped Alma would come, or that, by now, he'd have found another way. But there was only one option left.

'I've got an idea. But I don't think you'll like it.'

CHAPTER 30
LETTING GO

'Too blooming right, I don't like it.'

Luke had waited until they reached the relative safety of the cubicle to explain. He couldn't have risked an argument in the vents: the sound travelled too far.

'It's the only way, Jess. I have to find Alma up there, and she even told me how to do it.' He listed the steps on his finger. 'Think of the sky, then death, and let the End Place pull you.'

'She also told you it was dangerous, and hard to come back.' She blocked the door. 'No. This is crazy. Let's wait for Alma.'

'We fell out, remember. She said she'd never come again, and she's more stubborn than me.' He looked at his watch. 'Tabatha will be back soon and when she checks the tracker, I'm finished. I might as well go down fighting.' Luke tried a smile. 'Come on, Jess, silver linings, remember?'

'You want me to be positive?' Jess cried. 'Well, I'm 100 per cent positive that this is a stupid idea. You might die, for heaven's sake. Be logical, Luke.'

Luke shook his head. 'But whose logic, Jess? This place has a logic. It's all based on fear: it tells you to wait and to keep your head down, hoping for an amber ticket one day. But if we all ignored it, even for a day, if we fought back, the whole thing would fall.'

Jess didn't look reassured.

'I'm sorry, Jess.' He placed his hand on hers.

She brushed it right off. 'Stop it. I'm not some new kid any more, you need to listen to me. You haven't thought this through. What if Alma's not there?'

He tried to think. 'If she's not, I'll find her. Or fly straight to the Ghost Council.'

'But they don't like half-ghosts! And what if there's a ghoul?'

'I'll think of something.' He opened the cubicle door. 'It's a bad idea, I know, but unless you've got a better one . . .'

Jess stomped her foot, sending the cockroaches scurrying into their hole. They both looked at the floor. A moment passed. A cockroach peeked out, antennae twitching.

She sighed, resigned. 'I'm not good at being angry.' Her voice was quiet. 'And it won't make any difference. You'll do it anyway.'

She walked away, then turned back and hugged him, hard, as though her life depended on it.

'Promise me you'll come back.'

'I promise I'll try.'

'That'll have to do.' Jess let go. 'I'll leave you to it. I don't want to watch.'

Luke walked in silence back to his bunk. He climbed into Ravi's empty bed, breathed and closed his eyes. He tried to remember what Alma had said. It had sounded simple enough.

He thought of the sky. Of rain, of clouds, and the wind.

He thought of death. Of the end that was coming to them all, whether they liked it or not.

And he thought of the End Place. Of his mum, waiting there for him. Waiting to welcome him with open arms.

The darkness of the dormitory gave way to blurred shapes. Sounds became drowned. Then there was a sense of weightlessness, of drifting up, out of his body, into the air. A whooshing, a screaming, in a starlit night.

He felt the pull of the End Place, and it didn't let go.

Its pull felt like freedom. Freedom from the plant, from Tabatha, from all of the struggle. But also freedom from the burden of hope, which had hung for so long like a noose around his neck.

Light as feather, he rose ever higher. Everything was black, but he could feel the cold growing. His senses numbing. He was falling asleep, but for once, it wasn't difficult. He was ready for it this time.

But then someone spoke through the void, gentle, but firm. 'Luke, wake up.'

He shook his head. He didn't want to.

The voice spoke again. 'You have to wake up.'

Something stirred in him. He knew that voice. His eyes opened at once.

'Mum?'

But there was nothing, only a black night sky.

Ice crystals dotted in sheet-like clouds all around him. He shivered, suddenly, in the frozen air. He had risen so high. If it weren't for that voice, he would have kept on going, all the way to the End Place.

Had it really been her?

He looked up for some sign. The cirrus clouds shimmered in the distance, and beyond them, the stars. It was beautiful, that was for sure, and he could still feel its pull. But not as strong as before. It wasn't his time.

He remembered Jess's hug and its warmth on his skin. The memories of the last few hours and days, and all that was at stake: his sister, his family and his friends. His freedom. He had to find Alma and the Ghost Council and tell them what he'd seen. When they knew what Tabatha was doing, they'd stop her for sure.

He breathed out and his kite-cloud unfurled beneath him. He sank back towards the city and the world of the living.

*

He scanned the horizon. To the west and south, there was nothing – just an empty sky and purple haze. To the east, in the distance, there lay a smattering of clouds: a horse galloping through the air; a shoal of fishclouds; and a long, thin man-cloud of sorts. But no sign of Alma, no swans, or anything birdlike. He turned to look north. What he saw made him want to sink into his cloud. Over Hampstead Heath was a monstrous swirl of charcoal thunder. Swollen, dark and crackling with blue.

A storm. He could feel the tension in the air. Could Alma be in there? Or had she left the city when she'd seen it coming?

Alma had warned him against going to the Heath alone, even

243

on a good day. But with the sky like that, he didn't stand a chance.

But he had to do something. Maybe if he could speak to those ghosts in the east? Would they pass the message on? The council would act, if only he could tell them.

Luke looked in each direction — Alma could be miles away for all he knew. He kicked his cloud in frustration. A piece of cloud fluff drifted east, then swept up and fast along the river. The wind was still blowing east. Maybe it was a sign.

Without a word, he tilted his kite-cloud and let the wind take him.

The wind blew strong and steady, pulling him across the monstrous grey city. He breathed in the views as he went. From the streets and canals, to the soot-stained buildings, it looked wild, living and somewhat hungry. But no matter how fast he flew, he couldn't seem to catch up. The ghostclouds he'd seen disappeared on the horizon. The wind slowed to a breeze. He'd never reach them.

He passed the Tower of London — its prisoners looked up through bars, skinny and shackled — then the great Tower Bridge. Its halves lifted to let a riverboat through; Luke rose higher in the air, safe from its propellers.

Then he caught sight of the east, and time seemed to stop.

The east of London was like a foreign land. When the ice caps had melted, and the waters rose, the authorities hadn't finished the flood barriers in time, and the eastern streets had been flooded ever since. Now instead of streets, there was a network of waterways, bridges, islands and eccentric boats that rose and fell with the tides. Towering over it all was the Old Olympic Stadium. A doughnut shaped building, with once proud pillars now dirtied and rotting, covered in green-grey creepers and white-flowering bindweed.

In the dark waterways, rippling the cool evening air, the only colours he could see were the blue, white and red of the Union Jack, fluttering on every houseboat in sight.

They weren't patriotic – well, not necessarily – flags were just regulation. If they took theirs down, they'd be spotted and sunk. At least it looked pretty from above, he thought.

And then amidst the sea of flags he saw it: what he'd dreamt of each night for the last two years. A solitary splash of sunshine yellow nestling on the edge of a bridge-ridden islet. He saw his home.

CHAPTER 31
HOME

The boat had a low flat roof and was square in shape, with four nautical windows on each side. On the top of the house was a garden, with a tiny lawn, a football goal and some muddy flower beds with trellises of red and white roses.

He found himself drifting towards it. Like a magnet, it seemed to pull him closer. Every fibre of Luke's being wanted to look, but he knew he should be searching for Alma.

Luke tried to act normal, but his hands shook. He hadn't seen his family for so long. His heart swelled at the thought of Lizzy; he used to play, talk and fight with her every day. And his dad – if only they could talk for a moment. He knew his dad would be proud of how strong he'd been. Just a look, it couldn't hurt.

He descended until his cloud brushed the tallest trees and cast a thick, grey shadow across his home, and then further still, until his cloud was a glistening grey mist, licking against the walls of the houseboat. He slipped off and landed on the outer deck. A tingle of excitement shot up his body, as he ran his hand along the wooden exterior.

He peered into the first room. The wooden shutters were down but he could just about see through the slats. When Luke peered up close, his heart leapt: it was his sister Lizzy. She was asleep on the bed, turned on her side. Her dark hair was longer and her face thinner. She looked more grown up than before.

Lizzy's room, once full of film posters and trinkets, was now almost as plain as Luke's dormitory in Battersea. A desk and her bed were all that remained. It was strange, he thought. It didn't feel right.

He moved to the next window, his excitement now twisted into an anxious knot in his stomach. Had Lizzy changed so much? Why did the place feel so wrong? Perhaps coming here had been a bad idea.

He reached the next room – his father's room – and saw a faded curtain had replaced the shutters. A pattern of red roses, with plenty of thorns, wove in and out across the fabric.

Through the closed curtains, he saw a shadow moving inside the room. It walked back and forth. There was something strange about the way it moved. It was slow. Unsteady. Lurching even.

The shadow stopped. It turned to the window, gave a long rattling cough, then grew larger. It neared the curtain, until a stooping silhouette stood against the light. The curtains opened with a jerk. An old lady stood at the window. Her skin was dark, and her forehead furrowed. Her lips were thin, and from their edges, faint webs of wrinkles spun out across her sunken cheeks. But her eyes were lively and hard. They peered out the window, looking into the grey.

It was Nana Chatterjee – Luke's only living grandma, and the only link he still had to his mum. She'd looked after Luke and Lizzy when their mother had died, and a few times since, when his dad struggled to cope. She'd come down at a day's notice and cook and nag and clean, with a fierce kind of love. She'd fought in the war too and was as tough as nails.

Nana Chatterjee rubbed her brow, turned from the window and hobbled at pace towards the door. She wore a dark pink dressing gown and held a thin steel cane that rapped against the floor as she walked. A surge of fear ran through Luke. Where was his dad?

Nana Chatterjee tottered on. She turned left out the bedroom and entered the kitchen. Luke followed, watching through the steamed-up windows. She climbed up a ladder, opened the hatch to the roof garden and stepped out into the mist.

'The scoundrels,' she muttered, picking up a pair of garden shears. 'Foolish. Corrupt. Vindictive scoundrels.'

She began pruning the roses with vigorous snips, each cut was precise and as quick as a bird. 'But she's sleeping again. That's a solace at least.'

It didn't make sense. Luke clenched his fist, and the mist drew into him. *Relax*, he told himself. But it was hard, with the questions hammering inside his head.

Nana Chatterjee was talking again. 'Kidnap his son? His only son?' she spat. 'Utter codswallop!' Then she sighed to herself and moved onto the fuchsia. She plucked a flower and put it in her pocket.

A flash of anger crossed Luke's face. What had happened here? He suddenly had an idea. He lifted his cloud up above the boat and hovered it low in the sky. *Think of the rain*, that's what Alma had said. So that's what he did. He thought of it, hammering wet against the window, lashing Lizzy and her kite, soaking them both through their coats in the park . . . and all at once, he felt it coming. The droplets buzzed inside him and began to fall.

His grandma's face rushed towards him, he felt the water

touch her face, and his cloud burst into shimmering images of light.

They were not images he wanted to see. His dad crying at the kitchen table, next to a pile of 'missing' posters with Luke's face on them. A grim-faced policeman arriving at the door, with a pair of handcuffs, dragging his dad out onto the street. The last, and worst, somewhere dark and dripping. Nana Chatterjee held Lizzy's hand, as his father coughed, pale and gaunt, from behind a row of metal bars.

He broke off the rain. Pain stabbed in his chest and his eyes stung with tears. His dad was in jail. His sister alone. His frail grandma holding the fort.

It had to be Tabatha's doing. She had framed his dad, paid off the police, and left his family to rot.

But somewhere inside, he knew it was his fault too. If he hadn't been kidnapped, this never would have happened. Or if he'd escaped instead of waiting to be rescued, or for an amber ticket, he could have proved his dad's innocence long ago.

The image came back to him. The dripping, black bars. His dad coughing. *How long had he been there? How long would he last?* Luke thought.

Down on the roof, something stirred. Nana Chatterjee had barely moved, despite the downpour. Her dressing gown was now sodden and her black-grey hair dripped, and though she held her shears, she was not looking at the roses. She was looking up at the sky. Right at him.

'Luke?' she asked, peering into the mist. 'Is that you?'

Luke froze. How had she seen him? Alma had said people only saw you if you wanted them to.

Had he wanted her to? He looked down at his grandma. Her eyes were hard, but he felt nothing but love. He knew at once that part of him *had* desperately wanted her to see him. To have someone in his family see him again.

And now he'd broken the Ghost Council's first rule – he'd interfered with the living – and he might never get to see his family again.

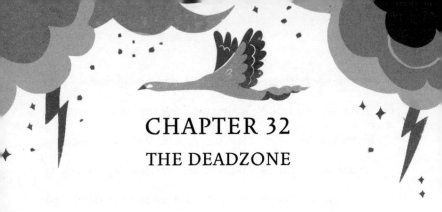

CHAPTER 32
THE DEADZONE

The wind swelled and changed direction, gusting leaves and water to the west. Was it the Ghost Council, coming? Had they seen what he'd done? Luke scanned the sky: no, still empty. It was just the wind. All the same, he felt nervous.

He heard a clatter below. Nana Chatterjee had moved, she was at the ladder. 'Pull yourself together, old woman,' she muttered, climbing down. 'It was just the sky, nothing more. Your mind playing tricks.'

She shook her head, then reached up, and slammed the trapdoor shut. The force of it sent a patch of roof tarp loose, spinning west on the breeze. Luke watched it dance through the air to the river.

He missed them so much, and he was still reeling from what he'd seen – his dad in that jail, his sister alone – but he couldn't stay. He had to find Alma, and quickly. Once the Ghost Council knew, they'd have to stop Tabatha.

Or he hoped they would. It was the only way his family would be safe.

But where was Alma? For all her talk, she'd shared almost nothing of herself, and no real clue where she might be. Who were her friends? Where did she go when she wasn't in the sky? It was obvious to Luke now that she didn't trust easily.

He looked to the river. The loose piece of tarp skittered down to it, then landed on some driftwood, like a makeshift raft. His thoughts stirred. It reminded him of something. Something Alma had said. Where had he seen tarp like that before?

The southern slums, that was it! The rooves were just like that – and Alma had said that the slums were her 'haunt'. She had to be there! Sheltering from the storm, probably, under all those tarps. It had been foolish to rush east, he saw that now. Alma was there, somewhere south, and he wouldn't rush this time. He'd be thorough, methodical, like a detective would. He'd been given a second chance and he wouldn't waste it. He turned his cloud and dived towards the river. Across its surface, a strong breeze blew west: west towards Battersea.

*

He'd been flying for some time – his cloud ash-grey with thought – before the station's chimneys rose up ahead. But it wasn't the chimneys that drew him, it was the tattered dwellings against the compound walls. The start of the slums. Teeming, leaning, and sprawling south – they were a patchwork of corrugated iron and tarpaulin.

He veered up off the river and towards them, and soon peered down over the edge of his cloud. Beneath him a handful of ragged families huddled around a firepit, hands held out for warmth, cooking meat and scraps and who knew what. Stray cats and dogs lurked in the gloom. The tang of burnt plastic hung in the air.

Violet had said the slum-dwellers knew things others didn't. Would they have seen a swan-cloud? There was only one way to find out. With a twinge of guilt, he moved close to one of the huddled groups, and thought of rainy days. A moment of nothing, then that strange splitting sensation again and the raindrops fell, splattering the tattered groups below. At once, images flickered into life on the surface of his cloud: hunger and cold, family and fatigue, long factory days and searches in the scrapheaps. But nothing of the sky. It didn't seem like the slum-dwellers ever looked up at the sky.

Then, as they rushed for cover from the rain, the images faded, leaving only a smouldering pyre and skewers of half-cooked meat.

Luke shook his head. He'd just have to look for himself.

At first, he scoured from above. But as the minutes passed, with nothing in sight, he sank lower and lower, until his mists filled the labyrinth of passages that wormed through the slums, to see if she was hiding, or sleeping, somewhere low to the ground. On another day, he would have enjoyed it all – his dad had never let him venture south of the river – but today, there was no joy to be had.

Another hour passed, and he began to lose hope. He glanced north to see the storm still raging. If he tried to find the Ghost Council in that, he'd be ripped into pieces. But if he didn't, who knew what Tabatha would do. She'd be back soon, he felt sure of it, and there was still so much of the slum to cover. He had to try something different. He rose back into the sky and scanned the horizon.

He had run out of ideas. A dog howled to the moon, a melancholy sound. Another dog joined, and a handful more, until the whole sky hummed with the howls of dogs.

Where were they coming from? He looked across and saw at once. He had stopped a stone's throw from Battersea Dog and Cats

Home. It was one of the few buildings that had survived the war intact. Its wire fences protected and homed thousands of strays. He'd often asked his dad for a dog. Not enough room on the boat, he'd always said, but after Stealth, Luke had wondered whether he might try for a cat.

Come to think of it, Alma had mentioned the dog and cats home. She said she loved it even more than London Zoo. Could she be down there? It was worth a look. He lowered himself down towards the building, filling the streets with a blue-grey mist.

'Awoooo!'

Another howl pierced the air, this time a greeting, quickly followed by a chorus of howls, as the dogs ran from their kennels and into the yard. They jumped, barked and scampered into his mist, wagging their tails and licking the air. It tickled. He couldn't help but smile.

It wasn't at all like he imagined. The dogs' coats were clean and they looked well fed. They ran about the yard, side by side, yapping happily. He rained down on them and a medley of half-formed dog-thoughts hit him, not as images, but as smells. It was a flood of aromas: fresh and rotten meat, cats and birds, water and earth, rubbish and drains. And, in the distance, a faint smell of smoke.

Luke shuddered. Not any old smoke, but a perfumed tobacco smoke, which he knew only too well: Tabatha Margate's pipe smoke. The smell was coming from the east – he turned and saw a black flash of sportscar in the distance, tinted windows wound down. Its tyres screeched as it tore round corners, away from the shelter towards the heart of the Deadzone.

Why was Tabatha heading there this late at night?

He had to find out. Luke puffed his cloud out and caught an eastward breeze, following the car from a distance, as it weaved in and out through empty streets. It never stopped once at lights or slowed on corners. It rarely needed to, to be fair, for the streets were deserted: it was the Deadzone, after all.

He tried to remember what his grandma had told him. Years ago now, the Europeans had invaded there. Under the cover of night, they'd burst through the Old Channel Tunnel with tanks and troops. Buildings still bore the marks of the attack: crumbling spires of brickwork and steel, pockmarked from the spray of bullets and shells. When it looked almost too late, their advance had been stopped dead in its tracks, by the mayor's ruthless counter-offence. He released poisonous nerve gas across the whole area. The battle was won, but that area of the city never recovered. Traces of the gas were still found today, and those who ventured there didn't always come back.

Why was Tabatha headed there of all places?

Her car came to a stop outside a giant brick building that had seen better days. It had great arches of woven steel and glass, but many had fallen, twisted to the ground. Underneath them, he glimpsed railway tracks, covered with rubble. It was Waterloo station itself. Once bustling with life, lay abandoned. Not even weeds grew here: the chemical traces had poisoned everything.

He looked down at the shadows. Craters were still visible, dotted around the buildings. One contained a double-decker bus with shattered windows, its red now faded, wheels long stolen. There was no movement he could see . . . except, in the corner, by the edge of a twisted steel column, was a familiar glow: the glow of a smouldering pipe in the darkness.

Luke lowered his cloud until it was a thick grey mist, blanketing the ground. Over the yowl of stray cats, picking at the rubble, he heard the whisper of voices. He needed to get closer. He stepped through the mist, keeping himself hidden, and watched from behind the rusting, double-decker bus. It was funny, he thought, even as a half-ghost, she managed to make him fear for his life.

'Have you got the goods?' said Tabatha, her voice quiet on the wind.

'Of course,' said another, with a strong French accent.

A second light appeared – the light of a torch – followed by a beast of a man with slicked back hair and stubble. He held a mud-coloured sack. He peeled back the fabric to reveal rods of blue-black metal.

'The rest of it's in the tunnel. What are you using it for, anyway?'

'It's none of your business.'

A pair of headlights flicked on ahead, so bright Luke's eyes stung. He squinted through a broken pane in the bus and his eyes adjusted. The lights came from a minibus, and behind the windscreen of the minibus sat Terence.

'There are fifteen,' said Tabatha. 'They're hard workers. Strong. Broken in. They follow rules.'

The Frenchman laughed. 'Yours always do. My van's in the tunnel. Load them up quick.'

Fifteen what? Then at once, he knew. He watched as Terence slid open the passenger door to the mini-bus and hoisted an unconscious child in a sackcloth over his shoulder. He felt sick.

The amber tickets were not a ticket out of Battersea. They were a ticket to Europe and beyond: to more hard labour, to a possible war or who knew what else.

Terence adjusted the body on his back. 'This one needs glasses. But he's a very good shoveller, and smart too. Keeps his head down.'

'We have glasses on the mainland. Chuck him in the back.'

Luke strained his eyes; it was too dark to make much out. Then Terence walked past the headlights, lighting for a moment a face he knew well. A face he'd seen every morning for the last two years: it was Ravi. His eyes were closed, but he was breathing.

Luke gripped the broken glass of the bus. Ravi had worked so hard. He'd dreamt of seeing his family for over four years. If he woke up in Europe – or who knew where – it would break him.

Luke wanted to run at Tabatha, he wanted to smash her with his fists, but that wouldn't help anyone. He had to think things through, think of a plan how to stop her, but there wasn't the time.

He shrugged. He'd just have to wing it a little.

He stepped out from his shelter, still cloaked in mist, and followed Terence through the night towards the Old Channel Tunnel.

CHAPTER 33
RESCUE

He wasn't taking any chances, even with someone as gormless as Terence. So, as Terence plodded ahead with Ravi on his back, Luke stayed a few paces behind, hidden within a haze of fog. As they neared the tunnel and the light petered out, a thick darkness took hold of the place. Terence didn't seem to notice. He stepped over tracks, rubble and broken glass, without even a glance down. He'd walked this path before, Luke was sure of it.

At the tunnel mouth, Terence flicked on his torch, illuminating arched brick walls in a faint, green glow. In the distance stood a wall of sulphur-stained rubble and twisted iron struts, where the once proud tunnel had collapsed, blocking the only path between England and Europe. Cracked water pipes lined the base of the barricade, gushing grey water across the muddy floor. A cluster of tabby cats drank from the puddles.

'Stinking cats.' Terence's boots squelched on, deeper inside, right towards the destruction. Where was he heading? 'Stinking kids,' he spat, adjusting the weight of Ravi on his back. Then at the last moment, when Luke was sure he would chuck Ravi's body on the floor, he turned sharply right. Through the light of his torch, he peered at the arched brick walls, and reached out his hand to touch a frayed rubber wire. What on earth was he doing?

Grunting, Terence pulled the wire down. There was a click and hiss, and a section of moss-covered brickwork slid open. Lights switched on from within, revealing a whole new section of tunnel, stretching into the distance, and a black painted van with a European number plate. Tabatha had reopened the Tunnel!

Terence wasted no time. He was already at the van, unlocking the door. Luke came close behind and peered in, flooding the secret tunnel with his mist. Inside the van, he made out yellowed soundproof padding and a set of manacles and rusting iron chains. A dank metal odour stained the air. Terence tossed Ravi in the back, then wiped his mouth. 'Stinking mist and stinking children,' he grumbled, then turned, and walked right through Luke back into the main tunnel.

Luke shuddered. *Still greasy*. At least Terence hadn't seen him, he thought. All he had to do now was get Ravi out of the van.

He grabbed Ravi's hand, and though at first his hands

slipped through, with some concentration, he lifted Ravi – still unconscious – to a floppy, sitting position. Then it hit him. He could hardly drag a sleeping Ravi out of the Deadzone, across the ground, rubble and broken glass. He had to wake him, somehow.

Alma had cleared Fat Elvis's sinuses, could he do something similar? But how?

Footsteps crunched behind him and he let go of Ravi, who fell without a sound to the padded van floor. A moment later, Terence arrived and dumped a pair of children in the back, before turning back to the mouth of the tunnel.

As soon as he passed, Luke stepped back into the van. He'd start with Ravi, then come back for the other two kids after. He leant down and put his hand over Ravi's face. The sinuses started in the nose, he knew that much, so with a grimace, he put a finger up Ravi's nostril.

'Yuk,' he said. Then his finger tingled. What was happening?

He pulled his finger out, but a tendril of mist had grown from it, and was flowing up into Ravi's nose. And he could feel it now, travelling deeper into Ravi's airways. And then suddenly he could see. In his mind's eye, an X-ray of Ravi's lungs unfolded, with every tube and vessel mapped out before him. And there, in the midst of the lungs, he saw the cause of the problem: the droplets of green Chlor.

Slowly, delicately, he reached his mist towards the green drops. The green mingled with grey, and then flowed back through the mist, out of Ravi's airways and mouth, into Luke's hand. He looked down. The index finger on his left hand glowed green from the Chlor. Luke grinned. It was gross, admittedly, but it was pretty cool.

Ravi coughed and sat bolt upright. 'What's happening? Where's my ticket?' Then he took in the van and the unconscious children. 'Oh.' He seemed to shrink as he said it. Like the air had gone out of him.

'It's OK.' Luke put a ghostly hand on his shoulder. It didn't look as reassuring as he meant it to be. 'We're going to get out.'

Ravi's words were a whisper. 'You were telling the truth. The tickets are a lie.'

'Worse than a lie. They're selling you abroad.'

'So why are here? To say "I told you so"?'

'No. I'm here to save you.'

'That's almost more annoying.' Ravi's face broke into a smile. A tired, cracked smile. 'Hold on, you're all fuzzy.' He stuck a finger out towards Luke, and it went right through his face. It wasn't the politest way to greet someone who was saving your life, but Luke let it pass.

'Wait?' Ravi blinked. 'What's going on?'

'I'm a ghost, temporarily.' He looked around. 'And if you don't get moving, you'll end up one too.'

Ravi swallowed. 'OK, lead the way.' Luke stepped out into the tunnel. Dripping, dark, and thick with mist. The only light came from the van, and that didn't stretch more than a few feet in front. Ravi stumbled out of the van behind him. 'My head feels like a spade hit it. Don't go too fast.'

In the distance, boots splashed through gushing water.

Ravi looked at Luke. 'Scrap that, go fast, just don't let go of my hand.'

Luke nodded and led Ravi into the darkness.

CHAPTER 34
ESCAPE

Churned up mud and broken glass crunched unhelpfully underfoot, as Ravi and Luke crept out towards the mouth of the tunnel. They stayed close to the wall, hidden in Luke's mist, as Terence's footsteps thudded past them, then became muffled beyond the secret door. It was only a matter of time before he saw Ravi was missing.

Luke would have to go faster, but the last thing he wanted was Ravi stumbling.

Behind them, the van door screeched open, followed by even louder man-screech.

'Come back now, you stinking wart of a child!'

The green beam of Terence's torch swung across the tunnel. Luke didn't look back. A minute more and they'd make it. Terence's muttering carried on in the mist, but thankfully sounded like it was getting further away, and they were now almost at the mouth of the tunnel. Luke's heart raced. He held tight to Ravi's hand, then suddenly Ravi clattered to the floor. What had happened? He looked down. A giant piece of twisted iron stuck up from the ground. Luke must have walked right through it and pulled Ravi into it.

'I'm sorry! Are you OK?'

'I've been better.' Ravi held his right leg. A small piece of glass stuck out from his shin. 'Does this balance out what I said in the plant?'

'I've forgotten already.'

But Terence's torch beam had not forgotten. It now pierced through the mist close to where they stood. They had to keep moving.

Luke pulled Ravi up. His friend gritted his teeth, unable to stifle a groan. It was quiet, but not quiet enough. Terence's footsteps grew louder and faster.

Seconds later, a greasy grip lifted Ravi in the air.

Terence sneered down. 'I've got you now,' Terence hissed, spraying Ravi with spittle. With his free hand, Terence pulled a vial of Chlor from his pocket and pushed off the stopper with his thumb.

Luke looked at the bottle. In a second or two, Ravi would be unconscious again. He had to do something. Then the light of Terence's torch, now slung on his neck, slipped down, lighting up Luke's arm. He saw a faint green glow in his finger, from the droplets of Chlor he'd removed from Ravi earlier.

It might not work, but he had to try. He leapt up and thrust his green index finger into Terence's mouth. Terence jerked back, breathing in the green droplets, then collapsed to the floor. Ravi fell to the ground.

'When did you become a ninja?'

Luke shrugged. 'Always was.'

They left Terence on the floor and were soon out of the tunnel. Where could they go? Tabatha would notice any minute that Terence had not come back, but Ravi couldn't go far with his leg hurt. They ducked behind a rusty train carriage while Luke tried to think. The carriage door flapped in the breeze, squeaking like a wounded animal.

'Terence? Where are you?'

The click of Tabatha's boot heels approached, followed by the heavy steps of the Frenchman. Luke turned to Ravi, he still looked pale from the fall. Could they wait it out here?

'Terence is down,' shouted the Frenchman from the tunnel. 'And the boy who needs glasses is missing.'

Tabatha sighed. The sound was so close it made Luke jump. 'It's always the smart ones. Stick Terence in the boot of my car. I'll get the boy.' Tabatha's footsteps grew louder, then she spoke to the darkness. 'I don't know where you are, but I know it's you, Ravi. You're the only one smart enough to escape.'

Ravi, smiled despite himself and mouthed to Luke. 'I'm the smartest.'

Tabatha hadn't finished. 'Too clever by half. That's why I fed you intel, via the guards, of course. I've found the children believe it more, if it comes from one of them.'

Ravi's lips went tight and pale.

'So here's some more intel,' her voice cut through the mist. 'Your parents are both in jail. They wouldn't give up looking for you – made a frightful fuss – so I had to deal with them. Your sister, however, is still selling incense in Waterloo Market. So I'll give you a choice.'

A sickly silence filled the air. Tabatha's choices were never good.

'If you don't come, right now, I'll sell *her* into forced labour in Europe instead.'

Ravi shook all over. Luke put his hand on his shoulder. He didn't know what to say.

'You've three seconds to decide. Three . . . two—'

Ravi turned to Luke. 'I'm sorry.' Then, before Luke could stop him, he stepped out from behind the van. 'I'm here, Tabatha.'

'Good.' Tabatha smiled and walked up to him. 'You know how I hate to see things wasted. Now hurry along to the van.'

Ravi turned to the tunnel and Tabatha whacked him hard on the back of the head with her bag. He fell to the floor, unconscious.

Luke closed his eyes. It had all been for nothing. Nothing.

'The boy's over here!' Tabatha shouted to the Frenchman. 'Move sharp. You've only got a minute or two before it comes.'

A minute before what comes? But Luke didn't know if he cared. All he knew was that his best friend was gone. That whatever he did – even dying it seemed – hadn't been enough to protect him.

Then he saw the sky. The dark of night, had now shifted to an ashy, pale blue. There were hints of pink along the horizon. What was happening? Whatever was coming, he had to get back: the kids at the plant would soon be waking up. Jess would be waiting.

He pulled his mist back into a loose cloud, clambered on and lifted into the air, up over the remains of the rusty train carriage. Below, the Frenchman lowered Terence's body into the back of the car as Tabatha spoke into her talkometer. Luke paused. If he could catch a glimpse inside her head, even for a moment, it might make the difference. He could find out where Ravi was going. Or what Tabatha was planning. It might help them stop her.

He had to try.

He concentrated and caught a breeze with the edge of his cloud and drifted over to where Tabatha stood, barely twenty feet below him, and thought of rain. He was quicker this time, within seconds that strange feeling came again, a tingling and then a splitting into tiny pieces, as his raindrops fell down towards the figure in black below.

As quick as a splash, before the drops hit the ground, Tabatha whipped out a wide, black umbrella and shielded herself from the water. Luke cursed under his breath. If there had been a stronger wind, he could have angled the rain under the umbrella, but there was nothing and, aside from her face, every inch of her body was covered in black.

Tabatha strode towards her car still talking into her talkometer. She unlocked the car with a loud beep and its lights turned on, casting an eerie glow across the grey. Her heels crunched broken glass and rubble underfoot.

'What do you mean, you think someone's been in the lab?' she shouted. 'Secure the place now, you idiots. And if you haven't found the culprit by the time I'm back from seeing the mayor . . .'

They'd found out. They would check the tracker soon. He had

to get back to his body before Tabatha did.

Below, Tabatha turned and scanned the deserted station, like she did with the lines of shovellers back in the plant. Then before turning to her car, she did something else – something unusual. For a fleeting moment, she looked up at the sky, right in Luke's direction.

Luke froze. Had she seen him? She couldn't have, surely?

Then she slipped inside the car. A dim glow flickered from behind its tinted glass as she lit her pipe. Through the glass, he saw her smile. She pressed a button on her dashboard.

A loud siren started in the distance. It was a deep, wailing sound. It echoed across the city, high and low, like the scream and sob of a dying animal. Luke knew the sound well. The smog was coming.

CHAPTER 35
THE SMOG

They'd been on the Heath the day it had happened. They always went on Sundays. The drive up at dawn, the flask of hot chocolate and the kites stowed in the boot. They'd climbed Parliament Hill in the blustery grey and set the kites to the sky.

His dad had stood with him, hands firmly rested on the back of Luke's shoulders, as though Luke might take flight too. Nearby, Lizzy flew her box kite by a cluster of oaks, whooping as it dipped through the morning air.

It was strange what he remembered. His dad's warm fingers. The tufty dewed grass under his boots. Lizzy's black ponytail bouncing in the breeze. Then his kite suddenly moving, with a mind of its own.

Luke shrugged off his dad. 'I want to see where it goes.' He liked to go with the flow, in those days.

'Don't go too far. Keep us in sight.'

Luke nodded and let the string pull him on. The wind shifted south, his kite insistent, teasing him over the brow of the hill.

He remembered the view. All of London spread out before him, his kite dancing higher than the buildings on the horizon. He took a few steps down the slope, and then a few more.

It was about halfway down when he felt uneasy. It was the sky; it had darkened a little. At that time of day, it should have been bright. He glanced up the hill: no sign of his dad. He'd gone further than he'd realised.

Then the kite went haywire. It ducked, dived, jerked, jumped, pulling hard at the string in his hands. Like it wanted to escape. Luke stumbled further, trying in vain to tame the thing.

'Dad?' he shouted, leaning into the hill. There was no response, only a row of black oaks watching from the hilltop. It began to rain, hard and cold, and then the string went slack. It was like the life had been sucked from the sky. The kite tumbled and the smog siren started.

The sound shivered his bones. He let go of the kite. He heard shouting and turned to see his dad's silhouette, and a wall of grey rushing towards him. The mist enveloped him, choking him with an odour of petrol and rot. His life as he'd known it was gone for ever.

Not this time, he thought. *This time, I'm ready.*

He pulled his mind back to the present and scanned the skies. There was no sign of the smog yet, but it must be near. He could already feel the wind dying, like it had with his kite. He had to think fast and move even faster. But how did a ghostcloud move without the help of the wind?

An engine revving interrupted his thoughts. Below him, Tabatha's sportscar lurched out of Waterloo station and swerved onto the road. She wasn't stupid. She was as desperate to get out of the smog as he was.

An idea hit him. It was crazy, he knew, but it just might work. He grasped tight to his cloud, tilted it to catch what was left of the dying breeze, and followed behind her.

Tabatha's sleek black car sliced through the streets below, dodging broken glass, dangling wires, and damp-cracked brickwork. She drove at breakneck speed, barely braking at the corners, but even with the wind fading fast, Luke gained on her. His advantage was simple. Where she had to drive round buildings and piles of rubble, he flew straight over. Within a couple of streets, he was flying directly overhead, and could make out the glow of her pipe through the darkened windscreen.

The wind gave its last gasp, then died altogether. He was ready. He sharpened the edges of his kite-cloud, and cut through the air, milking his momentum for all it was worth. He lost height rapidly, dropping past the caved-in heads of the tower blocks, the shattered slate roofs of theatres and bars, past the corroded metal of twisted lampposts, until he was gliding mere metres above the back of the car.

With one last push, he leapt down through the mist and pushed his hands through the grille on the back of her car. He gripped as tight as he could.

And it worked. The car pulled him forward through the backstreets, faster than any storm Luke could imagine. Air rushed by, a hum at first, then a howl and roar. It tore against his sides. Wisps of steam ripped from his person, like layers of skin. But at least he was moving, and away from the smog. Not even the smog could travel as fast as this.

The car swerved again, but he held on tight. He forced his head up, peering through the window into Tabatha's car. She was smoking her pipe, the steering wheel in one hand, the talkometer in the other, accelerating hard. She wasn't even wearing her seatbelt.

He tried to glean something – a word of what she was saying, something useful – but it was impossible above the howl of the air rushing past them. It made his head swim.

Then something cut through the blur: the scent of decay. It started faint but sharp, but within a street or two, it coated the air with a putrid musk.

Tabatha's car turned a corner and a shiver lurched down his body: a green-grey mist waited at the street's end. It stretched from the tarmac high into the sky, blocking the stars. Monstrous and impenetrable, it obscured the buildings. And Tabatha was heading right for it.

How could she drive through it? Nobody could see through that wall of grey. And yet, her foot pushed harder onto the accelerator.

He waited for her to turn a corner or take a shortcut back to the plant.

She didn't.

With metres to spare, Luke let go, and watched the car dive into the smog. There was a sudden, deafening silence as if the roar of the engine had been smothered. Then his head began throbbing from the stench.

He watched the smog. There was a stillness to it. Clouds shifted at the edges; but this grey was perfectly still – the stillness of a cat, waiting to pounce. And behind the wall of grey, there was something darker. Black, twisting shapes. The murmur of voices. He knew he should run, but he found himself peering closer.

A familiar figure stepped through the grey. Ebony hair tied back. Eyes wet-black with tears. Exactly the same as she'd been in the East Wing.

'You're not real,' Luke said. 'I know you're not real.'

His mother smiled sadly. The sound of sobbing thrummed in the air. Behind her, the grey wall slid greedily closer.

Luke turned and ran.

CHAPTER 36
CORNERED

Luke felt – unsurprisingly – light on his feet and stepping through rubble was almost fun. At least, it might have been, if there wasn't a deadly smog hot on his heels.

At least he'd put some distance between them, a street or two, buying him time to search for shelter. Crumbling buildings lined the street: derelict pubs, rusting shopfronts, and the once glorious theatre, whose peeling posters coated the pavement like leaf sludge. Everything was broken; you needed something sealed to hold out the smog.

He stretched his arms in the air – if he could get a flutter of breeze he might fly – but there was nothing. He'd never known the air this still. Maybe Jess had been right: he needed a plan. This improvising thing had been a total disaster. He'd lost his family, Ravi, and perhaps soon his life – it didn't get much worse. And yet, if he'd stayed in the plant, and waited, he knew he'd have felt worse. At least he'd tried, even if it had all come to nothing.

Luke cut down a side street. A disused water tower lay ahead on a tripod of rusted, dried-out stilts. A crumbling ladder ran up its side. *Could there be wind at the top?*

He scrambled up the ladder to the top of the tank. The smog had thickened at street level, but at the higher levels he could still just about see through the grey. It was strange, he thought, it was as though the smog was coming from the ground. He looked higher up. Right overhead, there were still patches of sky. He'd aim for those and leap the wall of grey, before it got too high.

A feeble breeze brushed his arm – a wisp of hope. He'd flown kites on less, even when his dad and Lizzy said he'd never manage it. He pictured them there, on the tower with him. His dad in his brown detective's coat and Lizzy wrapped up in as many layers as she could fit on: she never liked the cold. They'd be urging him on. He could do it, they'd say.

He pulled in the dregs of rainwater from the water tower and grew his kite-cloud beneath him. As carefully as he could, desperate not to waste a drop of the breeze, he lifted into the air.

The wind swelled, shifting him upwards in the smog's direction. There was enough uplift to carry him over the top. It was a risk, and he'd have to take it. He angled his kite-cloud and went shooting up into the air, higher and closer to the smog.

He was almost there. He could see the top of its grey wall, not far ahead now. If he could only reach the top.

Then suddenly, the wall leapt up, curving overhead, like a thin grey dome. What on earth? He thought. Could smog do that?

It didn't matter. He'd have to chance it and cut through where it was thinnest. He leant into the wind and shot towards the grey. He heard a cry from above.

'Don't do it!' Luke turned to see Alma high overhead, slipping through the last gap in the dome of smog. What was she doing here? 'Luke, wait for me!'

'It's thin. I can cut through.'

'Not this smog. It's different, I can sense it.'

What did she mean? Luke slowed and peered at the grey dome above. Then, out of the smog, shot a misty tentacle as fast as water. He dodged it, but it whipped round and grabbed his foot. It tightened ice-cold around his ankle.

'Hold on!' Alma shouted, cutting down fast through the air. But she wasn't fast enough. The tentacle pulled him out of her reach towards the grey.

A blade of blue lightning sliced past him, inches from his feet. and the tentacle faded into nothing. Alma grabbed his arm and pulled him onto her swan.

'Stay down, just in case.'

Luke nodded. His foot felt numb. 'Alma, since when did smog have tentacles?'

'I don't know! It never used to – and it was bad enough then.' She looked behind them, a wall of grey rose in the distance there too. 'We're surrounded. We need somewhere sealed to hide.'

Luke tried to ignore his foot and think, but it was no good. Nothing was sealed in the deadzone. Everything he'd seen was crumbled and ruined.

Then it came to him. 'The Old Channel Tunnel.'

Alma nodded grimly. She angled her cloud and swooped towards the centre of the Deadzone. Above them, the smog was now falling fast, a grasping dome of grey and black.

They landed by the tunnel. A pipe trickled water across its entrance. A solitary cat crouched lapping it up. The last time he'd entered, he'd left with Ravi. Now Ravi was gone. He hoped this time would end better.

A purring interrupted him. The tickle of fur against his mist.

He looked down. A brown and white tomcat waited at his feet.

'Stealth?' Luke bent down. It was first good thing that had happened all day. 'You're alive!'

'Alive for now,' Alma called back, striding ahead. 'Stop playing with furballs and get inside.'

Luke picked up Stealth — a bundle of warmth in his arms — and hurried after Alma into the tunnel. At the wall of rubble, Luke pulled the wire, like Terence had, and the hidden door slid open.

'Do you think we'll safe?'

Alma's eyes blazed. 'From the smog, maybe. From me, no. Do you know how dangerous it is for you to come out here alone? You, my friend, have some explaining to do.'

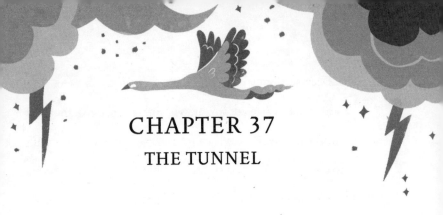

CHAPTER 37
THE TUNNEL

Luke and Alma sat with their backs against the walls of the tunnel, listening out for the smog through the sealed door. An hour had passed. The stench remained strong and the door rattled occasionally.

It had given him time to bring Alma up to speed.

'And the ghoul in the tank, how did it look?' Alma asked.

'Tired, fuzzy, fading away.' He stroked Stealth in his lap. 'Though still pretty ghoulish.'

Luke had explained about the lab, his family and Ravi's recapture. Alma had listened, at first surprised, then with growing horror. She asked question upon question. Luke racked his brain to remember all the details, from the propeller designs to the dark incinerators.

'This is serious,' Alma said. 'Even the council can't ignore this. It breaks all the rules. We'll go straight to them once this creepy smog clears.'

'If it clears.'

'Either way, you're in trouble.' She threw her hands in the air. 'I can't believe you came out here alone, looking for me. It's so reckless.'

'I know, but still.' He picked at a crumbled brick on the floor. 'Sometimes the reckless thing is the right thing too. You should know. You risked the smog to save me.'

'I didn't come here to save you. I came here to scold you.'

It was a lie, and they both knew it.

'OK, but I could hardly let the smog swallow you up. I did the decent thing. Anyone would have done it.'

'Methusaleh wouldn't. Most wouldn't, I reckon. I bet I could count those who would on one hand.'

'Well, then you're lucky. I could count mine on one finger.'

Her mouth smiled, but it didn't reach her eyes. That was the problem with Alma, she never talked straight. She always joked, but so often seemed sad. And though she spoke a lot, she shared so little.

'Alma, tell me something about yourself. Nothing funny, mind you. Something normal. Boring.'

'But no one likes boring.'

'You know what I mean,' he said. 'Like where you live? Or your hobbies?'

Alma picked at the hem of her dress. 'OK, fine. I live by Crystal Palace, in the southern slums. Not many ghosts like it there, because it's all smashed up.' She stopped, as if to check if she should continue. He nodded, so she did. 'But I like it down there. It's quiet. It's strange. It's beautiful too. And at night, the broken glass makes the moonlight dance.' She stopped herself. 'But that must sound silly.'

'No, it sounds nice.'

She dug her hands into her waistcoat pockets. 'Well, when we're out, you should visit sometime.'

'I'd like that.'

It was silent for a moment, then Alma spoke. 'Luke?'

'Yeah?'

'I know I'm annoying, sometimes.' She stared at the floor. 'But you'd save my life, wouldn't you?'

'Of course,' he said. 'Saving you from that incinerator was the best thing that's happened to me. I'd do it again in a heartbeat.' He looked down at his chest – he could see right through it. 'Though technically, I don't have a heartbeat right now.'

'It's the thought that counts.' And for once, Luke knew that he'd said the right thing. Alma sighed and snuggled up against some pipes. 'Well, we might as well get comfy.'

The pipes – they stirred something vague in Luke's memory. 'Alma, before the smog came, Tabatha pressed a button in her car.'

'So what?' said Alma. 'I love pressing buttons.'

'Not this button.' Luke joined the dots. It began to make sense. 'I think this button might have actually *pumped out* the smog. In the lab, Jess said that there were experimental fumes being piped out around the city. Tabatha must be controlling it. That's why the kidnapping map we found had precise smog timings on it. How else would she know?'

Alma swallowed. 'That would explain the tentacles. If the smog fumes are experimental, then it's not just pollution, but burnt up ghosts too – those tortured souls.' She looked to the door. 'The smog was bad enough before, but if those things are mixed in too, *bits of ghosts*, then it's no wonder so many of us are getting caught up in it.'

'Not just ghosts, people too. Jess said more people are getting sick. They won't see the tortured souls like we can, but they'll still be affected by the smog.'

A faint sobbing reached their ears from somewhere beyond

the tunnel. That ghoulish version of his mother was out there, somewhere in the smog. Luke shivered, then whispered. 'What happens if it gets you?'

'Nobody knows for sure, but it's not like a ghoul – it doesn't take you to the End Place. They say the smog goes right to your soul. It numbs your body, then your mind.' Alma stood up and peered warily at the door. 'Then it's too late. You're part of the smog. And you're never getting out.'

The sobbing grew louder. Alma put her finger to her lips and they watched the tunnel door in silence. From beyond it, came a splash of water. The rattle of rubble. A tinkle of something on broken glass.

A moment of silence.

Then the door shuddered, sending rock crumbling from the ceiling.

Alma blinked. 'Time for plan B.'

'Plan B?'

'We're going to Europe!'

She grabbed his hand. Luke shook his head. 'Wait, what? What about my body? The council? Or Jess? She's stuck in the plant!'

The door creaked again behind him.

'Did you put Jess there? No. Did the council listen to us? No.' Alma tugged his hand again. 'They're not your problem. And your body's no good either, if you lose your soul to that thing.' She forced a smile. 'We'll be back within the week, I promise. We'll fly back over the sea, it'll be lovely.'

'But that'll be too late for the others.'

The door groaned from behind them.

'Come on, Luke!' Alma scowled. 'We're no good to them if we're dead.'

'We're no good to anyone if we keep running away.'

The door shuddered once more. Stealth jumped up and began hissing at Alma.

'Great,' Alma said. 'Even the cat hates me now.'

But Stealth rushed past her. Tail raised. Back arched. Hissing wildly.

'What *is* he doing?'

Luke watched Stealth, hissing at the darkness of the tunnel towards Europe. Stealth, the cat who never made a sound. A lump of fear grew in Luke's stomach. 'Do you think someone's down there?'

'Of course not.' Alma wavered. 'It's probably just another cat.' Her fist glowed electric blue, lighting the cluster of old pipes where she and Stealth stood. 'But no harm in checking.' A burst of blue shot from her hand, deeper into the tunnel, lighting it up . . . until it was swallowed by a writhing wall of smog.

Stealth yowled.

'There's smog coming *up* the tunnel?' Luke cried.

'There can't be. Unless . . .'

They didn't need to say it. If Tabatha piped the smog around London, she could easily pipe inside the tunnel. It was logical, really, Luke thought. It'd stop any intruders trying to follow her tracks.

And now they were surrounded.

'What do we do?'

Alma swallowed, and before she could answer a wet black tentacle leapt out from the darkness. She rolled out of the way, but it curled back towards her, sinuous and sharp. She fired another bolt of blue. It lit up for a moment, then faded, leaving a stench of decay.

Stealth meowed desperately from the pipes.

'Can you zap our way out of here?'

Alma shook her head. 'I can only do it a handful of times before I run out of steam.'

Then her eyes widened, and she sent another bolt of electricity past him. He turned to see a tendril fading inches from his shoulder. Behind him, the sealed door had slid an inch open. Tentacles squeezed through the gap, spidering up the wall, like quick-growing ivy.

Luke backed away from the door, towards Alma. She looked exhausted already. He kept the creepers in view.

The lightning had slowed the smog tentacles, but there were so many of them. It was hard to think, through the stench and sobbing. And it didn't help that Stealth was hissing louder than ever.

Tentacles shot across the floor from both directions. Alma raised her hands and sent bolts of blue across the tunnel.

She staggered back against the wall. 'I'm out.' Her face was pale.

Luke stared at the tendrils of smog, creeping back through the door and out of the darkness. It was hopeless, they were trapped. 'I'm sorry, Alma. I didn't think it end like this.'

'I always thought I'd end up going alone. So the fact I'm with you is definitely a positive.' She braved a grin. 'And I bet the End Place would be boring, anyway.'

Luke remembered the End Place – the cirrus clouds shimmering high above. They felt so far away. 'This can't be it,' he muttered.

Alma didn't reply. Things must be bad, he thought, if Alma was quiet. Even Stealth had stopped hissing.

Where was Stealth?

He looked around. He'd been by the pipes, but now there was nothing.

Suddenly, there was a flash of brown and white. Stealth's head popped out from a pipe.

Luke squinted: not just any pipe – a green pipe coated in cat hair. A pipe he could have sworn he'd seen before.

'Alma, this pipe – I think I know it. We need to follow him into it.'

Alma looked ready to zap a lightning bolt at him. 'What? I've told you, never go down pipes. I ended up in an incinerator last time.'

Luke glanced at the tunnel mouth. Another tendril of mist skittered towards them. 'Let's face it, it's got to be better than being caught by that thing.'

She hesitated, then nodded.

He leant into the pipe opening. 'Here goes nothing.'

And with a squeeze and push, he shot himself forward, down the pipe into the darkness.

CHAPTER 38
CATS

Mewling, purring and growling. Soft fur swishing, wiggling whiskers and a prick of claws. The grey cleared. Luke and Alma stood between mossy grey walls that sloped up to a circle of light above. Steaming brass pipes lined the walls and every inch was covered in cats.

'The cat room – I knew it – we're back in the power station!' Luke jumped up and down. 'The cats must come here to hide from the smog.'

Alma leapt up and kissed him on the cheek. 'You were right!'

'Erm.' Luke rubbed his face, blushing. 'I guess I was.'

She shrugged. 'I guess the moral of the story is: listen to the half-ghost.' She tapped her head. 'You've got double the halves, so double the ideas.'

Luke groaned. 'That's not how maths works.'

'The point is, you've got options. You can choose which half to run with. The human half or the ghost half. The sensible half or the silly half.'

It had a certain logic, he supposed. Then he took a moment to savour the distinct lack of tentacles in his underground workhouse. There was no place like home.

'That was closer than I expected.' Alma brushed down her dress. 'And I should definitely reappraise my position on cats.' She knelt to stroke one; it turned and hissed. 'Or not. Anyway, we've got to act quick. You get your body and I'll find the council. They take ages to decide, so wait nicely, and don't do anything crazy, right?'

'I'll try.'

But Alma didn't rise. Instead, she put a finger to her lips in thought.

'What?'

'Oh!' She smiled. 'I was just thinking that I've never kissed a half-ghost before.'

Luke's cheeks burned. For once, he wished ghosts *could* fall through the floor.

A clang from the vents saved him. A scruffy blonde head appeared through a vent.

'Jess!' Luke said. 'I'm so glad to see you.'

'Thank God!' Jess said. A handful of cats rushed up to greet her. 'I hoped you'd be here.' She lowered herself down. Her hands fiddled with a loose strand of sackcloth.

Luke knew at once: something was wrong. Jess wasn't smiling.

She looked at Luke. 'They've taken your body. Two guards marched in, with muskets, and made a beeline to your bed. They must have had a tip-off.'

'They'll have checked the tracker.' Luke felt sick. 'Where did they take it?'

'I heard them mention the lab.'

Nothing good happened in that lab. For all he knew, he'd end up caged like those animals.

Alma turned to Luke. 'I'll come with you, to stop the guards.'

'Don't be stupid. Tell the council first. We can't risk you getting trapped. Worst case, I wait here and join my body later.'

Alma's eyes were firm. 'No, worst case, she experiments on you, and by the time I'm back you're some kind of smog-thing. You're my friend. I'm coming.'

There was no arguing with her, he could tell, and he was secretly relieved.

'I'm coming too,' said Jess. 'It's my investigation, remember.'

'No, Jess. They'll notice you're missing.'

'It's not up to you.' She bit her lip. 'I can help, I know it.'

Luke knew she could help. He'd seen Jess prove her value far too many times. But the last thing he wanted was for her to get caught.

'No, Jess. It isn't safe. Tabatha has no idea you're involved. Let's keep it that way.' He forced a smile. 'Don't worry. It'll be fine.'

Jess didn't smile back.

'No it won't,' she said. She bent down and stroked the back of Stealth's neck. 'You look after them then, buddy.' Then without so much as a wave, she disappeared down the vent.

Luke's throat was dry. 'It was the right thing to do.'

Alma climbed up towards the vent. 'Of course it was. We're heading into certain danger – a skinny, blonde plumber is the last thing we need.'

Luke wasn't so sure, but he'd made his decision. He pulled himself up and followed Alma into the vents.

CHAPTER 39
THE BODY

One thing was for certain, Luke decided: travelling through vents was easier as a ghost. No scrabbling. No knee scuffing. No claustrophobic crawling with Jess's feet in your face. Instead, they drifted effortlessly along, catching draughts where needed.

They reached the East Wing in minutes and lowered themselves into the unnerving, white cleanliness of the sick bay. The secret door had been left open. Voices from the laboratory echoed up through the opening.

'This kid is so heavy,' a gruff voice wheezed – the voice of Fat Elvis. 'Can't we stop for a snack?'

'No,' said the second guard. 'We've already had two.'

'Come on!' said Elvis. 'Tabatha's not back for an hour. What she doesn't know can't hurt her.'

'She'll find out somehow, she always does in the end. Let's seal him up, then get out. This place gives me the creeps.'

Then the clang of steel toecaps on metal drowned out the voices.

Luke turned to Alma. 'Are you sure about the lab? It's not safe there for a ghostcloud.'

'Can you knock out guards?'

Luke shook his head.

'Then I'm coming.'

They tiptoed through the opening onto the raised gangway. Luke looked around: it was larger and darker than he remembered. The teardrop grey lanterns swayed as they passed. The mist within swirled like a storm in a snow globe.

'It's like they know we're here,' Luke said.

Alma peered warily into one: it glowed grey like she did. 'If I end up a light bulb, please switch me off.'

He hurried ahead to the staircase and peered down. The guards had stopped halfway, Luke's body dangling over Elvis's shoulder.

'He'd better not drop me,' he whispered. 'Shall we get them on the stairs?'

Her nose turned up in disgust. 'Ghosts don't use stairs.' She stepped onto the railing and dived into the darkness.

'Drama queen,' muttered Luke.

Luke landed silently next to Alma in the shadows, at the bottom of the stairs.

Clang. Clang. Clang.

'I'll knock them out at the bottom,' Alma said. 'That way they won't drop you.'

Alma stopped, eyes locked on the rows of incinerators and their glass chambers. Most lay empty, but some swirled with grey and the glint of propellers. Her face paled. 'This place is a dungeon.'

'I know,' Luke said. 'Though the other side has puppies if you need cheering up.' A grumble came from above. Luke's body tensed. 'Will you zap them?'

Alma shook her head. 'I'm out of lightning after the smog, but I've a few tricks left.'

Clang. Clang. Clang.

The guards were almost there. Luke's skin prickled. What if his body fell and his head cracked against the floor? Alma sounded confident, but she looked tired. Her eyes weary. The smog must have cost her more than he realised.

Clang. Clang. Clang.

There was no time to think. The two guards had reached the bottom of the steps.

Alma darted out, in a fresh floral dress. 'Hello, boys!' She curtsied. The guards stopped, visibly shocked, but by the time they reached for their muskets, it was already too late. Alma thrust her hands over the guards' faces, smothering their mouths with a thick fog. They gasped for air then made a gurgling sound.

'Luke, grab the body!'

Luke snatched it from their arms, a second before the pair thudded to the ground, unconscious.

'What do I do now?'

'You left of your own free will, so you need to will yourself back. Think about the reasons you want to be alive.'

Luke reached down and touched his chest. He summoned the happy thoughts that kept him going when he was shovelling: his dad, Lizzy and his yellow houseboat; warm, windy days on Parliament Hill; his kite soaring through the hot blue sky.

Nothing happened. All he felt was cold skin and a fading heartbeat.

'It's not working.' He panicked.

'Try again!'

Deep down, he knew why. Those memories were a lie now. His dad was in jail. His sister alone. His home a shadow of what it used to be.

'I can't. My home, my family, it's all ruined now.'

'Then they need you more than ever.' Alma's eyes burned. 'We don't live because it's easy. We live because there's something, or someone worth fighting for. Even if it's just yourself.' She took his hand. 'You're lucky, Luke. People care about you. Your family, Jess, Ravi. Not everyone has that. Do it for them.'

Luke closed his eyes. He thought of Jess laughing in the room full of cats. Of Stealth rubbing against his leg. Of Ravi, Dad, his sister, his grandma – and the other children suffering throughout the plant – they needed him. He thought of Alma too.

His skin warmed under his fingers. His heartbeat picked up. The cold stone floor dug into his spine. And he found himself opening his eyes. His real eyes.

He looked up at Alma. She straightened out her sleeves and grinned. 'Well, I'd better be off then.'

'Me too.' Luke got to his feet and looked at the guards. 'Thanks for saving me, again.'

'It was my turn, I think. But let's not make a habit of it.'

As Luke climbed the stairs behind Alma, he found himself smiling. There were worse habits, he thought.

Then a noise from above wiped the smile of his face.

Click. Tap. Swish. Hissssss.

High above, the lab door hissed shut. The dark figure of Tabatha stepped out onto the walkway.

CHAPTER 40
TRAPPED

Click. Tap. Swish. Click.

Luke pressed himself into the shadows of the spiral stairs. His heart raced in his chest. High above, he made out Tabatha's slender, black figure as she strode across the gangway, a pipe glowing in her mouth. She removed her jet-black coat and draped it on the railing.

'Guards?' she called down, her voice dark and thick. She peered over the edge; her amber eyes flickered like flames under the lanterns. 'Where are you?'

No reply. She tapped her pipe on the railings, sending embers cascading through the air, lighting up part of the floor below. Tabatha stared, then shook her head. 'Idiots. Leaving the door open again.'

She walked across the gangway to the map of London and began making notes.

Luke whispered to Alma. 'You have to leave, now!'

'I can put an end to all this. I need to get closer.'

'Don't be ridiculous. She's not like the guards.' Luke paused. 'Back in Waterloo station, I think she might have seen me.'

'She's attuned?' Alma said. 'Well, big deal. I'll just stay out of sight.'

Alma leapt from the stairs and grabbed hold of the underside of the gangway. She inched her way along, swinging underneath.

Luke wanted to shout at Alma to come back, but he couldn't risk the noise. Either way, he reasoned, he couldn't stay on the steps – if Tabatha came down she'd bump right into him. Holding his breath, he took a couple of steps up, towards the door.

Tabatha sat at her desk and opened a file. Was she entering a new child in her record of workers? Or crossing one off?

He took another two steps. He wasn't far off now. Nor was Alma, she was only a few feet from the end of the gangway, moving one hand at a time. It looked like she might make it.

Tabatha put down her pen. Something had caught her attention. Her eyes narrowed, then she reached under the table.

Had Tabatha seen Alma? But there was no way she could have from where she was sitting.

Then he saw it: the lanterns above the gangway. Though Alma swung below, the lanterns still sensed her, swayed and swirling as she passed.

Tabatha must know. Whatever she was reaching for under the table could not be good.

'Alma, look out! She knows you're coming.'

It was too late. Tabatha darted to the railings, wielding a blue-black trumpet-like contraption, with a pipe trailing from it. Alma looked up, eyes wide, then Tabatha pulled the trigger. A deafening roar erupted from the thing, the sound of air ripping, and a second later, Alma vanished.

An incinerator chamber below flickered into life. Alma's stood inside it, banging her fists against the glass.

Tabatha smiled coldly, then dragged a nail along the railing – the *skriitch* of metal pierced the air. She locked her eyes on Luke. 'Now what am I going to do with you?'

Luke looked to the door. Could he make it in time?

'It's locked, dear.' Tabatha took a step closer along the gangway. 'Your ghost friend is locked in there too.' She waved down to the chamber where Alma was trapped. 'And you will be soon when I'm finished with you. A chamber of your own. A most interesting specimen: a boy *and* a ghost.'

Luke didn't stay to chat. He sprinted down the stairs and dived into the shadows where the guards lay. Glinting in the darkness, he saw what he'd hoped for: a loaded musket.

He heaved it onto his shoulder.

CRACK!

Something smashed into the musket, sending him flying. His shoulder throbbed from the impact, but the musket had suffered worse. It lay in pieces on the floor. On the railings above Tabatha reloaded her pistol.

'When I was little, my dad made me hunt the escapees. Looks like I've still got it.'

This was not a time for thinking, then acting.

It was a time for running.

Clang. Clang. Swish. Clang.

Luke crouched, sheltered behind a glass ghost chamber. Sweat ran down his back. His shoulder ached horribly, but he didn't make a sound.

'I saw my first ghost when I was about your age,' Tabatha purred, stepping down the stairs. 'It was around the time my mother died. She left me with my father. He wasn't a kind man.'

Luke's mind raced. She'd been like him once. How had they turned out so differently?

Clang. Clang. Swish. Clang.

'But no matter how I pleaded, the ghosts wouldn't help me. They said they couldn't interfere. And it got me thinking. The ghosts had all that power and did nothing. It was so inefficient. I thought, if only someone could harness that power – that eternal energy – it would change everything.'

Luke wiped his face with his hand. Tabatha's voice echoed around him; it was impossible to think straight.

'So I kept my head down, studied hard, and harnessed it myself. I've made my mark and a lot of money in the process. There have been sacrifices, of course, but there always are. Principles can't stand in the way of progress.' She sighed. 'But when I saw you in the sky, by Waterloo station, I knew I'd missed a trick. I'd been so focused on burning ghosts that I'd never contemplated *being* a ghost.'

Clang. Clang. Swish. Clang.

The clang of heels on metal echoed in his skull. He pushed it from his mind. There couldn't be many more steps left. When she left the staircase, could he make a break for it?

'Think about it,' Tabatha continued, 'ghost-travel could revolutionise transport. Or intelligence gathering. Governments would pay astronomical fees for the privilege. Or then again, I might keep the knowledge to myself. If I could travel as a ghost. I'd practically be a goddess.'

Clang. Clang. Swish. Click.

A click? She'd reached the bottom of the stairs. Where would she turn next? Left for the caged animals or right for the ghost chambers. He hoped against hope that she chose the former.

'So what I'd like to know, Luke, is how do you do it?' Her voice reverberated around the room. 'And if you won't tell me willingly, I'll have to *make* you.'

Click. Click. Swish. Click.

Luke frowned. It was impossible to tell where she was from the sound. The heel clicks echoed all around the room. They could be coming from anywhere. Was she closer or further? Should he risk a glance?

Tabatha sighed from the darkness. 'I forget, you're stubborn like your father.' She laughed. 'You know what? Even after I threw him in Pentonville Prison, he still wouldn't keep quiet. At least, not until I had him fall sick.'

She made him sick? Luke had an urge to run at her screaming, but he bit his fist and waited. She wanted him to do that. A true detective remained calm under pressure. A detective like his dad.

His mind drifted to happier times. To when they'd travelled to the countryside, up through canals between green-brown fields. Luke had been walking on the roof when a low hanging branch had knocked him into the water. He'd plunged deep, gasping in the dark, flailing and grasping towards the boat.

Then his dad dived in and everything changed. He grabbed Luke tight, but instead of swimming for safety, he laughed – big, snorting, reckless laughs – then promptly dunked Luke underwater. Spluttering to the surface, Luke found himself laughing too. The water wasn't scary any more. It was sweet on his tongue. It wasn't even that cold, once you got used to it.

For the next half hour, they flicked water and pondweed at each other in the afternoon sun. And when the sun finally sank, they'd swum on their backs, side by side, looking up at the sky overhead, a hazy orange-blue dome curving towards the horizon.

That was where he wanted to die. Not here, in the dark, hiding from her.

'I'm getting bored, Luke,' Tabatha growled in the gloom. Luke listened carefully. Underneath the growl, was that another sound he heard? Something high and squeaky ... mice perhaps? Or even puppies?

Had she gone to the other section, away from the incinerators? If she had, the path to the stairs would be clear. But he had to be sure. He listened desperately through the silence for one more sign.

*Click. Click. Click. **Crash!***

The clatter of metal echoed through the room, followed by a cacophony of squealing and yapping puppies. She must have knocked over a cage – she had to be in the other section. This was his chance.

He sprinted towards the staircase, ducking low in the shadows of the empty incinerators, his footsteps drowned out by yapping and barking. He reached the last row of chambers and the stairs came into view. One more stretch and he'd make it.

A long, black leg shot out in front, sending him tumbling. His head hit the stone floor with a crack.

Dazed, he looked up. Tabatha gazed down on him, pipe glowing in her mouth and a black heeled shoe in her hand.

'Oldest trick in the book. Misdirection.' She laughed, blowing smoke in his face. 'In the absence of a pebble, it seems that throwing a shoe works delightfully well. You, of all people, should have seen that coming.'

She put her remaining shoe back on, then stuck the heel deep into Luke's stomach. He winced in pain. 'Now, tell me before I have to get nasty. How do you become a ghost?'

CHAPTER 41
OUT OF TIME

Tabatha twisted her heel deeper into his stomach.

'I'll never tell you.' Luke's words came out in gasps.

Tabatha ran her tongue over her upper lip. 'I thought as much. You're the stoic type. Torture never works. So let's save us both some time and skip that part.' She bent down and dug her nails into his arm, then dragged him across the stone floor to the chamber holding Alma.

Alma bashed her fists against the glass, her hands glowing with electricity.

'Oh, do shut up.' Tabatha spat. She pressed a button on the chamber, and a blue-grey propeller emerged above Alma. Alma raised her hands to protect herself.

'Stop it!' Luke shouted. 'Leave her alone!'

'Oops,' said Tabatha. 'Too late.'

The propeller whirred at speed, and Alma disappeared

into a cloud of swirling smoke.

What had she done? Luke tried to sit up, but Tabatha's heel shot down again, this time on his chest, pinning him to the floor. She wiggled it, like she was stubbing out a cigarette, making his whole body convulse with pain.

And that was when he felt it. Something else hard was digging into his side. There was something in his pocket. What was it?

Tabatha sighed. 'It takes several days to finish off a ghostcloud like that. It's slow and painful, but they make quite wonderful light bulbs.' Tabatha looked back at the monitor. 'But this button here is much quicker. The ignition button. Do you know what that means?'

'Burn,' Luke whispered, though he was only half listening. His real focus was getting his hand down to his pocket. He'd remembered what was in there. And it might be the only chance he'd get.

'Exactly,' said Tabatha. 'And if there's one thing I love more than money, it's burning things.' She shrugged. 'Unfortunately, the incinerators weren't powerful enough for souls. I needed a bigger furnace, hence the third chimney. There, a single ghost could power a city for months.' She looked at the button. 'But in these incinerators, if I ignite, all I get is a half-burned ghost.

They're nasty, stinking, tentacled things. One escaped into the East Wing the other week.'

The tortured soul? Alma would become one of those? He looked up at the glass. Alma had formed again from the mist. Her eyes blazed with anger, but there was fear there too.

Tabatha pressed the button. 'I do love technology.' The monitor screen began counting down.

10 ... 9 ... 8 ...

Tabatha leaned in close. 'So unless you want her to burn, tell me the truth. How do I become a ghost?'

7 ... 6 ... 5 ...

'Last chance, my dear.'

Then the countdown stopped. The machine beeped. Tabatha scowled.

'What on earth?'

And two things happened at that moment. Luke's hand slipped into his pocket, round the bottle of Chlor, and, high above him on the railings, by the control panel, he saw a flash of blonde hair.

Jess had followed them after all! She must have found a way to pause the incinerator.

Tabatha tapped furiously at the buttons on the incinerator.

He couldn't risk it restarting. He had to distract her.

'Tabatha,' Luke whispered through his teeth. 'There's only one thing you need to do, to become a half-ghost like me.'

Tabatha looked away from the chamber, and knelt beside him, her eyes hungry. The smoke from her pipe clouded her face. 'What is it? Spit it out.'

'It's simple,' Luke said, slipping off the stopper from the bottle of Chlor. 'You just need to die.'

Luke kicked hard, sending Tabatha and her pistol flying, and threw the bottle of Chlor right at her.

The toxic green liquid splattered over Tabatha's clothes, face and glossy black hair. She staggered back, unsteady, gasping for breath. Then something unexpected happened: Tabatha's pipe glowed bright, and the Chlor vapour burst into flames. A ball of fire engulfed her face and she fell to the floor, shrieking.

Luke pulled himself up. Jess rushed up to him from behind, dragging the musket from the remaining guard behind her.

'Next time you leave me behind,' she said, passing him the gun, 'I'll aim that musket right at you.'

'Fair enough.' He heaved it onto his shoulder. 'Now let's just hope I can fire it.'

'Guards!' Tabatha screamed into her talkometer, clutching her face with her free hand. 'Come to the lab, now! EVERYONE.' Then she froze, seeing Luke, his musket locked on her. 'You wouldn't dare,' she hissed. 'You're too soft, like your father.'

Luke cocked the gun. 'In that case, I'll have to take after my mother.'

He pulled the trigger. The bullet shot an inch over Tabatha's head, smashing the glass of Alma's chamber. A rush of steam shot out of the laboratory, through the open hydraulic door. A second later, a troop of guards rushed in.

'Don't kill him!' shrieked Tabatha, standing up from the floor. 'He's mine.'

She removed her hands from her face and stared at Luke. An oozing, red and white burn covered half her face, in the shape of a flame.

'You missed. And even your ghost didn't save you.' She tried to smile, but the burn twisted it into a dripping sneer.

The guards gasped, but it didn't shock Luke. Nothing about her could shock him now.

Two strong, greasy hands lifted him into the air and carried him up the stairs, where another guard had Jess pinned to the floor.

Tabatha called up, her voice slow with anger. 'Assemble everyone in the furnace hall. I've something very special in mind for these two.'

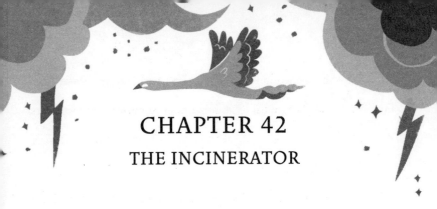

CHAPTER 42
THE INCINERATOR

It was all so familiar. The hungry flames licking the walls. The dancing shadows beckoning them in. The ceiling so high that the light never reached it. But there was a difference this time – it was one of perspective. This time, Luke was not a shoveller: he was the fuel.

Hands tied tight, feet tied tighter, he sat in a cage with his back to Jess, watching from the shadows as the stream of children marched into the room. They formed neat lines from the back of the hall, snaking up to the white-hot furnace.

Above the furnace stood a blue-black metal contraption – a cross between an enormous oven and a diving bell. The children gazed at it in awe and confusion. Luke recognised it at once. It was the incinerator, or at least a version of it, blown up one hundred times. At the top, rising up into the chimney itself, was a series of monstrous propellers.

Tabatha leaned closer and whispered to Jess and Luke from the shadows. 'When the chimney opens tomorrow, it will suck all the ghostclouds right out of the sky. There will be energy for all, even the southern slums.'

Luke tugged at his ropes without success. 'And when all the ghosts are gone, what then?'

He could almost hear Tabatha smile. 'Fresh souls, of course. The young ones burn brightest. Why else do you think I keep children down here? It's hardly an efficient way to get coal in a furnace.' She laughed and walked away.

Luke went cold. 'We have to stop her.'

'I wonder,' said Jess. 'Does she even have a soul?'

Tabatha walked out from the shadows, down the line of children, a black veil hanging over her face. Black heels clicked. A black coat swished. A black nailed hand clenched white with fury.

She climbed the steps to the podium by the furnace. A hush fell over the children and guards.

'Tomorrow is a special day. The launch of the third chimney will revolutionise energy production. It will transform our city. It will strike fear into the heart of Europe.'

Luke wriggled to get a better view, wincing as the ropes dug into his wrists. He'd never seen so many children there. She must have woken every soul in the plant, even those on the night shifts. Some rubbed their eyes, or stifled yawns, but they all stared at Tabatha with complete attention. You did not want to be caught looking away.

Tabatha's velvet voice continued. 'In ancient times, when launching a ship, you'd smash a bottle of champagne on the side for good luck – a little sacrifice to the gods.' She leant in, conspiratorially. 'I used to think it was wasteful. I've changed my mind.'

A spotlight shone down on Luke and Jess's cage, revealing them to the room. A gasp rolled down the hall.

'These despicable children tried to burn this plant down. They broke into my lab. They even attacked me.' Tabatha pulled off her veil, revealing the livid, red burn, still glistening with fluid.

Another gasp echoed round the hall. Tabatha wiped a tear from her eye, enjoying the attention.

'This terrible behaviour demands a terrible punishment. They will burn, like they burned me, and like they tried to burn you. Guards, now!'

Steel screeched on stone as the guards dragged chains down the length of each line.

'Now pull!' Tabatha screamed, her flame-shaped burn flickering in the firelight.

The children bent down, picked up the chains, and pulled to the familiar shovelling rhythm.

Clink. Clink. Clink. Clink.

With each clink, the cage jerked up and forward through the dark air, closer towards the mouth of the great incinerator.

Clink. Clink. Clink. Clink.

The children saw what was happening and began to whisper. Some looked up with undisguised horror.

Tabatha snarled, 'No talking in the furnace hall.'

But the whispering grew louder, and soon it thrummed like music in the air. A couple of children let go of the chain, but the chain moved on.

Clink. Clink. Clink. Clink.

'Silence!' shouted Tabatha, firing her pistol into the air. 'Any child that speaks will be shot by the guards.'

The guards cocked their muskets and pointed them at the children. There fell a deafening quiet. Luke and Jess's cage lifted faster, the heat thickening as they rose.

Clink. Clink. Clink. Clink.

Only the chain clinks and furnace crackles broke the silence. Luke found the quiet too much to bear.

'Tell me something, Jess,' Luke said. 'I need a silver lining.'

'That's a tricky one.' Her brow furrowed. 'I've got it. If we burn now, at least our souls won't burn, like the rest of the kids.'

It was morbid, but despite himself, Luke laughed out loud. A handful of children looked up from below.

They could hear him? His heart beat faster in his chest. Of course they had heard him, the room was practically silent after Tabatha's threat. They would have heard a pin drop.

Clink. Clink. Clink. Clink.

Luke looked at the furnace. He hated public speaking. There was no time to choose words. But with the guards at the door, it was the very definition of a captive audience.

He cleared his throat.

'The amber tickets are a lie,' he called down. A handful of children dared to look up at him. 'Tabatha sells us to Europe, through the Old Channel Tunnel.'

'Lies,' said Tabatha, her face unreadable. 'Ridiculous lies.'

Clink. Clink. Clink.

The pace had slowed. A shiver of doubt ran down the line.

More children looked up at Luke.

'If it's such a lie, why don't you bring Ravi back?'

'Out of the question,' hissed Tabatha.

Clink. Clink. Clink.

It was slower still. Yet more children looked up, and Luke realised something. The children's stares didn't scare him any more, he felt braver for them.

'It's only out of the question because you can't, because you sold him to Europe!'

'He's not . . . I . . . I'll bring him back, to prove it,' Tabatha called back. 'After the launch of the chimney, of course.'

Tabatha stood unbowed, but the children had heard it – they had heard her hesitate. For the first time, perhaps. And now, at least a hundred of the children were looking at Luke.

Clink . . . Clink . . .

The chain was moving slower still. But it was still not slow enough. The mouth of the incinerator loomed larger each second.

'It's working,' Jess whispered. 'Say something else!'

He knew what to say. The thing that had hurt him more than anything else. 'They don't just kidnap us, they ruin our families. My dad's in prison. Ravi's too. And yours will be too. She frames them for our kidnappings, so there's nobody left to fight for us outside.'

'Stop him now!' Tabatha shrieked. 'Someone shut him up!'

But by now, Luke and Jess were at least a hundred feet up in the air, and there was nothing she could do without bringing them down. And it didn't matter, he realised, because the chain had stopped moving. Every single child now looked up at Luke. Not in horror, or pity, but with a flicker of hope.

Tabatha wore a mask of fury. 'Stop looking at him!' she shouted. 'Anyone who looks will be shot!'

The children immediately looked down at the floor. But not one of them reached again for the chains.

'Weak, that's what you are. All of you, sit down. I'll burn them myself.'

Tabatha picked up a chain, and dragged it, lurching on her heels, across the stone floor.

Click. Clink. Click. Clink.

The furnace grew closer with each click of her heels. The heat stung Luke's eyes and stabbed his lungs when he breathed. Was this how his dad felt, coughing in jail? How was she managing to pull it alone?

Click. Clink. Click. Clink.

Tabatha grunted and wheezed, but she didn't stop. Luke couldn't tear his eyes from the furnace. *Think of happy times*, he told himself: his dad, Lizzy and his grandma in the boat. Alma in the sky and his mum in the End Place. But the thoughts didn't stick. They burned like paper. And the flames grew larger still in his mind.

Click. Clink. Click. CRASH.

Luke looked down. Tabatha had fallen to her knees. Lungs rattling. Face grey and soaked in sweat. Her hair unravelled and stuck to her face. She glanced up at Luke with wild eyes.

She dug her nails into the floor and pulled herself up to standing.

'Terence – don't just watch. Help me pull!'

'But ma'am,' Terence said, 'I can't do that *and* point the musket.'

'I don't care!' she shrieked 'Just pull this chain!'

Terence picked up the chain and pulled. They lurched an inch forward. Then another. The heat was unbearable. Jess began to whimper.

'Faster, Terence!'

Another inch closer. Then one more. Now Luke could see right down the mouth of the incinerator. Flames leapt out, singeing the bars of their cage. The heat scratched his skin like a hundred hot knives. He shut his eyes, but orange and crimson still seeped through his lids.

Jess shouted above the roar. 'It's not over, till it's over!'

'We did our best, Jess.' Luke squeezed her hand. 'But it's over now.'

A rumble came from above. The cage stopped.

Tabatha shrieked over the noise. 'It's only a storm, Terence. Don't stop pulling!'

The rumbling came again, louder this time, then grew into drumming, then a stampede. An ear-splitting roar burst from the chimney.

Luke put his hands to his face and peeked through his fingers.

An ocean of water exploded from the chimney, flooding the incinerator. Water and fire. Crackles and hisses. Then the glass shattered, and a swathe of boiling steam rushed through the hall. The steam rose as it went, passing just over the children's heads, but straight into Tabatha, Terence and the guards.

Shrieks from below. Then the sizzling steam rose up towards the cage. Luke braced himself, closed his eyes once more, and yet, when the droplets of steam touched his skin, they weren't hot, but cool.

He opened his eyes. Everything was grey. Had he died, maybe?

But it felt so real. He tasted the drops of water on his tongue. They were cool and fresh, like a mountain stream.

The mist cleared. The bars of his cage came back into focus. But something had changed. There was someone else standing in the cage with them: Alma.

'You did it, Luke.' Alma smiled at him. 'The council believed me because of you. You're safe now.'

Then, high above, came a resounding CRACK, followed by a creaking, grinding, tearing sound, as the ceiling of the furnace hall split wide open.

Rain poured down through the crack in the ceiling, cooling the air. For the first time in years, thousands of children saw the sky.

CHAPTER 43
FAMILY

It was another hot day in the east of London. A blue sky beamed down, while a little yellow boat drifted in the shade of the Old Olympic Stadium.

Nana Chatterjee snipped roses on the top of the boat, with intense concentration. Luke's sister Lizzy snoozed in her bedroom. The smell of burnt toast and buttery scrambled egg wafted through the houseboat, through the open porthole window, to where Luke sat with a fishing rod.

It had been two weeks since the roof of Battersea Power Station had fallen, in a freak lightning storm, the likes of which London had never seen. Blue lightning lashed the roof with such intensity that some claimed it was a blade from the heavens.

Most sensible people, however, agreed that weather was just weather. To think anything else was quite preposterous.

The result of the storm was what had made the front page.

When the water zeppelins had arrived to put out the fire, they'd found a thousand pale faces staring back out of the darkness.

Not quite so pale now, Luke thought, as he rolled up his sleeves. His grandma said he'd soon be as dark as her, if he didn't stay out of the sun. He didn't care.

A shadow flickered in the water. He lowered his fishing rod down a little, flicked it up, then whispered across to Jess. 'Like that, see? Quick, but gentle.'

Jess bit her tongue, jerked her rod up and down, in quick succession, sending her hook flying out of the water, flinging the bait high into the air.

'Careful!' Luke's grandma shouted down. 'I don't want any maggots in my roses. Let alone my hair!'

Jess put the rod down. 'So, how's your dad's case going?'

'They found Tabatha's car in the Thames. He said she escaped across the bridge, but lost control in the smog.'

'Are they right?'

'I don't know. They haven't found her body. But if she's gone, she can't have gone far. The lightning storm smashed up the Old Channel Tunnel, so she couldn't have left that way.'

Jess smiled. 'The "storm", really? What a coincidence . . .'

Luke grinned.

'My uncle's checking the sewers,' Jess said. 'Every night, they go looking. They found a few of the guards, and one had a tip off on Terence. Said he was hiding in a fish and chip shop somewhere up north.'

'We'll get them both. Everyone's looking for them.'

A shadow passed over them – a shadow in the shape of a giant swan. Luke smiled up at the sky and pointed to his watch. 'You're late! Again.'

They watched the swan sink down through the sky, until it was a misty haze, then a wisp of steam on the water. A moment later, a girl with dark curly hair swam up out of the water and pulled herself up onto the boat. She wore a bright green dress, which somehow wasn't wet at all. She curtsied, then grinned.

'A lady is never late, Luke,' said Alma. 'Everyone else is simply early. Deputy Councillor is a serious job! I'm so busy. I barely have time to do my hair.'

'Isn't your hair made of mist?'

Alma raised an eyebrow. 'Anyway, moving on.' She pulled out a pen and sketched a watery map of London on the dried-out wood of the boat. 'We've rained on every nook and cranny of the city, and not a word on Tabatha. The council has no jurisdiction if she makes it to Europe – so they've gone to the coast to watch the ports.'

Luke looked up at the expanse of blue above. 'I wondered why the weather was so good. My grandma's roses are suffering a bit.'

Alma winked. 'I can sort that, if you want.' She stood up and leant against the boat window, and a gentle mist from her hands covered the parched roses. 'We're asking ghosts up and down the country – it's not normally done, but these are exceptional circumstances. Everyone's a bit spooked.'

Jess laughed. 'Well, if even the ghosts are spooked, I feel a bit better. I keep waking up at night, thinking I'm down in the furnace hall.'

'Me too.' Luke nodded. 'I think I shovel in my sleep.'

'I wonder what Ravi's doing,' Jess said.

For a moment, they were silent, looking at the water. Luke had seen Ravi's sister in the newspapers the other day, she was searching for news of her brother. She looked so much like him.

'There is something,' Luke said. 'Dad took me back to the lab and I found something for you, Alma.'

'From the lab?' Alma frowned. 'I hope it's not some horrible specimen.'

'No, it's a file.' Luke pulled a white leather-bound volume, with the letter A on the back. 'It's a list of children who worked in the plant. How they died. Their families. That kind of thing.'

Alma stared at the file, then wound a strand of hair round her finger. 'And I'm in it?'

Luke nodded.

Jess put her hand on Alma's. 'You don't have to open it. It's up to you.'

'It's only that . . .' Alma sighed. 'Things are just getting interesting. What if this changes things? Or worse, resolves things!' She looked up at the cirrus clouds high above. 'I don't think I'm ready for the End Place, yet.'

'Then don't go,' Luke said. 'Why rush to the End Place if you like it halfway? Stay with us a while.'

Jess leaned in. 'We could go to Europe and find Ravi!'

'I had been thinking that. Even though he's a grump, I liked him.' Alma weighed the file in her hands. 'But logically, Luke, surely I should read it. It's my family, in there . . .'

'They'll always be there, ready for when you need them. But Ravi needs us now.'

Alma chewed her cheek, then pulled up a swan-shaped mist

from the surface of the river. She stepped out onto it. 'So you're telling me to put it off?'

'I'm telling you not to overthink it. Trust your instinct, and all that.'

'OK.' She saluted. 'Sounds like a plan.'

She chucked the file back to Luke and her swan-cloud began rising. 'Don't lose it. I'll see you tomorrow. And start planning that trip to Europe!'

Luke watched her cloud drift into the sky. It joined a group of other bird-shaped ghostclouds and drifted south.

When she was gone, Jess looked at the file. 'What happened to her? If I can ask.'

'It was the bomb. The one that destroyed the third chimney. Alma was shovelling that day. Her and five hundred other kids.'

'I'd want to forget that.' Jess sighed. 'There's nothing positive about that.'

'Actually, there is. If she hadn't died, she couldn't have stopped it happening to us. To the whole sky, in fact.'

They heard a purring sound. Stealth leapt out from the port-hole window straight into Jess's lap. She grinned.

'Breakfast is ready!' shouted a voice from the kitchen.

'One minute, Dad!' Luke turned to Jess. 'You coming for breakfast?'

'I'd better go home. My parents are waiting.'

Jess stroked Stealth one more time, put him down, then crossed the gangway to the island, and ran off down the street by herself. You could do that now, Luke thought. There hadn't been a kidnapping in weeks.

He pulled up his rod and released the fish he'd caught. He always set them free. Then he headed inside for some burnt toast and eggs. To a place so full of hope, that the dark never reached it.

ACKNOWLEDGEMENTS

To all the pupils I've taught, who are a constant inspiration, at the Harris Schools Federation (Coleraine Park forever!), Newport Primary in Leyton (Sosali forever!), Walthamstow's wonderful St Mary's CofE, all the Ark schools and my Olga Primary beta-readers. You're the future and I'm counting on you all to keep writing.

To my own brilliant teachers at CityLit (Barbara Marsh, Jonathan Barnes, Conor Montague, Neil Arksey), Katy Darby at City University (where I wrote the first chapters), and Catherine Johnson at Curtis Brown (where I wrote the last).

To the writing organisations that gave me hope: Spread The Word and SCBWI's Undiscovered Voices for believing in me, and for invaluable advice – this book wouldn't have happened without you. To the Liars League, Faber's FAB Prize, YouWriteOn, Lighthouse Literary, PRH WriteNow the Writementor community.

And of course, all the SCBWI volunteers, whose agents' party and brunches (complete with a baby-holding service) were invaluable.

To my super-agents Steph and Izzy – who overcame lockdown and COVID-19 to make this happen. From ghoul-origins to the great cigar vs pipe debate, the book is so much better for your input and working with you both has been an absolute joy.

To the dream team at Hachette – your enthusiasm and brilliance never fails to wow me. Special thanks to Samuel Perrett and Chaaya Prabhat for the gorgeous cover; to Flic, Lucy, Katy, Nicola, Tracy, Hilary and Alison for all your amazing work (and my favourite zoom backdrop ever); to Jenna for sparing my darlings and to my warm, wise and wonderful editor Anne, for making this book the best it can possibly be.

To Piers Torday, Mike Bedo and Kate Oliver – you are the wisest. To my LWA, CBC and UV fellow writers – you are lovely (and also wise). To the schools (and teachers) that taught me to love reading: King Alfred's, St Joseph's and St John Fisher's.

To the fantastic Shanks family for their unfailing support. To Sarah, Chris, M & L (and SUK) for our bundle of joy. To my Jack, Dunc and Rosie for the love and the bonkers home movies. To Grandad Luke, Diane and Ryan. To Dad and Shani for wise words, edits, and the best writing refuge (seaside+childcare!). To my mum – for having the biggest heart, for inspiring me to write, and always being there for me and my family.

Finally, to Joe and Juliet for everything else. For sleeping through. For tidying up (sorry). For being rocks. For being sparks. Love you both to the sky and back.